WILDE WOMEN

KIERSTEN MODGLIN

BITTER HOUSE
PUBLISHING

WILDE WOMEN is a work of fiction. Names, characters, places, images, and incidents are products of the author's imagination or are used fictitiously and are not to be construed as real. Any resemblance to actual events, locales, organizations, or persons—living or dead—is entirely coincidental and not intended by the author. The scanning, uploading, and distribution of this book without permission is a theft of the author's intellectual property. No part of this publication may be used, shared, or reproduced in any manner whatsoever without written permission except in the case of brief quotations embedded in critical articles and reviews. If you would like permission to use material from the book for any use other than in a review, please visit: kierstenmodglinauthor.com/contact
Thank you for your support of the author's rights.

The name and trademark KIERSTEN MODGLIN® and any other related logos used in this book (collectively, the "Author's Marks") are the exclusive property of Kiersten Modglin. Unauthorized use of any of the Author's Marks or of any word, term, name, symbol or device that is likely to cause confusion or mistake with respect to the user's connection or association with Kiersten Modglin, or her approval or sponsorship of the user's products or services, or that is likely to dilute any of the Author's Marks is strictly prohibited by law.

Copyright © 2025 by Kiersten Modglin.
All rights reserved.

Cover Design by Kiersten Modglin
Copy Editing by Three Owls Editing
Proofreading by My Brother's Editor
Formatting & Graphic Design by Kiersten Modglin
Foxglove Sketch © Charlee Modglin

First Print and Electronic Edition published in 2025 by Kiersten Modglin and Bitter House Publishing, LLC.
kierstenmodglinauthor.com
bitterhousepublishing.com

*To the wild women who inspire me to use my voice—
Margaret Atwood, Jodi Picoult, Taylor Swift, Shonda
Rhimes, Alice Hoffman, Hilarie Burton, Sarah Dessen,
Lois Duncan, Sophia Bush, Glennon Doyle, Jenny Han,
Jensen McRae, Gracie Abrams, Dolen Perkins-Valdez,
Kelsea Ballerini, and Maisie Peters.
And to the wild women yet to come.
We aren't going anywhere.*

CHAPTER ONE

CORINNE WILDE - 1994

The sky is strange as we return to Foxglove. Gray, like after a storm, even though it hasn't rained today. It gives me a funny feeling deep in my gut. Something I can't explain. Like when I know something bad is going to happen before it does.

Like the earth here knows it, too.

It's July, so I'm out of school, but this entire summer has had that strange edge to it—like it already knew fall was coming, like it'd been preparing since the final weeks of spring.

Today, as we loaded the car for our trip, there was the kind of wind that lifts the hair at the nape of your neck. The kind that makes the trees sound funny, like they're whispering secrets you're not meant to hear.

Mom and I have driven all day without saying much. I don't even think she's noticed the radio isn't on, but I can't bring myself to point it out. She's trying not to cry, and I'm afraid to break the spell.

So we drive up the long gravel road in silence.

I haven't been here in years. Not since I was a little girl—nine or ten, maybe. But even if she hadn't told me, I'd have known where we were going. I felt it under my skin, crawling like ants, even before I saw the old cedar tree, the rusted mailbox half-devoured by goldenrod and pokeweed.

Foxglove looks the same as I remember.

Haunting. Formidable. And somehow still cozy.

I have always loved that about the old stone cabin. She looks like she can take care of herself. Like the witch's hut from the stories Grandma used to tell me when I was little. Fairy tales about magical houses and powerful women.

I can't explain it, but it feels like she's been waiting for us. Or maybe I've been the one waiting. Seeing Foxglove again makes me feel like I've been holding my breath all this time.

Despite my time away, the meadow still knows me. The tall grass, lush with wildflowers, sways in the wind like it's waving hello, as if welcoming me back. Welcoming me home. As we step out of the car, I resist the urge to wave in return.

I'm glad to be home, I say, only in my mind. I don't need to say it out loud for Foxglove to know.

The old house doesn't smile, but it doesn't frown

either. It just waits, the way it always has, as we unload our bags and make our way onto the porch. The air smells of rosemary and lavender, and I brush my fingers over a strand of wisteria hanging near the porch as we approach the door.

Mom doesn't knock. What would be the point? There's no one here to answer.

That's why we're here. My grandma is dying.

Mom says she can't make it to the door anymore. A man who lives nearby checks on her, makes sure she eats—but even he can't fix this.

Mom didn't want to bring me. She said it would be too hard, that I'm too young. But Grandma asked, and Billie Wilde has never been able to say no to her mother, even after all the years and distance between them.

The small house smells of campfire smoke as we enter, and my eyes immediately find the charred logs in the fireplace. Once, when I was little, Grandma let me make s'mores there using sticks we collected in the yard.

Now, that same grandma—the one who once seemed so full of life and invincible—lies in her bed, wrapped in a quilt the dull color of old leaves. It makes me sad, like the color has drained from her, too. Her skin is thin like the tracing paper Mom keeps in her desk at home, and her body looks like it has sunken into itself—concave and terrifyingly empty.

But her eyes, I'll never forget them as long as I live—they are still sharp as ever. The kind of eyes that find you the second a bad thought crosses your mind. Before you ever have time to act on it. As we enter the room, they find me before they find Mom.

"Corinne," she says, and her voice carries the distinct rustle of dry grass. "Oh, honey. You came."

I rush to her side, tears already stinging my eyes and making me feel foolish. I sit by the bed on the old wooden stool I used as a child to see in the mirror when I brushed my teeth. The same one I used to climb on to reach the cookie jar hidden away behind the toaster. Thinking back, it was never a great hiding spot, and I have to wonder if she meant to truly hide it at all. Maybe it was always just a game.

"Of course I came," I say, my voice cracking like ice on a frozen pond. I promised Mom I'd be strong, but I'm failing.

She smiles at that. Slow and quiet. Thoughtful. I'm grateful she doesn't acknowledge my tears. "Good. You belong here. Always have."

Mom stands by the doorway, arms folded tight. Her eyes are as dry as a bone, but she's pale. Scared.

Grandma reaches out her hand—not to Mom, but to me. She grasps me tight. Under my warm palm, she's cold as ice, and I'm horrified by how thin her skin has become. I refuse to let it show, holding her hand tighter, more fully, out of spite. Like if I hide my fear well enough, the reasons to be afraid will disappear.

Like if we don't acknowledge that we're losing her, we won't.

"When this is over...when it...*happens*, you'll need to bury me in the field," Grandma says, not wasting time. "With the others." Her voice is matter-of-fact. How can she possibly talk so casually about this? About...dying.

Mom flinches at her words, and it's clear she's as unprepared for them as I feel.

"Do you remember the place?" Grandma goes on, her eyes no longer as sharp as they were mere moments ago. She looks as if she might fall asleep. "Billie? Tell me you remember. Under the willow tree, where the lilies come up in May. There's a row of markers I showed you when you were young. They're there, though they might be covered in moss. Crooked. You might have to look, but you'll see them. They're waiting for me. Your grandma Ruth. My gran, Martha. And her mother before her. All of us."

Mom steps forward, hands clasped together. "But you'll want a funeral. A casket. You haven't told me—"

"I don't want any of that." Grandma cuts her off with a heavy breath. "Just put my body in the ground. Return me to the earth. To my mother and sister. My gran." It's the first time I hear her voice crack, and when I look from Mom to her, Grandma's eyes are squeezed shut. "Corinne should help. She needs to learn our traditions."

"She's a child." Mom's voice turns to steel, her cheeks pale.

"She's a Wilde." Grandma's thumb runs over my knuckles, and her gaze spars with Mom's. I love the way she says our name. It always makes me feel powerful. As if it's a spell. A promise.

There's a long pause, and it feels as if they're still talking without moving their mouths. Still arguing, though only in silence and flicks of gazes.

Finally, Mom takes half a step back. When she speaks, her voice is flat. "I remember the place." When Grandma isn't looking, I catch her rolling her eyes.

"Good." Grandma turns to me again. "You remember the meadow, don't you, Corinne?" She pats my hand, and my breathing catches in my throat. "It's special. Sacred. Guarded by generations of Wilde women, but played in by those same women as they grew." She lifts her hand, popping a finger on the end of my nose. "The earth needs both, you know? The laughter and the bones."

She pauses, studying me. "You were a child who played there, and one day...one day when you play, you'll stop by and say hello to me again, won't you? You'll visit me? In the meadow, where I'll be waiting." She lifts her wrinkled hand and brushes a stray tear from her weathered cheek. Then, a smile. "And someday, your grandchildren will visit you, too." She draws in her lips, eyes closing once more. I don't know if she's looking for an answer, but I can't bring myself to speak.

When she opens her eyes again, I nod softly, afraid the memories of the meadow will make me feel too much, miss too much. But it's clear I have no choice.

Without warning, the memories flood back into my

mind without much care for my feelings. Long days in the tall grass. Weaving flower crowns from the wildflowers. Befriending the bugs and making bouquets with the dandelions. The sunlight warming my tangled hair. Chasing shadows with a stick for a sword and dancing with the fairies. Pretending the wind could talk. Imagining it could tell me secrets and keep me safe. I used to lie in the middle of that field and feel the ground breathing beneath me.

"I thought it was a fairy garden," I admit. "When I was little, I thought it was magic."

Grandma's eyes soften. "Who says it isn't?" She squeezes my hand once more.

"We should let your grandma get some rest," Mom says, touching my back gently.

I wait for Grandma to argue, to say I should stay right here with her, but she doesn't. She nods her chin toward the door with a look I'll never forget.

I think she knows.

I think maybe she is trying to burn the image of me into her brain.

Somehow, she knows it will be the last time she ever sees me. That this is it for us.

"Foxglove is yours now, Billie," I hear Grandma whisper as we walk out the door, talking to my mom. "Don't forget about her."

"I'll get you some tea and another blanket." Mom doesn't cry as we walk away. She just nods once, her body tight as a fist, and shuts the door.

As we watch her sleeping peacefully that night, Hazel Wilde—mother of Billie Wilde, grandmother of me—takes her last breath.

Death is silent, I learn. Hers is, anyway. She doesn't make a sound. She just goes eerily still, her final breath slipping out between her lips like smoke from a chimney, barely there, then gone all at once.

Two days later, we bury her in the meadow under the willow tree.

In the end, Mom honors Grandma's wishes. We find the largest stone we can to mark her grave, then begin digging. As we work, I silently promise to visit her, just like she asked.

Mom lets me help with every part of the process, which surprises me.

Maybe she needs my help, though.

I can't stop watching her. Worrying. Taking stock of the slight wrinkles around her eyes, the streaks of shimmering silver starting to appear in her hair, the heavy way she breathes.

She's getting older, and for the first time in my life, that scares me.

The earth is soft and pliable from the lingering effects of yesterday's unexpected storm, and we work slowly and carefully beside the other grave markers Grandma talked about—flat stones covered in moss, wood slats with mushrooms peeking out of the deep cracks, an old iron doorknob hammered into the ground. Though a handful have been carved with names or initials, most don't have any identification. Just signs. Just honor and memory.

Grandma made it clear she didn't want a priest. She didn't want prayers. She wanted to go back to the land, the way all the Wilde women have.

Someday, this will be how I go, too. It's my legacy.

Mom won't carry on the tradition herself. She'll have a proper funeral in a building, surrounded by friends and family. She'll want a real gravestone—one carved with her full name, the one she reclaimed after the divorce.

She doesn't have to say it; her bitterness as she carries out Grandma's bidding makes it clear. She thinks it's silly. Strange. I'm pretty sure I heard her mutter the word *barbaric*.

I'll admit it feels weird to put her straight into the earth like she asked, but it also feels…right. It's what she wanted. *Dust to dust.*

When it's done, Mom goes back inside. Alone, I can't fight my tears as I collect wildflowers the way we used to when I was a little girl. Grandma taught me to identify every plant in the meadow, taught me how to tell the dangerous ones from the harmless.

When I'm finished, I lay a braid of wildflowers at the base of the tree—Queen Anne's lace, goldenrod, and a little foxglove for the name of this place. They were some of her favorites, from a time that feels so far away now.

As I step back, the wind picks up, and the tall grass bends low, like it's bowing. Like it's honoring her, too.

I stay with her, refusing to leave, refusing to say goodbye until Mom calls me inside. By then, it's dark, and I try not to think about Grandma, cold and alone under the dirt.

I say goodbye to her but promise to be back soon. Even though I know it's a lie.

With Grandma gone, Mom doesn't want to remain at Foxglove for another second, let alone for another night. The house is too quiet, and the silence makes her skin itchy. She doesn't stop pacing, stop twitching and fussing, until everything is packed.

In the car, as we pull away, I turn in my seat and watch the cabin get smaller and smaller until it vanishes behind the trees, swallowed whole by the earth around it.

"When will we come back?" I ask.

Mom doesn't answer.

"It's ours now," I remind her of Grandma's words. "We could live there. I could switch schools, and we could plant a garden. We could take care of it, just like Grandma said. I could—"

"No," Mom says, cutting my hopes off at the root. There's no negotiating with her when she's this way. It's firm. Final. "Foxglove is not our home."

I don't understand. "She said we belong there." My voice is soft, weak. I'm not fighting the way I know Grandma would want me to.

"She says a lot of things," is all I hear before she turns up the radio.

I turn back to my window, pressing my hand against the warm glass. As we turn off the winding road, with no guarantee of when or if we'll return, I make a plea to the trees. To the flowers. To the land, to Foxglove.

Don't forget about me. I squeeze my eyes shut, willing the earth to hear me now like it seemed to when I was young. It's childish foolishness, but if there was ever a time I needed to believe in the magic of this place, it's now.

Please don't forget.

Eventually, my longing for Foxglove fades. My time away does what Mom hoped it would do, distracting me. Distancing me. I forget about the wild fantasies of childhood and the magical meadow that once fascinated me.

The cabin sits empty. We don't talk about it. Don't visit.

Still, every once in a while, a dream will sneak up on me, catching me off guard. A dream about the meadow or the willow tree, about the little creek that runs through the woods. About the flowers and the sunshine that feel so different there. About the wind, and the roots, and the stones sunk so deep in the dirt only the earth remembers their stories. Bones with names long since forgotten.

And, foolishly, when my mind wanders back to that girlhood innocence and whimsy, the place where fairies are real and the good guys always win, I wonder if the ground is still breathing.

If the house remembers me.

If it's still waiting.

Still listening for a Wilde girl to come home.

CHAPTER TWO

CORINNE WILDE - PRESENT DAY, 2025

Foxglove is a memory box, so filled to the brim with the past I sometimes feel as if there's no room for the present. My mother grew up here, and her mother, and hers. Centuries of Wilde women have survived on this land and within these walls from the moment it was built.

This is what I tell myself—that others have done this before me, and that I can do it too—as I pull up next to the quiet, old cabin the day after my divorce is finalized.

Despite Mom paying a neighbor to keep the land tidy, the yard is overgrown in patches near the cabin, like he's been skipping the weed-eating. I guess he thought no one would notice either way, and until now, he'd be right.

The old cedar tree is still here, and that rusted mailbox still stands—now even more covered than I remember by the goldenrod and pokeweed trying to swallow it up.

I put the car in park with a heavy breath, bracing myself.

A glance at the back seat tells me Taylor is glaring out the window with her AirPods in, still angry with me.

When her blue eyes lock with mine, I put on my bravest smile. "Home sweet home."

She doesn't bother arguing with me or pointing out that this place is not and has never been our home. Instead, she rolls her eyes and shoves open her door, stepping out of the car.

The sweet scent of lavender hits my nose in an instant, and the tall meadow grass dances in the breeze. The stone cabin remains. Untouched, unbothered. If the years of emptiness have affected it in any way, it's unclear. It looks just as I remember it, and my throat feels itchy at the thought.

Though I try not to look, not to reminisce too hard, my eyes find the willow tree off in the distance, and I nod softly to myself. To her. *I'm here.*

"Mom, unlock the trunk," Taylor says, hitting the back of our vehicle with her palm.

I blink away the fog over my eyes, getting down to business. This is not the time for nostalgia. We have things to do. Together, we unload our luggage. What luggage we brought with us, anyway. The movers are on their way with our things, but a good bit of our stuff will be stored at the old house with Lewis until I figure out something more permanent.

As picturesque as this place may be, as much as I

loved it once, I can't argue with Taylor's silence. Foxglove isn't our home. It isn't the place for a teenager, out here in the woods all alone. I've taken her away from everything she knows and loves, and the guilt of that is stronger than any attachment I once had to this place.

Still, moments later, I turn the key in the brass lock and push open the door with a bright grin, hoping that if Foxglove gets a sense of my happiness, it will get on board with making itself a happy home for us.

Lord knows it would be the first happy home we've had in a long time.

The air smells stale, like dust and damp wood. It's the scent that lingers after it rains.

My face is enveloped at once in a spider's web. I step back, swatting and gasping as I work to wrangle the silk-like threads from my skin. When I'm free, I look back at Taylor, who is staring at her phone rather than looking my way.

Not that I'm surprised to see it.

Not that I can blame her really.

We put our bags down in the space between the kitchen and living room as I take in the sight of the cabin. My first impression of the outside of Foxglove after all this time still seems to be true inside. Despite being empty for the better part of the last thirty years, it's held up quite well. It needs to be tidied up, for certain, but the bones seem strong.

Bones.

I swallow, forcing away the thought.

My eyes travel over the stone fireplace, the inside stained black from years of use. The mantel carries the word someone carved into it years before I was born. A legacy I studied and traced with my fingers over and over as a child.

It must've taken forever. My once-tiny voice rings in my head, and without moving, I can feel the cold, rough stone beneath my pointer finger.

Some things are worth taking the time. My grandma's warm yet vague response had come from behind me. Was she sitting in her chair, knitting a blanket? Or perhaps she'd come up from behind me, whispering the response in my ear. Maybe she'd answered from the kitchen where she was baking cookies or peeling potatoes.

Try as I might, I can't remember. The memory disappears like smoke. My young mind was only focused on the stone. On the word.

WILDE.

Did the woman who carved it know that her future granddaughters and great-granddaughters would stand next to it one day? That they'd cook their s'mores and warm their house under the letters she carved? Take Christmas photos gathered around it.

It could've been a man, I suppose. A great-great-grandfather of some kind, but in my mind, it's always been a woman.

"Are you okay?" Taylor asks, and when I look over at her, her brows are drawn together. She doesn't realize the ghosts this place holds for me.

I shake the memories out of my mind, setting to work. "The movers will be here soon with the furniture. Do you mind sweeping up in your room so they can get your bed set up?" I reach across the small kitchen island and grab the wooden-handled broom resting covered in cobwebs against a chair.

I remember the day we left it here, when Taylor was just a baby.

The neighbor has been checking on the place, but it's still just as we left it, and I'm struck with a thought all at once. *It didn't forget.*

Tears hit my eyes, and I clear my throat.

Taylor stares at me as if I've lost my mind, waiting several seconds before she takes the broom from my hand with two fingers—as if it were a bug. "You want me to sweep my room? I'm going to get tetanus."

"Come on, honey. Please. Do you need me to show you which room it is? It's the one on the right. Bathroom's directly across from it."

She glances down the hallway. There's a bathroom, two bedrooms—one on the side and one directly at the end of the hall—and a staircase in the back that leads to a loft so small it hardly qualifies as a room. My grandma had a rocking chair up there when I was young. A dollhouse. I used to paint pictures and read books on the red floral rug during particularly rainy days. Back then, even that dusty little hideaway felt special and magical. Now I'm realizing just how cramped and plain it all is.

With a sigh, she turns away, muttering something

under her breath that sounds like, "Oh gosh. How ever will I find it in this maze of a house?"

Once she disappears down the hall, I move over to the counter and squat down, opening the cabinet under the sink carefully, half expecting a mouse to jump out at me. To my relief, though, there's no mouse. Or at least, not anymore. The evidence they have been here is scattered across the old newspaper placed down as shelf liners.

I lean in cautiously, turning the valve connected to the old brass pipe. It creaks and groans. I lift up, closing one eye as I turn on the faucet. When the water sputters with air then releases into the sink, my eyes line with unexpected tears.

This time, it's not because of a memory. For whatever reason, this feels like the first sign everything might actually be okay. That, somehow, we'll make this place work. At least for the summer. After that, we'll figure it out as we go.

With that bit of good news, I flick on the light above the sink, letting out another short breath as it comes on without issue, and glance around the room, trying to decide where to start first.

My eyes find the small, clay cookie jar tucked back in the corner, and I pull it forward slowly. The stone rattles across the wooden countertops. I place it in front of me, wiping dust away from the black, hand-painted letters.

The jar is worn in a pattern from years of use, proof of the fingers used to pry the lid off. My little fingers and so many others. I never thought to ask how old this was, but looking at it now, I know my grandma wasn't the first to use it.

It's funny, the things that are unimportant as a child, and how much they mean as you get older.

"Uh, Mom?"

I'm startled by Taylor's wary voice, drawn back to the present again. I hustle down the hall on my way to her. "Is everything all right? What's wrong?"

She's standing on the far side of the bedroom, a pile of dust next to her foot as she stares down at the hardwood floor. "How long has it been since anyone stayed here?"

I breathe out with relief. She's okay. "A while. Thirty years." It feels impossible. "But your grandma always had someone check in on it. A neighbor, I think. The one who mows the grass for her. He stops by and looks in the windows every few days, drips the faucets when the temperature drops down too cold. Why? Is it a dead mouse or something? We're bound to see some critters—"

She scoots something across the floor with her foot, and it takes me several seconds to register what it is.

"A Reese's wrapper?"

"It looks new." Her eyes meet mine. "Like someone has been in the house recently."

"Well, who knows how long these things last," I mutter, but deep down, I worry she's right. This wrapper looks as fresh as if someone dropped it on the floor today.

"There's more." She points farther back in the corner, to a space hidden by an old box of items we left behind when I was a child. Stepping toward her, I see a pile of trash. Candy wrappers, empty soda cans. Upon closer examination, I realize there's a banana peel in the pile, too. It's dried out and brown, but not so much that it looks as if it's been there for months or even weeks. If I had to guess, this is just a day or so old.

A lump forms in my throat as I force myself to keep calm, to not scare or worry Taylor. "Probably just the neighbor. I'll ask your grandma."

She eyes me. "The neighbor who is supposed to 'look in the window now and again and drip the faucets' has been coming into the cabin and leaving his trash? Yeah, sure. Okay. Seems legit."

I muster my best smile. "I'll get it sorted out, okay? Why don't you start going through any clutter left in my room instead? I'll finish sweeping yours."

She rests the broom against the wall with a groan, moving past me. "Fine, but if there's a squatter here, can we just, like, let them have it?"

When she's out of the room, I inspect the pile of trash closer, wondering if, in the strangest turn of fate, she's right.

Has someone been staying in our new home?

CHAPTER THREE

CORINNE WILDE - PRESENT DAY

An hour later, I've just finished sweeping and dusting Taylor's room when my phone rings. I'm hoping for a return call from my mom, but instead, it's the movers letting me know they made a wrong turn but are pulling up outside Foxglove now.

It will feel good to have our things here with us. It's only a small piece of home, a tiny piece of our new normal, but I'm relieved to have whatever we can get.

When they arrive, I walk them through the cabin, showing them where everything will go. I wish it were better. This place used to be something I was proud of.

Growing up, I loved this little cabin. There was something magical about it. Safe. Whimsical. I could play in the forest surrounding Foxglove for hours—turning fallen trees into castles and the fields of wildflowers into my kingdom. From a young age, I was allowed to run and play and explore to my heart's content, rarely returning home until the sun set, when my sparkling woods turned into a shadowy ghost land.

Back then, this place was my kingdom of wonder. Now, I just wonder where my life went wrong.

As the movers unload our furniture and boxes—the bed from our old guest room, a dresser we've never actually used, the small desk I wrote my novel at before upgrading. I'm downgrading now, as this one is the only desk that will fit the space in my bedroom at Foxglove.

They unload Taylor's bed, nightstand, and dresser while I work in the kitchen, scrubbing the countertops and sink until my fingers are raw and the surface looks clean.

There's a scorch mark on the wooden countertop near the stove that's been there longer than I've been alive. I vividly recall running my finger over the dark burn as a child, obsessed with the way it almost perfectly encircled my finger. I trace the spot now though, and my finger covers it easily. Somehow, while everything else in my life has changed—myself included—this cabin, this place, is still a touchpoint. Unchanging. Completely still.

Once the movers have left, I open my phone, searching for enough service to place an online order for a new lock. It's probably an unnecessary expense, but with the evidence someone's been here, I'd rather be cautious. I won't take chances with Taylor's safety. I'll replace the lock to give us peace of mind, whether or not Mom can tell me why the neighbor might've left a pile of trash.

What is his name?

I'm blanking. When Mom calls back, I'll ask her. *If* she calls back, anyway. Before, that was never in question.

It was always Mom and me against the world. Then, my dad died. Even though it was years after the divorce, it changed something fundamentally in us. I pushed Mom away.

I think, for a while, it felt like she was the reason I had less time with him. Like she robbed me of half the time that should've been spent with him under one roof.

We recovered slowly, but that was before her new boyfriend—*now husband*—came along to steal her attention. And then came my divorce and my return to Foxglove, which seems to truly have been the nail in our coffin.

I force the thought away. It's not like it matters. It's not like any of it matters. Not the neighbor and not the fact that Mom isn't speaking to me. Now that we're here, there's no need for anyone to check in on the place. And whether or not she can understand why I needed to return, why I could no longer stay in a marriage that was suffocating me, it *was* my decision.

And just like Grandma told me what feels like a lifetime ago—Foxglove is mine now.

Of course, I'm reminded of one of the many inconveniences that comes with living at Foxglove as I spot the delivery date for the new lock—two days from now. In the city, we were spoiled by getting most things the same day. But Foxglove is miles away from town.

I'll just have to get used to it. It's not the end of the world.

We can manage for two days, and if anything strange happens between now and then, I can always run into the nearest town and get a lock there. It's just that the only hardware store nearby is around an hour away, and very small. I'm sure I could find a new lock there should I need it, but looking around this house, I think there are better uses of my time.

Taylor walks into the room, AirPods in. She pulls one out to say, "Dude, you need to call and get the Wi-Fi setup scheduled."

"Dude," I repeat, pointedly, "I'm aware. I'll call first thing tomorrow."

She groans. "Watch it take like a month for them to get out here. Nothing works."

"I warned you service is spotty this far out of town. That's why I brought our old DVDs. There's a player in one of these boxes. We'll just have to make do with what we have."

"DVDs?" She balks as if I've suggested she go down to the stream to collect our drinking water. "Seriously? What is this, the nineteen hundreds?"

I knead the space near my elbow, releasing a breath through my nose. "Honey, I know it's not ideal, but I'm really trying here, okay?" My voice cracks, and I hate it. I hate myself for letting it happen. None of this is Taylor's fault. She's just a kid who has lost everything she's ever known because of her parents' stupid mistakes.

"I'll look to see if they have a service number that's available twenty-four seven and try to call. Maybe I can get someone out here tomorrow."

Without a word, Taylor turns on her heel and storms out of the room. I start to follow her, to ask her to come back, when I hear a noise from outside. Taylor stops in her tracks, and it's clear she heard it, too.

She glances back over her shoulder, a cautious look in her wild eyes, blonde hair falling across her face. "What was that?"

I'm quiet, thinking. I definitely heard something, but before I can answer, I hear it again. Footsteps outside the cabin.

Someone is tiptoeing around out there.

Someone is outside.

CHAPTER FOUR

SARAH WILDE - 1630

For as long as I can remember, I have always been drawn to the massive forest surrounding Foxglove. To the ancient trees that seem to whisper in a language I can't quite understand. My bare feet know the land and all her secrets better than I do, as if they have walked it for centuries before. As if their destiny is right here among the weeds and brambles.

Every corner of my home and its surrounding wood holds something new and unexpected, some hidden mystery just waiting to be discovered. It's something understood deep within my bones, within the very rawest parts of me, though never spoken aloud. This—this place where I was born, this place where I will die—is a place of secrets, of untold stories, of silence and of whispered messages, warnings, passed down through the generations of Wilde women. The ones who came before me.

While the meadow has always been free for me to

roam, echoes of my mother's stern voice can be heard in every corner of the house, warning me to stay close, to keep near her. Still, as I've grown, so has my curiosity. After all, what harm could possibly come to me in our home? This place where I help Mama clean, help her cook, where she tells me stories and braids wildflowers into my hair.

Countless times I have been told fairy tales about Foxglove—that our home is filled with hidden places, packed to the brim with passages and tunnels. Secret, sacred places meant only for Wilde women.

The stories aren't real. They're folklore. Folly. Tales mothers tell their daughters to keep them from wandering too far.

This is why I'm not afraid tonight as I creep into the kitchen. I've done it many times before when the house is quiet. Though it's been hours since Mama sent me to collect firewood, her voice still lingers in the air. She has always been protective. Like my gran before her. Her sharp eyes follow me around as if she can see through the very walls. Perhaps she can. But in this moment, the house is silent, and I am alone.

The kitchen smells of herbs and smoke, and the warmth of the crackling fire in the hearth fills the space with a comforting heaviness, as if Foxglove were wrapped in a warm blanket.

In the drawing room, my hands trace the worn stone of the fireplace as I watch the orange embers crackle and dance, pulling me into a haze. I blink away from the fire as a strange tug stirs somewhere in my stomach. It draws my eyes to the floorboards, to a place where the grain of the wood seems to shift in a way I'd never noticed before.

Mama's voice rings in my head, warning me to retire to my bedroom. Reminding me I should be asleep, that my chores will come early in the morning.

I ignore her. Ignore myself, rather. She's sound asleep, not here.

I kneel down, pushing aside the corner of the worn rug that covers the floor. It takes me a moment to understand what I'm looking at—what I'm looking *for*, perhaps, but there it is—a small crack in the board, barely noticeable. My heart races, excitement bubbling up from within me as if I've found some ancient treasure, some hidden cove. Like the Wilde women from the stories.

I press my fingers into the crack, feeling the old wood give way as I carefully pry it open. There's a loud groan and my heart seems to stall in my chest as I hold my breath, listening for the creak of the floorboards beside her bed, for the swish of her bare feet along the dusty floor.

There is nothing.

I release a long breath, steadying myself before I look closer at what I've found. Beneath the broken floorboard, hidden away like some forgotten treasure, I've found a narrow passageway. Just three steps down into the cool dark. I can't see where it leads. Can't see anything.

My heart goes mad in my ears, wild like the rabbits Mama catches in the traps in the back of the meadow.

It smells of earth. Of things buried long ago.

I feel the pull again—a sharp tug, stronger now, so strong it makes my stomach queasy. It urges me forward like a fierce wind pushing through the trees.

Without thinking, I lower myself into the dark space, one step, two, then three. My feet scrape against the old wood, and I gather my skirt in my hands, trying to see what lies ahead. Dust fills my lungs, along with the scent of the earth. It reminds me of afternoons spent by the creek in the woods. Of muddy toes and muddy knees.

Mama would never approve. That thought makes me smile as I press forward.

I am a Wilde woman. This house and all its secrets belong to me.

The shadow-filled passage spreads out before me, narrow and winding, never-ending. It feels almost as though it were meant for someone much smaller than me, so tight in some places that I have to turn sideways or duck my head to fit through.

The air grows colder as I venture farther, deeper into the darkness, but the pull within me only grows as I explore. It's like a voice, like a hand somewhere deep inside my soul guiding me through the dark. Telling me everything will be as it should.

There's no way to know how long I wander or how far the passage stretches. I move only on instinct, like a wild animal—as if I've sprouted whiskers and can sense everything around me.

That's how I feel down here. Wild and free.

Eventually, I find myself standing in a small chamber deep in the ground. It's as if I've come out of a trance, as if my feral senses are warning me of danger. I've wandered too far.

I look back the way I've come, and I feel sick. If Mama finds out, I'm terrified of what she'll do. Tears sting my eyes as I take in my surroundings.

The walls here are covered in moss and ivy, and the stones are cold and wet. Running my hand along the stone, it's as if I'm in the bottom of a well, and I suddenly feel very trapped indeed. This must be the secret place my mother warned me never to enter. This place is the reason for all of her stories.

The weight of what I've done presses in around me so tightly I can't breathe, and I sink down to my knees.

I should turn and go back, but I can't breathe even to stand. My head hurts, my chest aches, and I feel very strange. Like the walls are closing in around me. I see no way out except back through, and *my heart... I... I can't... I can't breathe... This space is too small for me. It's too... I'm too...*

Darkness creeps into my vision like droplets of ink.

"Sarah!" Mama's sharp voice echoes through the air above me. Then...*light*. Moonlight hits my eyes all at once, and I hear footsteps overhead, followed by her calling my name again. "Sarah Elizabeth Wilde! You answer me this instant!" The panic in her voice sends a shiver down my spine.

In mere moments, the air seems lighter. I can breathe

again. I scramble back to my feet, heart still pounding. My body is a trembling mix of fear and relief. I don't care what she does to me, only that I am alive. Only that I can fill my lungs once again.

"I'm here!" I call, clasping my hands as I wait.

In front of me, I begin to make out a tall, spiraling staircase, and then my mother. She descends the stairs, holding her skirt in one hand. The moonlight illuminates her from behind like an angel, and as she gathers me in her arms, I'm convinced she must be.

She scoops me up like she hasn't done since I was very young and carries me up the stairs. I close my eyes against her chest, listening to the *thud, thud* of her footsteps, the heaviness of her breath.

The moonlight hits me fully when we reach the top of the stairs, and she sets me down on the ground. My bare feet hit the damp grass, and I stare around.

We're in the meadow. To my left, I can see Foxglove, the firelight illuminating her windows, smoke rising from her chimney and leading us home.

We're at the base of the oak tree, and I watch as Mama closes an iron door before covering it back with stones and leaves. A secret door in the earth.

Just like the stories.

Mama takes my hand without saying a word, and, together, we make our way through the meadow. The moon casts shadows across her face so I can't prepare for what's coming. Instead, I just walk, head down, awaiting my punishment.

The weeds in the meadow catch my dress, scratching at the skin on my ankles and feet, but I don't dare complain.

She waits until we are back inside before she speaks. She stands me in front of the fire and strips my muddy dress from my body, so I'm standing there in my shift, shivering despite the warmth from the hearth.

Her eyes find mine for the first time, and there's something behind them I don't understand. Not the anger I expected, but something sad, I think.

She eases me down into a chair, then disappears into the kitchen, opening the cupboard. She digs into the back where she keeps her salves and tinctures, eyeing bottles and tins before she finds what she's looking for.

When she returns, she kneels in front of me, wiping my legs and feet carefully with the hem of her skirt. It stings something awful, but I don't dare complain.

Then, she unstoppers the bottle and pours a bit of brown liquid onto a cloth. She gives me a warning look with her eyes, one that tells me this will sting more. She doesn't need to say a word for me to understand.

When she's done, she wipes a salve across my wounds with gentle fingers.

The waiting for her to speak is almost worse than if she'd just taken a switch across my backside. The silence is heavy, full to the brim with disappointment.

"Mama, I'm sorry," I tell her softly, my voice breaking the silence. Breaking the spell.

She looks up from my feet, brushing a bit of hair

back from my eyes. "Sarah," she says softly, her voice low but steady, "do you know what you've found? Do you realize where you were?"

I open my mouth to speak, to explain myself, why I did what I did, but my words catch in my throat as if I've swallowed a bug. She knows why I did it. She probably knew that I was going to before I'd left my bed earlier tonight. She knows everything, like she always has.

Her lips rub together as she casts a glance toward the rug, and I see she already moved it back into place. Like it was never disturbed at all. Perhaps she was waiting for me to try to return that way, but when I didn't, I frightened her. Her lips go very thin, like they do when she's worried. Like they did after Grandma died and when Father was ill last winter. There's no anger in her eyes, just a quiet understanding.

"I just wanted to know what it was," I answer softly, guilt eating away at me.

"I know that. Perhaps it was foolish to keep the secrets from you for so long." Her cheek rounds with a soft, one-sided smile. "You're growing up on me, after all."

She draws in a long, deep breath. "Sarah, I want you to listen to me. Foxglove is not like other homes. And you are not like other girls. I have told you the stories since you were a little girl. I've warned you about the dangers here, warned you to listen to me."

"I didn't mean to—" I stammer, but she holds her hands up, silencing me with a single move.

"It wasn't so long ago I was your age, sneaking around to learn the secrets too, you know?"

My eyes go wide. It seems impossible that Mama ever broke a rule.

She gives me a little laugh. "You are a Wilde, my love. You are part of me, and I...you." She closes her eyes with a soft nod, and when she opens them, her gaze hardens for the briefest moment. "All I've ever wanted to do was keep you safe. You and your sisters, and now your baby brother, too. This house, Foxglove, has kept us safe for generations. It knows who we are. It knows our blood. Our scent. Our strengths and our weaknesses."

She stoppers the bottle and closes the salve, spreading her hands across her skirt. "But the secrets it holds must be kept in our family, do you understand me? Really, really understand. You must never tell a soul."

I swallow. Her voice is deadly serious, and it scares me more than I'd like to admit. "I didn't tell anyone. How could I? I was alone. I just...I saw the door, and I wanted to know where it went."

Her eyes go soft, and she takes my hand in hers, pulling me down to the floor, to her lap. She rests her cheek against mine so we're both looking into the fire, and her voice is in my ear. "I know, child. Oh, do I know. But Foxglove...it is not a place for curiosity. Not until you're old enough to understand it all."

I lean against her cheek with more of my weight, and she rocks us back and forth like she did when I was a child. As in those days, my body is heavy and tired in her arms. My mother. My safe space. "When will I be old enough?"

"Soon." She kisses my cheek. "Too soon, I'm afraid. For now, just know that this place will always protect you as long as you are of our blood. But that protection comes at a price."

"A price?" I don't understand.

Her next words sound strange to me, old like the earth and the wind and the skipping stones my sisters and I play with. Like she's reciting an incantation.

"Only Wilde women can know the secrets Foxglove holds. Never men. Never outsiders. If they do...if we reveal her secrets...the house demands a price. I will tell you the way my mother told me, and her mother before that. Foxglove is one of the only places in this world that does not belong to men. And it never will. If they try to take her, it is our duty to protect her. She is our responsibility. She is ours, and we are hers."

A chill creeps down my spine as the weight of her words hang in the air, heavy and confusing. "Not even Papa?"

"Or your brother," she tells me, though I hadn't thought of him. I hadn't thought he'd count.

"But...why? Why can't we tell them? They are Wildes, too." And it's true. My father goes by my mother's name, even if it's not biblical. Even if people in town whisper about it.

"Because they are not the same," she says, her voice barely above a breath. "It is not the same. Someday you will understand." She places a hand on my chest, over my heart. "Foxglove protects the Wilde woman. She has always protected us. It's why our ancestors built her. Why they chose this land, these stones. It's why they gave her secrets. But this was the cost, that no man could ever take that power. Her power. Not even when we love them."

I still don't understand. She eases me off her lap, though, standing and brushing the dust from her skirt, from my legs. "Now, I won't punish you for tonight if you'll promise to forget what you saw. If you vow to never speak of it again and never enter the passage unless I tell you to."

"I promise." I grasp the fabric of my shift in my fists at my sides.

"And you promise never to tell your sisters, never to show them?"

"I promise."

"And your brother." Those words don't sound like a question.

"I'll never tell anyone, Mama. I promise you."

She brushes my arms with her palms, tucking a finger under my chin to get me to look at her once more. "I know it feels like a punishment, my darling, but I promise you'll understand all of this one day. Foxglove has its secrets, and those secrets will be yours one day to protect."

Those words seem to glow in the air like fairy dust, and I feel as if I'm watching them in the air as they travel straight from her lips to my chest and settle into a warm place. I feel the truth of her promise, the weight of it as it sinks into my bones, into my flesh as real as if I've been branded by a hot iron. As if the house itself is reminding me of my promise. Of the deal we've just made—Foxglove and myself.

Whether I like it or not, I have responsibility in my blood. The house chose me. I am its protector, and someday, her secrets will be mine.

CHAPTER FIVE

CORINNE WILDE - PRESENT DAY

Unlike our old home's front door, with a large glass pane and windows on either side of it, Foxglove's door is solid wood. Practical out here, affordable when it was built, but now, standing at the door with someone knocking on the other side and no way to look and see who it might be, I'm regretting it. It will be one of the first things I change as soon as I can manage it.

I cross the room into the kitchen and peer out the closest window, but I'm too far down the cabin's wall to see who's standing there. If they drove, I'd be able to see their car parked behind ours, which it's not. Whoever it is has walked here.

The neighbor.

The answer comes to me at once. This must be the neighbor checking in on us. Surely Mom has told him we're moving in by now.

With a deep breath, I hurry past Taylor again. Whoever it is hasn't knocked again.

"Who's there?" I call, my voice shaking.

It takes several seconds to get a response, but when I do, a chill runs over my spine.

In a deep, gravelly voice, the person responds, "Your worst nightmare."

My body stills, and I scowl. "Oh, you asshole."

I swing the door open and stare at my best friend. Her friendly face—copper hair cut short above her shoulders and the warmest brown eyes—shines back at me in the dim porch light.

Her arms are full of bags and boxes, so I can't hug her as I step back, trying to take things from her as she moves into the house.

"What are you doing here?"

She hands me a package of paper towels and a grocery bag, and I peer inside. It's full of snacks, and it looks like the one in her hand is filled with cleaning supplies.

"I wanted to surprise my girls." She drops the rest of her things on the floor and hugs Taylor, then draws me into a longer embrace, holding eye contact as she pulls away. "How are you?" She's asking more than those few words, and we both know it.

I nod. "I'm great. You didn't need to come all the way here. Don't you have showings this weekend?"

"Rebecca's covering for me." Carrying the bags across the room, she places them on the kitchen counters. "I figured you guys could use some help getting settled in and..." Her eyes travel the room. "Cleaning."

"It's been a while since anyone was here," I admit. "I'm surprised Mom didn't sell this place years ago."

"Well, be thankful she didn't. You're sitting on a gold mine at this point." Her gaze flicks up over the wall. "The land, anyway. When you're ready, you could sell it and make enough to buy a house in cash somewhere else. Somewhere closer to me." She bats her eyelashes at me playfully.

Taylor bounces up on her toes with hope. "Yes. Yes. Let's do that." She claps her hands together.

"You know we can't sell this place." The cabin seems to droop with relief, as if it were holding its breath waiting for an answer, like it's grateful to know where I stand. This place has always felt otherworldly to me.

Despite the dust and disrepair, I can still see the nail holes my grandparents and their grandparents once put into the walls. I can feel the worn spots on the floor, where someone down the line paced up and down the hall worrying about a problem that has long since been forgotten.

There are decades of height marks written in shaky, fading ink on the wooden doorframe of the broom closet. Most have vanished with age, but I can still make out a few: Lyddie, *I think*. Hannah, Josephine. Katherine. Martha. The baseboard in my bedroom has the letter H for Hazel carved into its wood.

There's our last name on the mantel and the words

WILDE WOMEN carved into a board and nailed above the living room window. This house is a memory box, not just for me, but for every Wilde woman who came before me. And I am now the keeper of the memories, even if most of them aren't mine to begin with.

This home breathes my family's air. It holds every piece of our past and our legacy. This land may be worth much more than the house ever was at this point, but it's not just a cabin. It's not even just a home. It's a piece of our family. A piece of the blood, sweat, and tears generations of Wildes put into it. To walk away from it now—to say goodbye to it for good—feels wrong.

As far as I know, I'm only the second Wilde woman not to raise my daughter here, though that was more about practicality than tradition. Foxglove was too far from civilization for Lewis and me to commute to work, or for Taylor to go to a decent school. The guilt of staying away when we knew this was here, of abandoning the piece of the world always intended for me, has been heavier than I realized until I returned.

Despite what I know selling it would mean for my life currently, it would be a betrayal of everything my ancestors did for our future—not just me, but my daughter, and any generations that come after us.

I can only hope that staying here, living here, even if only for a while, will help Taylor understand why I feel so strongly about this place. Why I feel we must protect it.

"Your mom's right." Greta comes to my rescue, bumping Taylor's hip with hers as she unpacks the bags on the counter. "I wish my family had something like this to pass down through generations, rather than just high cholesterol, good hair, and that weird gene where cilantro tastes like soap." She sticks her tongue through her smiling teeth as Taylor rolls her eyes. "This place is special, you know? You'll see."

"Well, I'll have nothing to do *but* see if Mom doesn't get the Wi-Fi hooked up soon." She drops her phone on the counter and clasps her hands together, begging. "Can't I please just come back with you? I'm not meant for the wilderness. I need civilization. I need Starbucks. I swear I'll be the best roommate ever."

Greta eyes Taylor with a look of pity. "Sorry, you can't, because I already had the best roommate ever. Twice." She wrinkles her nose at me playfully. "Okay, now, we're officially having a sleepover, so someone go set up the TV and pick out a movie, and someone else tell me which of these delicious snacks we're going to pig out on first."

"Tay, why don't you pick the movie," I offer. "We'll get the snacks ready."

Without a word, she drags her feet across the room and begins sorting through the boxes, searching for the one with all our old DVDs inside it.

Moving closer to Greta and lowering my voice, I say, "You didn't tell me you were coming."

"I knew if I did, you'd tell me you were fine. And I knew that would be a lie, but I also knew if I pointed it out, you'd say it wasn't, and…" She huffs out a breath. "It was just easier if I surprised you."

"You mean if you left me no choice."

"Tomato, to-mah-to," she teases, booping my nose with her finger. She looks over my shoulder. "How's she doing?"

"About like you've seen," I say, my voice even lower than before. "She hates me. Hates us both, I guess, but I'm the one she's stuck with."

She presses her lips together, nodding. "Have you heard from him?"

"Not since we signed the papers. He wasn't at the house when the movers came by. I guess he assumed I didn't want to see him."

"What do you know? Miracles happen every day." She rolls her eyes. "I still can't believe you let him keep the house. It should've been sold and split. I could've gotten you both enough to start over."

"Yeah, Mom said the same thing about EJ."

Greta's eyes search mine as she fights against an angry smile. "It's not enough her new boy toy is trying to steal her away, now he's going after my business, too?"

"It's not like we would've used him. You're the family realtor."

"Well, I would be if you sold anything." She tears open a bag of mini oatmeal cookies, popping one into her mouth. "You guys are like a realtor's nightmare. You know, most people move houses every three to five years."

"We can't sell the house, and you know it."

"Yeah, yeah..." She wags her hand, pretending it's talking as she mumbles, "Sentimental stuff and important memories and good parents and yada yada yaaaeeeech..." She pretends to gag, pointing a finger toward the back of her throat.

I wave her away, slipping past to grab bowls from the cabinet. "It's the house we brought Taylor home from the hospital into, you monster. I couldn't let him sell it."

"Yeah, but now it's his."

"If I pushed the issue, he would've never given in and let me keep it. He had nowhere to go. Selling would be the only option, and that would've killed me. At least this way, Taylor can visit him there. Her children can see it. It's still hers."

Her expression goes skeptical, and I know she wants to point out that I can no longer force Lewis to keep the house, but it was the only sort of power I had, and I leveraged it. I don't want to believe he'd screw me over.

"So, want to hear something weird?"

"Are you just trying to change the subject?" She pops another cookie into her mouth and holds out the bag for me. I take one and tear open the bag of M&M's, splitting them between our bowls before adding popcorn and mixing them.

"Maybe," I admit. "But I think someone might've been coming into the cabin. We found trash in the bedroom."

"Ew, what?"

"Weird, right?"

"Probably some local teenagers. Lord knows we used to find random houses to get drunk in back in the day." She gives me a pointed stare, then her gaze travels the room again, and I know she's right. "This place is perfect for that."

I laugh, reaching next to her to pull a bottle of wine from one of her boxes. "You're probably right."

"Did you figure out how they were getting in? Surely the door wasn't unlocked. The place is dusty, but it's not destroyed. Did they break a window?"

"No, not that I saw. I ordered a new lock for the door, just in case. Maybe the neighbor lost the key...or maybe his son steals it or something."

"Does he have a son?"

"No idea."

"Does anyone else have access? Besides the neighbor."

"Mom. But other than that, just me and Lewis. And he never cared about this place one way or another. I can't exactly see him sneaking off out here."

She takes in a deep breath, thinking. "Well, when does the lock get here?"

"Two days. We'll be fine until then."

"Of course you will. But I'll stay until it's changed, just to be safe."

Most days I have no idea how I got so lucky to have her. "You don't have to do that."

"I know, but I'm the best, so..." She takes her bowl, shoveling a handful of popcorn into her mouth as she calls out to Taylor, "What are we watching?"

CHAPTER SIX

CORINNE WILDE - PRESENT DAY

Like when we were kids, Greta and I lay my mattress on the living room floor to sleep for the night.

"Now, don't think I'm going to let you hog all the covers just because you got divorced or something," she teases as we slip under the blanket.

"Ah, cool. I was worried that would make you start being nice to me."

"Please, my friend. It would take a lobotomy."

I pretend to jot something down. "Lobotomy. Noted. Not ruling it out."

She laughs, staring up at the ceiling, arms resting across her chest. "Man, I miss visiting this place when we were kids. How many times did we sleep right here? Your grandma would be asleep. It would be storming." She wiggles her fingers toward me playfully. "It was like we had our own little island."

"Too many times to count."

"I remember we used to look for patterns in the grain of the wood like we were looking for shapes in the clouds." She turns her head to look at me. "Do you remember that?"

The memories come back to me at once. "I remember...making up things I could see to keep up with you. Same as when we were older and *actually* looking at the clouds."

She hums a laugh. "Well, I might've been making some up along the way, too."

"So, you didn't really see Jake Jagielski's eyes up there?"

She snorts and swats my arm. "Honey, I see those eyes everywhere."

After a few moments, she rolls over, propping her head up in her palm. "So, real talk for a minute, how are you doing? This week has been a lot."

I start to answer, but pause, forcing myself to take stock of how I'm feeling underneath all my attempts to bury my emotions. "I'm...sad," I admit, my voice cracking. "I never thought it would get to this point, you know? It sounds stupid, but I guess I always thought that right before we signed, he'd realize this was all a mistake, and we'd make up and go home and pretend it hadn't happened. I kept waiting for something to change, but it didn't."

"Did you ever tell him that?"

I give her a look that says she knows the answer.

"Obviously he sucks, and we hate him, and you're so

much better off, and yada yada, but also...none of that. People hit rough patches, you know? People change. I always liked you two together. If there's no hope for you guys, I'm not sure there's hope for any of us."

"I don't hate him," I say, agreeing with her. I could never hate Lewis, the man I've loved since I was seventeen. The man who gave me our daughter. Who was by my side through so many life changes. Loss, sickness, grief, love. "We just aren't the people we were."

She gives me a small, sad smile. "Because, obviously, you got much cooler than he ever was. He couldn't keep up."

"Obviously." I smile, though I'm drying my eyes.

"When is he going to see Taylor?"

"I asked him for some time with her. I worry if she goes home, she'll never come back to me." At that, my voice cracks, and tears well in my eyes. I brush them away as quickly as they fall.

"Of course she will," Greta promises me, though we both know it's something she can't guarantee. "You're her mom."

"I'm the woman who—as far as she's concerned— just broke up her home and took her away from everything she's ever known."

"No." She pokes my chest. My heart. "You're the woman who showed her that your happiness—*her* happiness, someday—matters. She may not realize it yet, but you just showed her how to take care of herself, even when it hurts." Greta's sleepy eyes search mine, trying to make me believe her words. And I do. Deep, deep down, I know she's right. I just wish I could feel it right now.

At some point, during one of our late-night fits of giggles over a ridiculous memory, I realize how much I needed this. How much I needed her to be here. To remind me that some things aren't changing—that this friendship, this constant I've had my entire life, is still here. I don't know how she knew I'd need her, but somehow, she did.

The next morning Greta and Taylor are baking cinnamon rolls together, which allows me a chance to step outside and take a walk around the cabin, through the meadow, past the giant oak tree and the old willow.

I stop by Grandma's grave and pull the weeds that have sprouted up around her stone. I wonder if she knows I'm here. Back. That I've returned to Foxglove, for however long. I can't help finding comfort in the idea she's still around, like she promised. Watching me. Protecting me.

I think she'd be happy to have Foxglove occupied again. I sit next to the grave and twirl stems of wildflowers together, my fingers stiffer than they once were, the movements less fluid. Still, I manage a loose braid to lay on her grave as I promise to visit again soon.

I stroll through the meadow of my childhood,

running my fingers through the tall grass. The weeds grab at my jeans and ankles, scratching my exposed skin.

The air here feels different. Charged. I'd forgotten how much I love this place, how alive it makes me feel. The more I explore, the more I want to see all of it again. The more I want to feel the way I did when I was a child walking this same path. Wild, free, safe. Home.

Soon I will take Taylor through the woods, show her the creek that runs through them and the little paths I used to walk. I wish I had brought her here as a child, and for the first time, all the reasons and excuses I had not to bring her feel irrelevant. Every child should have a place like this.

The world surrounding the cabin is filled with sounds, the dry branches of the willow tree swaying in the wind, the leaves from the oak brushing up against each other as if whispering about my homecoming. Crickets chirp and frogs croak, and a metallic green beetle buzzes in the air, landing on my shoulder for only a brief moment. I resist the terrible urge to brush it away.

The air is heavy and damp with morning dew, and it clings to my clothes. Looking back, I survey the house and the property, deciding how much work I have ahead of me. The stone cabin appears as sturdy and strong as ever, but it could stand to be power washed and the wooden support beams along the porch need to be stained. I should probably have the metal roof inspected soon for any damage or rust.

Greta's black Lexus is parked next to ours in the

driveway, partially in the grass, which explains why I couldn't see it through the window last night.

I cross the rest of the meadow slowly, feeling an odd mixture of stress and peace, as if they're fighting inside of me to take up space.

At the edge of the woods, I stop.

Up ahead, a flash of movement catches my eye.

My breath lodges in my throat as I try to think, to process. I'm out here alone. If I try to run, I might fall. I might not be fast enough.

It could be an animal.

It could be a person.

It could be a killer.

It could be whoever was in my house.

I weigh my options. I could call out, or I could turn away and pretend I didn't see or hear anything.

When I see the movement a second time, someone up ahead, I clear my throat, raising my voice. This is my home. I don't deserve to feel unsafe here. I've never before felt unsafe here. "Is someone there?"

For a moment, the person is still. Then I see them moving again.

"Hey there. Sorry if I startled ya." From the shadows, a man emerges. He looks to be around my mom's age. His face is worn and weathered from the sun, and he's got odd-colored hair—I can't tell if it's gray or the ashiest shade of blond.

He moves closer, and I take a step back.

"Can I help you?"

A small smile tilts one corner of his lips upward. "I'm Conrad. Guessing you're Corinne."

I'm silent, trying to piece together who this is and why he knows who I am.

"Your mom has me watch over the place. I live just down the way." He points over his shoulder. "She mentioned a few months ago you might be moving back in soon." His gaze trails along the cabin over my shoulder. "Guess that's now."

"Right. Yeah," I tell him, snapping out of my trance. I hold out a hand. "Nice to meet you. Sorry, you just...I wasn't expecting you."

"Yeah, guess you wouldn't expect to see a stranger lurking around, would ya?" he says with a laugh. "I was collecting hedge apples. Hope you don't mind. Your property's covered in 'em."

He points to a pile of bumpy, green orbs on the ground. I recognize them immediately. I used to pretend they were goblins in disguise as a kid. That one touch would turn me to stone.

"Keeps the spiders away," he explains. "You'll notice I've been keeping 'em around your foundation for ya. You should keep doing that."

"Thank you. I will. I—"

Before I can finish my thought, everything stills. Across the meadow, I hear a sound that takes me only seconds to register. It's the sound of my daughter's voice.

And she's screaming.

CHAPTER SEVEN

MARY WILDE - 1642

The fire crackles and pops across the room, its warmth spreading to every corner. Outside, the wind howls and rattles against our windows, like someone is trying to get in. But they're not. The first storm of the season is upon us, and I think that might be worse.

I've hated storms for as long as I can remember, hated the way they make the air feel, the way they light up the sky too bright and make everyone—the animals and the people—act strangely.

The walls of Foxglove groan against the pressure of the wind, but inside, Mama keeps telling me we are safe. Gran sits in her rocking chair, rocking, rocking, and I listen to the slow and steady groan of the legs against the wood floor.

The fire fights against the darkness creeping in through the gaps of the house, giving me just enough light to see my doll.

As the first log crumbles, spitting a gust of smoke, Mama takes Anna off to bed. The storm wears on, and I scoot closer to Gran, nearer to the hearth. I pull my knees to my chest and watch the flames dance and twist.

My gran smiles at me from her chair, her fingers deftly working yarn into a pretty pattern in the firelight. She doesn't even have to look at what she's doing.

I've always loved watching her as she works. Mama has tried to teach me, but she doesn't have Gran's patience. Her quiet, steady concentration and the way her fingers seem to know just what to do without even pausing to think. She works as if she's knitting more than a blanket, more than fabric. She moves with such beauty it's as if she's stitching history, tradition…magic. Something much older and wiser than I am.

"Isn't it about time you went to bed, Mary?" she asks, watching me with wise eyes that always make me feel like she knows what I'm thinking. Maybe she does.

"I'm not sleepy yet."

"Your mother will need your help in the morning. The storm brings extra work."

I dance my doll along the hearth, not saying anything. I can't sleep during storms, I just can't.

Mama appears in the doorway to the parlor, hands on her hips. "You're next, my darling," she says.

"Can't I just stay up a little while longer?"

"A little while longer?" she repeats, her voice soft. I can't tell if she's going to agree.

"Yes. For a story."

Mama looks at Gran, who just nods her head. "'Tis okay, Sarah. I've got her."

Mama takes a long moment to think, and for that moment I worry she'll send me to bed anyway, but eventually, she brushes Gran's shoulder with her hand before pointing to me. "Straight to bed after the story. Promise me."

"I promise."

Once she's gone, I wait for Gran. She doesn't look up from her work straight away, but I can see a slight smile tugging at the corner of her mouth, like she's pleased with me.

Gran has always indulged me when I ask for stories or sweets, especially when the storms outside rage. She's never said as much, but I suspect she knows what I've kept to myself all this time. The storms make me feel like the rest of the world has disappeared. Like it's just us. Just Foxglove.

It's not a very good feeling.

"So," she says, her voice soft and warm. "What kind of story shall it be tonight, my love?"

My hand rests against the warm stone of the fireplace. The scent of rain fills the air, even inside. The wooden wall is rough behind me, solid and old. Twice as old as I am at least. I tap my chin in thought. "Tell me...your favorite story."

"My favorite?" Her smile grows bigger for a moment, her hands working faster. "Oh, I'll have to think about that."

Then she pauses.

There's a shift in the air around us, just slightly, as if my question made her think of something sad. I worry I've said something wrong, but just as quickly, she goes warm again.

Her smile returns, that knowing smile that tells me everything is okay and that it will continue to be okay as long as she's here. Slowly, she returns to work. I wonder whom the blanket will be for once she's done with it. Probably Anna, my new baby sister.

When Gran speaks, it's as if she's lost in a memory, no longer here with me but in another time. Another place. I don't think I like the feeling.

"Well, there is one tale I don't believe I've told you, though it's not one of mine. Not really. This story is an old one—one that came from well beyond my time."

"How did you learn it?" I ask, my voice raspy and dry. It feels as if there's lightning in the air, and not just outside.

"Oh, I don't remember. It's as old as the earth. You might find it boring."

I sit up straighter in my spot, clutching my doll to my stomach. "Tell me," I beg. She's teasing me, I know. Her stories could never be boring.

She gives a slight nod of her head, and I settle in.

Her voice goes deeper, the way it always does when she tells a story. Like she's trying to put me to sleep. Like she's speaking directly to something deep inside of me. Or, perhaps, inside the earth itself.

"This was a long, long time ago. There was a woman—very smart, very beautiful—who lived alone in a patch of woods not much different from our own. This woman was a healer, a wise woman, who knew tricks from the earth that others did not. There were whispers about her talents, about what she could do, and many came to her—many trusted her—when they needed help."

"What was her name?" I ask, mesmerized.

"She went by many names," she says simply. "A name could get her into trouble, and so she changed it often. Kept it a secret. Secrets are the most powerful thing a woman can own, Mary. You'll do well to remember that."

She pauses her rocking and looks me in the eyes. I tuck my lips into my mouth, nodding.

"She lived in a cabin," Gran says, returning her attention to the yarn in her hands. "A little cabin that was hidden deep within the woods where the trees grew so thick that sunlight barely touched the ground. The home was simple, built out of wood from mighty oak trees in the forest and stones from the river. The home came from the earth, from her own sweat and blood, but once it was built, the woman knew there was something special about it. Some people might even say there was a magic to it. Things that could not be explained, not by the woman nor by anyone else who came upon it."

My heart beats faster as I listen, absorbed in the rhythm of her words, the hum of her voice. Outside, I can hear the patter of the rain against the windows, the howl of the wind, but inside, the cabin is still as stone. Even a beetle pauses to land near my hand on the hearth, his back shining in the firelight like a bit of green glass. It's as if everything inside Foxglove, maybe even the walls themselves, are listening to the tale right along with me.

Gran continues her story, her gaze distant and fuzzy as if she's watching the story unfold, not just telling it. "The woman was known for how much she understood the land. People said she could speak to the trees, that she listened to the wind and could understand the waters. And when the storms came—storms like this one tonight—when the wind howled like a wolf on a full moon and the rain flooded nearby villages and killed crops, why... her cabin would remain untouched. As if it had never stormed at all. Some people said it was the trees...that they were so thick they protected the house, but the woman knew the truth. She had seen the way the trees bent, the way the wind blew the rain away. As if the land itself, the earth around her, had made it its job to keep her safe. No matter the storm, no harm seemed to come to this woman as long as she stayed in her woods."

When Gran looks at me, the hairs on the back of my neck stand up, and it feels as if a spider has crawled across my skin. I rub my palm against it, just in case, but there's nothing there, just the magic of Gran's story settling into the room around us.

"But powerful women are very rarely appreciated by our world, my love. There were some who didn't understand the woman's power. They were afraid of her.

Afraid of what she might do. What she was capable of." Her voice goes low into a soft whisper, as if she doesn't want anyone to overhear her, even the walls, even the beetle, still sitting next to my hand. "They called her dreadful names. Witch. Devil's child. They demanded she leave the land. Leave her home. They wanted her cabin, her secrets. They wanted to own the magic that protected her. For centuries before us and centuries after, I'm afraid, powerful men have called women witches as a means of control. They have used that word to take their land. Take their money. Sometimes...sometimes to take their lives. And that's what they wanted to do to this woman."

"Did they get her?" My stomach feels strange, like I need to lie down.

Gran shakes her head. "She refused to go. Refused to give in. Many, many women before her had tried the same, and they'd lost, but this woman knew the land would protect her. She trusted it like it trusted her to keep it safe. She said, 'For as long as my blood takes residence on this earth, no man, no town, and no crown shall ever own it. This place is mine, as long as I stand upon it, as long as my bones rest below it.'"

"And that worked? They left her alone? Let her stay?"

Gran chuckles. "You're getting ahead of me, my dear."

"I didn't mean to."

"The woman stayed, but they did not leave her alone.

Not for the rest of her days. They tried to take her cabin, force her out. They tried to tear it down, to burn it to the ground. But every time, they would fail. The rain would pour and extinguish their flames. Wild animals would arrive and chase them off. The ground would soften, so thick with mud they couldn't make it across her land. No matter what they tried, the earth stopped them in ways they couldn't explain. And soon enough, they stopped coming. The woman stayed safe and the cabin—the woods—remained. Unchanged. Protected. Steady as the sun."

Her words are heavy in the air, like the blanket forts I make with Mama sometimes, and I get the feeling I can't quite catch my breath. The story seems to swell to fit the room, like there's no more space for my questions. The beetle flies away, and we sit in silence, just the sound of the crackling fire and the wooden chair rocking against the floor once again.

The wind outside howls so loudly it chills me, but it's just the cold of it seeping in through the cracks in the stone. There's no fear this time. It's just...sound. Like music, almost. It's the sound of something ancient. Something that has always been there, will always be.

My eyes go to the fire, my mind wandering, tracing the lines of her story again in my head as I picture it, as real as if I can see it, too. As real as if I'd lived it. The flickering flames cast dancing shadows across the walls, to every corner of the room.

My heart pounds in my chest as I wait for my gran to

go on, to tell me more, but she doesn't. The story is over, and it's time for me to join my sister in bed.

Still, my body is buzzing with something curious. A strange thought flutters in my head—a butterfly on the wind in the meadow, plucked petals tossed into the air.

"Gran?"

"Yes, Mary?"

"Is that story about Foxglove?" My voice trembles with a feeling I can't name. "Was the woman in the story… Did she live here? Was she real? Are you…her?"

At that, my gran lets out a soft laugh that shakes her belly. Her fingers stop working. "Oh, my dear. The only magic in my life is getting to be your gran." Despite her words, her eyes search mine as if they're looking for something. An answer I don't have.

"I just thought—"

"But," she interrupts me, her voice barely above a whisper, "the only thing that matters is what we choose to believe. One day you'll be the one telling stories to your children. Your grandchildren."

I make a face, and she laughs.

"You will. Some stories are meant to be remembered and shared, told to your daughters and theirs. And some stories are better left alone. Meant to be forgotten."

I don't understand what she means, but when I look her in the face, searching for answers, she doesn't meet my gaze.

"You'll understand in time." She leans back in her

chair. "The earth has a way of keeping her own secrets. She shares with you what she wants you to know."

I wrinkle my nose. "You talk about the earth as if it's real. Alive, I mean."

"As real and as living as any one of us," she says with a firm nod. "She has secrets and stories too, you know? Better than any of mine." She pats her knee. "Come on, then. Give me a kiss good night. You'd better run off to bed before your mom has my hide."

I stand, easing onto her lap and kissing her cheek.

Before I go, she takes my hand and looks me in the eyes. "The question is never whether the story is true, Mary. That doesn't matter. Not really. The question is only whether you're ready to hear it." She presses a thumb to my cheek, running it over my skin like she's memorizing the pattern of my bones. "Whether you believe it."

With that, she nudges me off her lap, her hands returning to work, moving quickly. Her face is solemn, tired. She makes no move to acknowledge what happened, what she has shared with me, but I feel it.

She opened a door. The weight of the secret is in the room with us; the smell of the dust she brushed off the mystery lingers as real as the smoke from the fire. One day I'll understand. One day I'll know the truth.

I glance back at Gran just once from the hall, and she sits, eyes closed, a small smile on her lips. It's the smile of someone with answers—answers I vow one day to have myself.

CHAPTER EIGHT

CORINNE WILDE - PRESENT DAY

I burst through the door, moving as fast as my legs will carry me. Taylor and Greta are no longer in the kitchen. I follow the sound of her scream down the short hallway and reach her bedroom. Inside, Taylor and Greta are standing facing her bed.

They're alive.

Safe.

Breathing.

I scan the room. "What happened? What's wrong?"

Taylor turns back to me, a horrified scowl on her face that makes my stomach twist. Before she answers though, her eyes lock on something—someone—over my shoulder. I glance back to see that Conrad has followed me into the house. I was so panicked I hadn't noticed.

He offers me a sheepish look. "Sorry if I overstepped. I heard the scream and followed without thinking. I can go—"

I turn away from him and back to Taylor. "What's going on? Why were you screaming?"

"My stuff." She moves toward the bed, lifting her comforter. At once, I understand. The comforter is a shade darker than before and obviously heavier.

It's soaking wet.

She grabs a pile of clothes from the floor, tossing them onto the bed. Droplets of water splash up from the impact. She picks up her laptop next, the silver machine absolutely dripping with water. "Someone destroyed all my stuff."

I move forward, gathering her things in my hands, trying to understand what might've happened. A glance at the ceiling tells me nothing there appears wet. If there was a leak in the roof, there would be signs.

With a look back at the door, I realize Conrad is gone, though I didn't hear him leave. Greta disappears from the room and returns a few seconds later with her arms full of hand towels. "This was all I could find."

Of course. Because our larger towels are packed away somewhere in some box that might take hours to find.

"Thanks. Here." I take half of the towels and toss a few to Taylor. Together, the three of us begin working to dry up what we can. There's very little use, though. Her blankets and clothes will have to be washed, and her mattress will take hours to dry out. There's no hope for her computer. She looks hopeless and angry, so utterly defeated it breaks me. "Honey, we'll get you another computer, I promise."

I have no idea how I'm going to swing it. I don't exactly have MacBook money lying around, and I refuse to ask Lewis for help. I can't.

But I'll manage. Somehow.

Carefully, I lift one of her shirts to my nose, wincing. I need to make sure it's only water, not something worse. It smells of nothing but our detergent.

"How did the water get in here?" Greta asks, looking at the ceiling too.

"Someone did this," Taylor tells us, waving her hand toward the bed as if it should be obvious. "Whoever has been squatting here—leaving trash. They clearly did this. Come on, Mom. Are we seriously going to just pretend like everything is fine?"

I press my lips together, looking around. "That doesn't make any sense. Even if someone was here before, no one has been in the house since we got here. There's only the front door, and you guys would've seen them come in or out. And if you didn't, I would have. I was just outside." Technically, I was distracted there for a minute or two talking to Conrad—being scared by him—but still, between the three or four of us, surely one of us would've noticed someone breaking in. And who would do that in broad daylight, anyway? And why? "You slept in here fine last night. No one bothered us. There has to be another explanation."

"Like what?" she demands, staring at me. "What explanation could there possibly be, Mom? This is insane. I'm *not* staying here. They ruined my stuff."

Splotches of scarlet stain her cheeks, so bright with fury and frustration I can practically taste it in the air. I step forward, and the floorboard groans underfoot.

"Honey, I—" I try to think, to offer some reasonable explanation for what could've caused this. Slowly, my eyes trail the walls, looking for evidence of a leaking pipe or something else, but there's nothing. Nothing in this room is wet except for the clothes, her bed, and her laptop. It's as if someone poured water directly on her things. But that's…impossible.

How would it have happened? Even if I want to believe her, how would it be possible for someone to sneak in here unseen, manage to somehow get—what, several glasses? A pitcher?—of water without being heard, and then leave without being noticed?

I cross the room to her window and run my fingers along the seam, pulling up gently, then with more force. It gives with a loud groan in protest, and after another tug, the window lifts.

My breathing catches as the breeze hits my skin, the scent of the lavender. It wasn't locked.

"Okay, so call me Sherlock, but maybe someone came in through the unlocked window," Greta offers, wincing.

It's a stretch. As we just heard, opening the window isn't exactly a stealthy task, and I still don't know how they would've gotten water into the room without drawing attention to themselves. But when I look back at Taylor, I know my arguments and excuses are pointless.

If I want her to stay here, I have to find the answer. I need to know what happened.

"I'll call the police," I say finally. "We can let them check this out, just in case."

It feels extreme, but I also don't really know what else to do. Adding a security system to my mental to-do list, I pull my phone from my pocket and dial the local number.

It takes around an hour for the police to arrive, and when they do, it's clearly the most exciting call this town's gotten in quite a while. There are four officers who arrive on scene, which I suspect might be the entire police force. Three women, one man. The Black woman who introduces herself as the sheriff is shorter than I am, her dark hair pulled back in tight braids.

She meets me at the door and asks us to replay everything that happened again. I tell her about the trash left in the room and the water this morning.

"And the neighbor who keeps an eye on the place? Where is he?"

"Conrad. I don't know a lot about him, other than that he's a neighbor, and he watches over Foxglove for Mom. I met him this morning, but he sort of...disappeared after we found the water."

"Disappeared?" She eyes me.

"Well, not disappeared, but he left. It was kind of

chaotic there for a minute, and I'm sure he felt like he was in the way."

"Right." Her gaze travels the room slowly as she thinks. "Can you describe Conrad for me?"

"He is in his late fifties or sixties, I'd say. Blondish-gray hair. Not too tall, definitely under six foot, but not too short, either. Average build. Tan."

"And where do you think he lives? Which direction? We'll want to talk to him. He might've seen someone lurking around."

"I'm...not sure. He was coming from this way when I saw him. There's a little path near the back corner of the meadow. There are several piles of hedge apples, unless he's already cleaned them up."

She nods, then turns to the officers behind her. "Cruz, you and Fox go try to find this neighbor. See if he saw anything."

The male officer, probably in his thirties with stark black hair and tan skin, steps back, following the lead of the woman who walks out first, her blonde hair pulled back in a tight bun that sits atop her head. It reminds me of the ballerina buns I used to struggle getting just right for Taylor. She always hated having her hair brushed.

Once they've left, the sheriff turns back to me. "Now, show me where the water appeared."

I take her down the hall, where Greta and Taylor are still working to get water out of her mattress with the towels we finally found. They stop what they're doing and stand up, turning to face us with straight spines and fearful expressions. Taylor's eyes find me as the sheriff gets closer.

She walks the length of the room, scanning the perimeter. Then she looks at Taylor. "And you were the one who first found the water?"

Taylor nods, hands clasped together in front of her waist. "I, um, I...got food on my shirt while we were cooking, so I came back to my room to change. That's when I saw the water. My laptop's ruined. My clothes, my bed...everything's drenched." She leans over and pushes in on the mattress, and a trickle of water gathers around her hand despite the amount of water we've already dried up, proving her point.

The sheriff looks up at the ceiling, then at me. "And there's no water in any of the other rooms? No signs of a leak?"

"No," Greta answers for me. "We checked right away. There's nothing. We have no idea where it could've come from."

"The window was unlocked," I add, reminding them all, searching for an explanation. "So someone could've come in through there and left." I pause. Though it's the most reasonable explanation, I know the logic doesn't hold up. "But they would've had to bring the water with them to not get noticed, and this is...a lot of water." I gesture to the pile of wet towels on the floor.

The sheriff steps out into the hall slowly, glancing into the bathroom. "Is there a back door?"

"No, just the front door. No other way in or out."

She clicks her pen, pointing up. "And what about upstairs?"

"There's a loft," I tell her. "But it only has one small window. No doors or anything."

She does a quick wave of her hand, which seems to mean something, because the remaining officer quickly shuffles past us and down the hall, poking her head into the bedroom that was once my grandma's but will soon be mine before she enters.

While she looks around, the sheriff draws my attention back to her. "Have you had any trouble like this before? Anyone hanging around at night?"

"To be honest, I don't know. I haven't stayed here since I was a kid, and I've visited fewer than a handful of times since then. My grandma used to live here, but she and my mom had a falling out when I was young, and we stopped visiting as much. The cabin was left to my mom after my grandma passed, but we only came back once right after Taylor was born. Mom had the neighbor, er, Conrad, check in to make sure the lawn is kept up and everything—essentially make sure the place doesn't burn down—but until now, no one has lived here. Conrad didn't mention any trouble when we spoke, but again, we didn't get to talk for very long."

The sheriff jots something down in her notepad. "We'll want your mother's phone number."

"Of course." I rattle it off to her, and she writes it down. I'm just relieved she doesn't ask me to call her. I don't want to have to dive into that trauma right now.

She scans the room silently. "It looks like someone's either moving in or moving out."

"In. My daughter and I." I gesture toward Taylor. "We found some trash in her room that looked recent when we arrived yesterday, and it worried us, but I ordered a new lock just to be safe. And then, of course, this morning I met Conrad, and now we're dealing with...the water."

She looks bored, and I realize I'm rambling. Repeating myself. "Have you spoken to your mother? Asked her if there was anyone else who might have a key?"

Great. Here we go. "I tried to call, but...we're not exactly on the best terms right now. She's not been returning most of my calls."

"Because you moved into the cabin?" she guesses.

"What? Oh. No." I try to decide how to sum up Mom's current issues with me. I missed her wedding, for one thing. A courthouse ceremony at the last minute. She surprised me with it, and asked me to attend on the day I was scheduled to meet with my lawyer a final time before the divorce decree was signed. And then there's the divorce itself, which she desperately didn't want me to get. Leaving Lewis, moving in here...it all feels like a betrayal to her, one that I can't undo. And then, of course, there's the new husband. The one closer to my age than hers. But somehow, I'm the one making the "life-ruining decisions." Those were her words in the last text she sent me.

I force the thoughts away, realizing the sheriff is still waiting for an answer. "She's got a lot going on right now. I'll try to call her again, but I really don't think anyone else has a key. No one else is really out here. I don't even know how close Conrad is, to be honest. We own the property, which is...forty acres, I think."

"It's secluded," the sheriff agrees. "But it helps to know your neighbors. When you need a cup of sugar or someone to look after things. Sounds like your mom got that part right." She opens her mouth to say something after a pause, but we're interrupted.

"Morris, you're going to want to see this."

The sheriff straightens as the officer calls to her, then moves forward past the three of us. I follow her quickly, not sure if I should, but it's my house, and—whatever it is—I need to know.

She steps into the bedroom at the end of the hall and looks to her left. "What is it?"

We follow her as she crosses the room to where the other officer is standing near the edge of the room. At first, I think she must be looking out the window, but then I realize she's looking down. She brushes her foot against a floorboard, pressing the toe of her boot into it so the board wiggles. "I noticed this was loose."

"This place is going to need some TLC," I say, wondering why on earth a loose floorboard is relevant to their investigation. "The flooring is original, as far as I know."

Without responding, the officer bends down, followed by the sheriff. She lifts her flashlight, which I'd hardly noticed she was holding. Then, before I realize what's happening, the sheriff grabs hold of the floorboard and tugs. Four additional boards go with it, all at once, like it's a...

"It's a door," Taylor says softly.

The officers don't look up. They stare down into the space.

"What's down there?" My stomach fills with ice-cold concrete as I hesitate to step forward.

Taylor moves around me to look, and I grab her arm on instinct, trying to stop her. Every hair on my arms stands on end. The air fills with the scent of mud and earth, something alive and dead all at once. It's so thick I can taste it on my tongue.

"Did you know you had a cellar?" The sheriff looks back over her shoulder at me.

My throat is dry as I move forward, past Taylor, to hover near the officer. "No. Are you sure that's what this is?"

"Looks like it." She leans her head down into the darkness, shining the light around. Through a mass of cobwebs in the corner so thick it may as well be a blanket, I see a dirt floor below. The part above the stairs has been torn. She uses her boot to knock down the remainder of the cobwebs, clearing our line of vision. "Looks like there are a few boxes down there, some old canning jars." She brushes cobweb strands from the toe of her boot. "If I were you, I'd figure out a way to put a lock on this door, too."

My blood freezes in my veins. "You think someone came in through the floor?"

"I wouldn't worry. The cobweb probably tore when we opened the door. I don't see any other doors leading outside down there, and the space is small enough that I don't think anyone could hide without you hearing them. But if I were you, I'd do it just to be safe. Get a little sliding lock or something to bolt it closed when you're not using it." She shivers, looking around. "When does your new lock for the front door get here?"

"It should be here sometime tomorrow. I'll order one for this door, too. I'm sure I can figure something out."

"If you run into town, check Randy's Hardware. He'll have what you need," she tells me. "It's on the square." Her urgency for the lock worries me, and I can't help thinking this must be exactly how someone got in, even if she won't say it.

"Thanks."

She nods. "As for the water, if there's no other way in or out, I'm guessing you had someone come in through the window, like you mentioned. I'd make sure all the entrances are locked now. We may be a small town, but that doesn't mean we don't have our fair share of issues." She pauses. "Though I can't say I've really ever heard of trouble this far out of town. Family squabbles, that sort of thing, sure, but nothing like this. I'll, uh...I'll file a report and see what we can find out about the neighbor, but whatever's going on, make sure everything's locked up, at least until people figure out the cabin is occupied now. Should get you fixed up. Seems like a harmless prank, either way." She glances at Taylor. "I realize that doesn't fix your laptop, but it could be worse, you know?"

Taylor shoots me a look, like she can't believe she just said that.

"Thank you, Sheriff Morris." I hold out my hand to shake hers. "We're sorry you had to drive out here."

"It's no trouble. We've got your number. If we learn anything interesting or concerning from your neighbor, I'll give you a shout, okay?"

With that, Greta walks her to the door, and I stand there, staring down at the cellar door I never knew existed. What other secrets is Foxglove hiding?

CHAPTER NINE

CORINNE WILDE - PRESENT DAY

With the police officers gone, Greta comes to find me in my bedroom. Without a lock, I've piled several heavy boxes on the cellar door for now.

She folds her arms across her chest, studying me. "You really had no idea that was there?"

"No. We never came in her bedroom, really. And the few times we did, she had furniture all along the walls, plus that big rug that covered most of the room, remember? If Mom knew about it, she never mentioned it. I can ask her next time we talk."

There must be something in my voice that hints at more than I've said because Greta turns her head toward me. "She's still not speaking to you?"

"I mean, we've spoken a few times, but she's short with me. She hates that I've let this happen, and she's convinced I could fix it if I tried. She loves Lewis. Sometimes I think she loves him more than me."

I try to make a joke of it, but we both know it's not one. From the moment I brought Lewis home to meet Mom, she has been completely taken by him. She finds him charming, funny, and outright perfect. And I'll admit, most days, so do I. But what is it they say? You don't divorce the same person you married, or something like that.

The divorce brought out the nastiest sides of us both, and now it's hard to see him or hear his name and not remember how we fought across that table, via our lawyers, for the scraps from our marriage. For the china cabinet and our record collection and every piece of furniture we bought together.

I still know, deep down, that we are the good parts of our marriage as well as the bad. The happy days and the date nights and the family vacations. The times he took care of me when I was sick and how he cheered me on during my book's publication. The times we drank champagne to celebrate his promotion to regional manager of his office, and the weeks I held us together after his mother passed. When we were good, we were really, really good. But when we were bad...when times got tough, neither of us was willing to fight for it anymore.

My mom—widowed but first divorced—would've rather I stayed where I wasn't wanted, had me fight Lewis as he decided to leave, than to give in, give up, and walk away.

"Well, I love you enough for the both of us," Greta

teases, crossing the room to wrap her arms around me and plant a kiss on my cheek.

I hum a laugh and rest my head against her shoulder. "I know you do."

"Besides, I'm sure she's just distracted by her new hubby."

I fake a gag. "Don't remind me."

"Does he expect you to call him Daddy now?"

I pull back and swat her arm. "Don't be disgusting."

She snorts and turns away, moving to leave the room, but she stops. "Hey, you know what? Why don't you and Tay come and stay with me for a while? Until your new locks can be installed and things calm down."

It's tempting. Greta has a house big enough for the three of us to live comfortably together. It's closer to all of Taylor's friends, her school, everything. But part of me knows that if we move in with her, it will be too hard to leave. To return here. It would be too hard to drag Taylor away from her home and previous life for a second time.

"I would love that, but we can't." My face wrinkles with sadness that seeps into my core, like a cold stream of water. I can picture it—the three of us curled up on Greta's couch watching a horror movie with all our favorite snacks. Midnight ice cream sundaes in the kitchen where we have dance parties all night and talk about boys. The two of us giving Taylor relationship advice and celebrating as she opens her college admission packets.

It could be a beautiful life for all of us. I'm not blind to that fact.

"You can. I have plenty of room, and it would be no trouble. Honestly, you'd be helping me out. You can feed Mr. Whiskers when I'm out late at work. You know I'd love having you both there."

"I know, but I can't do that to you or Taylor. Or myself, if I'm being honest. I promised myself after the divorce, I'd learn to stand on my own two feet, be an example for Taylor. If we move in with you, it'd be the opposite of that. I'll love you forever for offering, but I just can't."

She chews on her bottom lip. "I don't like the two of you being out here alone."

"We're not alone. We have Conrad." I have no idea if that's true. Nor do I have any idea if Conrad would help us should we need it. But he's nearby. He's been watching this place for Mom. And he did come running when he heard Taylor scream. If nothing else, it feels better knowing we have someone else in the vicinity. That it's not just us and the trees.

Greta gives me a knowing look but doesn't push the issue. "Well, the offer's always there if you change your mind."

CHAPTER TEN

MARY WILDE - 1649

It's strange, the way men have begun to look at me. To notice me, wherever I am. Not bad, necessarily. Just... strange. Try as I might, I can no longer miss the admiring glances, the shy smiles, and the whispered conversations between them whenever I enter a room. Even the boys I've befriended over the years have begun to act differently.

I try not to let it bother me. Honestly, I do. I'm fourteen, and my mother has prepared me for womanhood. For being a wife someday. I know some of what will be expected of me when I marry.

Still, I didn't think it would be so soon. When Mama mentioned I would have a visitor yesterday, I thought it might be Margaret or Jane. Instead, it was Thomas Bingham. He will be the first of many, Mama has said. Suitors from the village, some may even come from towns far away. I can't disappoint her, and I won't, but I can't help feeling like a cloak has been ripped off my head, like I'm no longer as hidden and safe as I once was.

Tonight, after the sun has gone to rest below the trees, Mama calls me into the parlor. The air in the house is thick with the scent of the evening's wood smoke. The fire crackles softly, lighting Mama's face and casting shadows across the room.

When I was a young girl, I was fascinated by the shadows. I'd sit for hours watching them dance before they eventually faded away with the dying fire. Lately, I realize I haven't had the time to be interested in such childish things.

I drag the blanket I've been quilting behind me as I take a seat next to the fire, studying Mama. She's beautiful, her long, wavy hair draped down over her shoulders. She sits in the chair knitting a scarf, her eyes steady on her work, but still as piercing as ever.

She reminds me of my gran more than ever now, since we've lost her. Her skin is softer, lines appearing where they once were not, and the slightest hints of silver have begun to lace through her hair.

"You're nearly finished," she says, looking over at the blanket in my lap. My hands set to work again, the way she and Gran taught me. Upstairs, I can hear Anna running circles in the attic. She loves to play up there, but Papa doesn't always let her. Tonight feels different. Important. He retired to bed early, and now I suspect I know why.

"In time for winter, I hope," I tell her.

Her smile is soft, but it doesn't reach her eyes. Outside, the wind whistles through the trees, and I can hear it from right where I sit, feel it coming in through the cracks of the old house.

"What did you think of young Mr. Bingham?"

My fingers stop moving. "He was...polite."

Mama seems positively delighted by my comment, though I'm not sure why. "I suppose there are worse things a young man can be."

"I suppose there are." Slowly, my fingers start to work again, and I rock in my chair. The sounds of the chair against the wood floor fill the room.

"Sit still, child," she says, her voice low but firm. "We need to talk."

A strange sort of feeling fills the air, but I don't know what it is. Tension, maybe. Worry. Dread. I sense something is coming, but I have yet to figure out what it might be.

"Thomas Bingham's family is decent," she says softly. "He would treat you well. Keep you close to us, until Foxglove becomes yours."

I turn my head slowly. "I'm not yet ready to marry, if that's what you mean."

"I don't know if anyone is ever ready."

I study her, and there's that odd feeling again. "Were you ready when you married Papa?" She must've been. They're so happy. Not at all like other parents I've seen in the village.

She lets out a long breath, setting her knitting down

on her lap. Her eyes meet mine, warming, but when she speaks, there's something heavy in her tone. A truth, a wisdom that feels like a secret. "You're nearly fifteen, Mary. Growing up. And with that comes responsibility."

I frown. "I am responsible. I clean and cook and help Papa with the animals. I mend our clothes and help Anna with her reading."

"All of those qualities will make you a brilliant wife." She pauses, leaning back in her seat. "And mother, someday."

I don't dare argue, though my hands are icy, and my stomach feels like the time we were all bedridden with sickness, when only the warm whiskey Mama prepared would stay down.

I know it's coming, but that doesn't mean I'm ready.

"There's more to it than that," she tells me, her voice gentle and low. Her words carry a weight that I feel in my chest, like she's covering me up, tucking me in. "Being a Wilde woman comes with its own set of responsibilities, you know. This house and everything that comes with it is a part of who you are, my darling. And it will be yours —to protect and to tend to—someday. Whatever man you marry will have to understand that."

She picks up her knitting again. "You've seen how the village treats your father for his choices. You shall need a strong man to stand by your side just as well."

I open my mouth to ask if she thinks Thomas Bingham could possibly be that husband. I don't see it— he's rather nervous if you ask me, not all like Papa—but she holds her hand up and I go quiet. Her eyes lock onto mine, and I get that feeling again that tells me she can see straight through my thoughts, can split the earth and pierce stone.

"There will be others. Suitors who come to court you. Men who will say kind things, sweet things. Many of them will promise you love and safety. Some of them may mean it. You will be the lady of the house, and you will leave Foxglove—and me—to build a life with the man you choose. But you must listen to me, my love, and remember what I'm telling you."

A shiver crawls up my spine like a line of ants, and I tremble at her words. The way she's looking at me now, I feel as if nothing will ever be the same. Whatever she says next, *I* will never be the same.

"No man can ever know what we know. About Foxglove. About her secrets."

Though she's never said it outright, my mother and Gran have both hinted at variations of this. The secrets of our house belong to Wilde women alone. "I know the rules."

"You think that it has been hard, keeping the truth from your father, but wait until it is the man you love from whom you must keep secrets."

"But why do we have to? Don't you trust Papa?"

She stops knitting again, this time clasping her hands together in her lap. "It is not about trust. Or even love. I know it is hard to understand, but you must. You must understand. Foxglove has rules, rules that came long before you or I were ever thought of. If you break the rules, if you tell anyone outside of our blood—any man especially—you will pay a price." She pauses, letting the words wash over me. "And so will they."

Bewilderment passes through me. What she's saying can't possibly be real. It's like the bedtime stories she once told me to keep me in bed at night, meant to scare me from wandering the house. "This all sounds like rubbish," I admit. "Unfair, even if it is true."

Her eyes go distant, her gaze softening as though she's looking right through me, though her face hasn't turned away. "Foxglove chooses us. Protects us. Keeps us, and us alone, safe from the world outside. A world which has not always been kind to women like us. And because of that, as a thank you for that, we protect her secrets. Fair or not, that is the life you have been given. The burden and the blessing."

"What if I don't want to stay here? What if the man I marry has a grand manor, or a whole estate—like Joan's husband?"

Her eyes darken with something old and fierce, something that frightens me, seems to frighten her. "When I am gone, you and your sister will decide how to protect Foxglove. I trust that you will do what is best for the both of you. And your families. But, Mary, there have been men in the past...men who thought they could hold our hearts and therefore Foxglove herself. Her power. Her secrets. Our ancestors, the Wilde women who came before us, some of them thought love would be enough."

She looks down, and I know this isn't going to be the happy ending I was hoping for.

"People in this world get consumed by power. By greed. Even the men we love. Even we ourselves. The very magic that keeps us safe can be a curse in the wrong hands."

"Magic?" The word feels heavy and thick on my tongue. "Not real magic." My words lift, like a question, but I'm not sure there is one. I'm not a child anymore. I don't believe in such things.

A slow, grim smile touches her lips, but there's no warmth to her expression. She leans back in her chair and closes her eyes. "Love is magic, my darling. Hope. Trust." Her eyes open. "Hate. Speaking your wishes out loud to the trees, that's magic. The way your Gran planted rosemary in the garden, the way she spoke to the plants to nourish them. The way I weave flowers into your hair to make you feel brave. Magic isn't always fairies and magic spells. Sometimes it's just choosing to believe in something. Sometimes it's just knowing."

I swallow, my throat itchy. "What happened to the men? The ones who wanted Foxglove? They died?"

"Sometimes." Her voice is as dry as the leaves in the fall. "But there are fates worse than death. Foxglove does not allow her secrets to be stolen, Mary. I don't tell you any of this lightly. I tell you this because, someday, you will need to know. Someday, you will pass this knowledge down to your daughters. And someday, I may not be here to tell you myself."

A strange, cold weight settles in my chest, and I think of Gran. I wonder when she told this to my mother. Wonder if Mama wishes she were here now.

"Is there love without trust?" I ask her softly. "Can you really love Papa if he doesn't know you? Doesn't that just make you ache with sadness?" A soft pain fills me as I think of my friends who won't share this burden. Who will marry men who love them and who will not be forced to keep secrets. It makes me feel dreadfully alone.

Mama stands from her chair, crossing the room to look out the window at the forest. The moonlight outside illuminates her face, the cool blue cast warring with the orange reflection of the fire on her cheek.

"I love your father, yes. The way I hope you and your sister will love your husbands someday. He has been a good man to me. A good father to you. But you must never forget that Foxglove is your true love, Mary. She will never betray you. Never hurt you. Never lie to you."

"But Papa hasn't hurt you."

Her hands go to either side of the window, to the stones holding our house together. "If you let her, my love, Foxglove will teach you the most valuable lesson any woman could ever learn. One that neither I nor your gran could ever teach you alone. It is not a lesson in being a wife or a mother, but a woman. A woman existing in a world that will do everything to control you. No matter how much you wish it so, Foxglove will never share its full self with a man." She looks over her shoulder at me, and I hold my breath, waiting for her next words. "And neither should you."

I nod as her words sink into my bones, chilling me. I don't understand. None of this aligns with everything she has told me about love and marriage. I am supposed to find a husband who will love me, who will take care of me. Who will protect me. Still, because she is my mother and because I know it's important to her, I hear myself saying, "I understand."

She reads me like always, like the primer from which I learned in the village school. "No," she says, turning her back to me again to look out the window. "No, you don't. But you will. In time, I'm afraid you will."

CHAPTER ELEVEN

CORINNE WILDE - PRESENT DAY

We spend the rest of the day cleaning and organizing, and Greta strings a clothesline across the house to dry most of Taylor's things. We blast music and dance around while we unpack, but the mood is less than happy. Taylor is angry over her ruined belongings and frustrated by the lack of answers, while Greta worriedly chews the skin around her fingernails when she thinks I'm not looking.

I'm just trying to keep them both calm.

The next day, Greta stays until the new lock arrives so she can help me install it.

"You two should really come back with me," she says again as I stand back, admiring my handiwork.

My hands on my hips, I look at her. "What? You don't think I installed it well?"

"No." She shakes her head, hands in the air. "It's not that. I just...with all of this going on—"

"You know we can't come back with you. We live here now."

Her incredulous gaze scans Foxglove, and I'm almost offended. "Even if you can't stay with me forever, just come to ride out the storm tomorrow. It's supposed to get really bad."

"Hey, at least we have a cellar now." I shrug one shoulder, teasing, but it's true.

She puffs out a slow breath. "Maybe you should call him."

It takes me a second to realize what she's said, a second longer to decide whom she means.

"No."

"I'm worried about you both out here. I don't like this."

"We're going to be fine," I promise her. "I'll keep her safe."

She bumps my arm with hers, her eyes going soft and filled with worry. "Sure, but who's going to keep *you* safe?"

Her concern makes my chest ache. Throughout the divorce, it's been easy to feel as if I'm alone. That I've lost the person who was supposed to care about me, to protect me. But here Greta is, once again, reminding me that that person has always been her.

"I promise we'll be okay." I have no way of knowing that for sure, but even as I say it, it feels true.

"And you ordered a lock that will work for the cellar door?"

"Yes," I confirm. "And I'll keep boxes on top of it until the lock gets here."

She stares at me long and hard, her eyes bouncing back and forth between mine. I know there's so much she wants to say, so much I want to say to her.

"Thank you," I whisper. For so much. For everything. I don't say that, though. I can't speak, but she seems to understand.

She pulls me into a hug, her arms going tight around my shoulders.

This goodbye feels heavier than ever. Before, we saw each other nearly every day. Whether we were meeting for lunch, she was bringing something over for Taylor or me, or she was popping by for dinner, it was rare more than a day would go by without seeing each other in some form or another. We found excuses. It was easy enough to do when she was just a quick thirteen-minute drive across town. Now, we're half a day's drive apart. It feels like crossing an ocean to get to the person who has never been more than half an hour away from me our whole lives.

Still, as we load her bags in the car an hour later, I put on a brave face and hug her again. "Be safe going home."

"I don't want to leave," she says, looking around. "I wish I could stay a few more days. Are you sure you don't need me to? I could have someone else do my showings."

I press my lips together, knowing what she wants me to say—what I want to say—but I can't. I have to do this on my own, or I never will. "But then EJ might get a chance to outsell you this month."

She points a long, painted nail at me. "Blasphemy."

I cover my lips with a laugh. "You're welcome to stay as long as you'd like, but no, we don't need you. Go home and get some rest on something other than a mattress on the floor."

"I didn't hate the mattress on the floor," she tells me, bottom lip pressed out. We're grown women fighting against tears at the thought of leaving each other.

"We'll come back home and visit you soon." We both know it's a lie. I will avoid that town until I have no other choice. I have no desire to return to a town that reeks of Lewis, a town where I can't unsee him the way I can here.

To rid my thoughts, I suck in a deep breath. The calming scents of the lavender and rosemary plants near the porch hit my nose, my throat. I close my eyes as tears fill them.

"And you'll call about a security system?" she asks, her voice tight and stiff.

It's about the hundredth time she's asked. "Yes."

"Today?"

I groan. "Yes."

She hugs me again, then Taylor, drying her eyes when she pulls back. "Ugh, okay. Fine. Kick me out, why don't you? Call me if you need anything, okay? And please make sure you lock everything up."

"We'll be fine," I assure her, nudging her toward her

car. "We love you, and we'll miss you. Watch your speed on the gravel, okay?"

"Now it's your turn to worry, hmm?" she teases, pulling her phone out of her back pocket to check the time.

"Always." I squeeze her hand and blow her a kiss.

With a final look, she slides into the driver's seat and returns our blown kisses as she drives away. A tickle itches the back of my throat as I watch her leave, that lonely feeling sinking into my gut once again.

I throw an arm around Taylor's shoulders as I lead her inside. "What do you say I make pasta for dinner?"

"Sure. Whatever."

She's sad Greta's leaving too, even if she won't admit it. Greta's the closest thing to an aunt she has on either side of the family, the closest thing I've ever had to a sister. She's been there for every milestone for Taylor, every school holiday pageant and every science fair.

The guilt I feel over separating the two of them, even if it's just by extra miles, is heavy. Heavier maybe than my guilt over the divorce itself.

Inside, while Taylor lounges on the couch, I return to my bedroom. The cellar door draws my eye like a siren's call I can't turn away from. Everything about it keeps nagging me. An itchy feeling has taken root under my skin that I can't ignore, a pull from somewhere deep in my gut.

Carefully, I slide the boxes away from the door. It's heavier than I imagined as I lift it and stare down into the darkness. Using my shoe like the sheriff did earlier, I clear away the remaining cobwebs, holding onto the wall for support.

I grab my phone from my back pocket and turn on my flashlight, staring down at the dirt floor below. That damp scent hits me again, mud that seems to cake my throat. It's as if I'm lying in the dirt myself, the rank scent enveloping me. Dirt and dampness and stale air. Below the door is a set of stairs I could take to lower myself down into it.

My heart picks up speed in my chest at the thought.

I lean down farther, trying to get a better look at what might be waiting for me. There's a stack of boxes in the far corner, though they look as if they've gotten wet and are falling apart. They're very old, probably older than if my grandma had been the one to leave them.

There's a shelf along the back wall with a few jars on it. The only other thing I see in this cellar—aside from whatever bugs and rodents might be lurking—is dust.

I wonder who the last person to be down here was. I picture my grandma—or her grandma, even—coming down to the cellar to get vegetables canned straight from the garden for her family. I imagine how the cool, damp air must've been a nice respite from the hottest days of summer.

I can't resist the temptation to explore the space, the opportunity to feel closer to the women who came before me in whatever way I can. Slowly, I place my foot on the first step, pushing down with as much weight as I can muster. The wood creaks underfoot, but it remains steady. Steady enough I feel confident it can hold me.

I move down to the next step, sucking in a breath of stale air. It reminds me of summers spent climbing over fallen logs and hiding inside the hollow trunks of trees in the woods.

As I ease down into the darkness, the possibility that someone might've come in the house this way knocks on the back of my skull like a pulse. The sheriff said it wasn't likely, but that doesn't mean impossible. There are shadowy spaces down here, hiding places. For a brief second, I pause, shining the light around once more, and I have to choose.

To decide.

I look back at the safety of my bedroom, my two options swirling in my mind, but in the end, it doesn't feel like a choice. I have to know.

The first and second steps hold me well, but as I put my weight on the third step, I hear it crack. Feel it start to give. Panic seizes my lungs. There is only a second to process that it's happening as the wood splits completely underfoot. My foot slips forward. I reach behind me, then sideways, grasping for the wood of the stairs or a rail that doesn't exist, trying anything—everything—to stop my fall. I slam into the next step, then the next, my tailbone on fire. I tumble forward, launching off the stairs and into the dirt.

I land with a thud, my nose scraping against the hard ground before I roll to my side with a yelp. For a moment, I lie in the stillness, catching my bearings. My stomach roils with fresh fear as hot as soup. I inhale deeply, puffing out a breath between my lips slowly, trying and failing to slow my heart.

I'm alive. I'm okay.

My hand goes to my nose first. It stings white-hot from the gash across the bridge, and warm blood dots the wound already. I'm okay. Nothing's broken as far as I can tell, but it burns terribly as I fan the blood.

I'm sore. My body feels worn and broken as I try to sit up, radiating fiery pain in some places and seeming to vibrate with dull throbbing in others.

I look around for my phone and find it a few feet away, wincing as I slip it into my pocket. The ground below me is damp and hard, and the air is stale and heavy, as if it isn't quite air at all, but something thicker, heavier. I check the stairs, my eyes flitting with fear as I remember it's my only point of exit. The third step is busted in the middle, but the rest seem unaffected by my fall.

Carefully, I stand and cross the shadowy cellar, my muscles and bones stiff and sore. I'm definitely going to be bruised by morning, if I'm not already.

I'm not trapped down here. I can make it up using the stairs that haven't broken, I just have to be more cautious when testing them. I got too confident, too trusting of the old wood. Still, being down here fully makes each breath feel a little bit more difficult. My body is as tight as a stretched rubber band—both from the fall and from the fear of this place. Of being trapped, though I know I am not, and of what I might find down here.

It's like the quintessential basement in every horror movie, and though I have to know what's down here, there's a part of me that wonders if I'll regret looking. I breathe in the dusty scent of the cool, damp air as I make my way to the row of old, wooden shelves. There are a few old jars, labeled in a scratchy handwriting I don't recognize.

Beans
Carrots
Pickles
Tomatoes
Beets
Corn

I'm shocked by how well the food appears to have held up over the years, though I wouldn't dare eat it. Still, it's a little time capsule left for me, most likely from my grandma. A piece of history I'm grateful to have. Once, she must have had meals planned for these foods. I wonder what happened. Why they weren't eaten.

It's hard not to picture the shelves filled with vegetables from the garden—meals just waiting to be made. Grandma was always a brilliant cook, and she was never afraid of the hard work it took to run this house on her own.

I'm tossed into my memories of her suddenly.

I remember the chickens she kept on the property and the large garden she tended. I remember how she'd wake me each morning with a kiss to the head, telling me the sun was waiting for me to come outside. I remember eating tomatoes right off the vine, or slicing them up, adding mayonnaise on a slice of bread, and eating it as a sandwich. I remember how she'd pour lavender and rosemary oils into my bathwater, how she'd sprinkle it with flower petals and tell me to call the fairies to come and play. How she'd serve every drink in a teacup, just because she could. I remember sitting on her porch learning to braid wildflowers, repeating each of their names and the special things they could do.

Wisteria for deep pain.
Valerian for sleep.
Lavender for stress.
Chamomile for the belly.
St. John's Wort for sadness.
Marigold for infections.
Yarrow to stop bleeding.

She said it to me often, as if she wanted me to memorize it. And I guess in the end I did. She made the most mundane things feel special, and that will forever be her legacy for me.

Passing the shelves, I move on to the boxes sitting in the back corner of the room. To call them boxes at this point is generous. As soon as I touch the cardboard, they deteriorate under my fingers, damp clumps falling to the dirt.

I wonder if Mom knows this is down here. Would she want any of it?

I pick up a white onesie, stained brown across the front. It might've belonged to Mom once, which is strange to think about.

I've never seen any of Mom's baby clothes, nor much from her childhood. From what she's told me and what I remember, Grandma was incredibly frugal. She used to take all the old bars of soap that had been worn down to slivers and put them in her soap dispenser, mixing them with water to make a concoction that could be used as liquid soap.

Shirts were torn to make rags, and jars were reused again and again for one thing or another. She made everything last, only bought what she couldn't make herself, and donated anything she didn't need.

That's why it feels odd to find this box of things they clearly meant to keep. Under the first layer of old clothes, I spot a stack of old photographs. They're covered in a film of dust, but once I dust it off, I'm surprised to see the first one is of me as a child.

I'm...maybe three or four here. Dressed in a strawberry dress and matching bonnet. In the next photo, I'm a little older. Or, at least, my hair is a little longer, tied back in pigtails. I'm standing in front of the cabin with my arms around a child I don't recognize. A baby. She's around a year old, maybe two, with hair so stark blonde it's almost invisible in the bright sun.

I bring the photo closer to my face, trying to discern who this baby might be. She's not anyone I recognize. Maybe a cousin. I believe there are a few on my great-aunt Marie's side, but it seems unlikely there would be any photos of us together. Grandma's sister died before I was born, and as far as I know, her kids didn't stay in touch. So who is this baby standing next to me, and why don't I remember her?

I place the photo to the side, digging through the rest of the stack quickly. There are a few more photos of the two of us, all around the same time and age before I reach the bottom of the stack. The rest of the box contains an old wooden dog that must've been a toy at some point, a soft-bristled baby's hairbrush, an empty trinket box, and more clothes. Standing up, I brush off my knees and the seat of my pants and cross the cellar again. There's nothing else down here—just shadows and dust.

Still, I take one of the photos of the young girl and me.

I climb the steps out of the cellar slowly, easing my weight onto each one before I commit. Once I'm out, I suck in a deep breath of the fresh air and study the photo again. I wait for the memory to come back to me, for me to recall who this baby is. A friend of the family, perhaps. A child Grandma babysat.

I pull my phone from my pocket, already knowing

she won't answer, but I have to try. Maybe if the police have reached out, she'll finally speak to me.

To my surprise, after a few rings, the line connects.

"Hello?" It's not my mom's voice that answers, though.

"I need to speak to my mom."

EJ's pretentious tone is like nails on a chalkboard. He thinks he's better than me, that he's more important to my mom than I am. The problem is, he's not wrong about that part, and I hate him for it. "Sorry, Rin. She doesn't want to talk to you."

His use of the nickname I've never liked and certainly never gave him permission to use sets my chest on fire. "I didn't ask that. I need to speak with her."

"She's unavailable," he says, his voice calm and casual.

I hate him, I hate him, I hate him. "I know she's mad at me."

"She just needs some time. You really hurt her."

I want to scream, to yell, to lash out, to grab him through the phone and throttle him, but I don't. "EJ, can you please put her on the phone?"

In the background, I hear her voice, though I can't make out what she's saying.

"Sorry. She says she'll have to call you back."

"We both know she won't."

He clears his throat. "Take care, Rin."

The call ends, and I toss my phone onto a pile of clothes, opening my mouth to scream though I don't allow a sound to slip out. I fling my arms down at my sides, throwing a silent tantrum just to make myself feel better.

And it does. Slightly.

I pick up my phone again once I've calmed down and scroll through my contacts, looking for my great-aunt's number.

If Mom wants to keep being childish and petty, fine. She can talk to me when she's ready, but I refuse to beg.

If anyone besides Mom would know who this baby is, it would be Aunt Lydia, my grandma's sister-in-law and one of the last living members of our family. She takes so long to answer, I'm preparing to leave a voicemail when she finally picks up.

"Heya, honey."

I smile at the sound of her voice. It's soothing at a time when I need it most. "Hey, Aunt Lydia. What are you up to?"

"Oh, I was just getting in from the grocery store. I've been meaning to call and check on you. Are you at Foxglove already? All settled in?"

"Yep, yeah. We got here a few days ago."

"Your mom said you were going to be there this week. How are you...?" Her words trail off, like she was going to add more—*doing, settling in, feeling, perhaps*—but the question isn't about the house or settling into a new place, and we both know it.

"I'm good," I promise her. A lie, but she doesn't push me on it. "It's weird...being back, you know?"

"That place is a little slice of magic right here on

God's green earth," she tells me wistfully. "I think it's good you've gone back. And besides, I shouldn't say this, but I always thought you were too good for Lewis."

I pause, hearing her words. I want to thank her, but she's wrong. And though she doesn't mean to be, it feels cruel. I was never too good for Lewis. And I would hope no one would call him too good for me.

Once, we were perfect. Happy and silly and beautifully perfect. The only thing we're guilty of is growing apart. Growing up. Being different people at forty than we were at seventeen. I have loved him longer than I was ever without him, and a signed paper and months of arguing doesn't change that. At least not for me.

"Have you heard from Mom lately?"

She hesitates. "Is she still upset with you?"

"No," I say, attempting to cover the truth. The last thing I need is for her to let it slip to Mom that I've been gossiping about her. "We just keep missing each other, so I haven't had a chance to check in since we arrived. Actually, that's partly why I called you."

I grip the photo, holding it out so I can see it clearly. "I found an old cellar at Foxglove I didn't know existed. Did you know we had one?"

"A cellar?" she asks, her voice soft. "You know, now that you mention it...I do think your grandpa might've said something about a cellar once. I never thought too much about it. Storm cellars were common back when Foxglove was built." She releases a soft hum.

"What did he tell you about it?"

She clicks her tongue. "I'm not sure. Maybe just that it existed. Honey, I'm sorry, I don't remember exactly. That was right around the time he died, now that I think of it." She lets out a soft breath. "I'd forgotten about it until now. Why do you ask?"

I start to tell her about the cellar, but something stops me. She called it a storm cellar, but that's not what this is. Whatever my grandfather told her, she doesn't know about this place. Not really. Until I say something, this secret that would have otherwise died with Grandma might only be mine. There's no reason *not* to tell Aunt Lydia, it's just a room of old, dusty shelves and dirt, but the words catch in my throat, and I can't. More than that, I don't want to.

"It's probably nothing. I found some old jars of vegetables and a box of photos."

She hums. "I'd love to see the photos, especially any of your grandpa Charles. It's like a time capsule. Gosh, I miss him some days." She laughs. "You remind me a lot of him, you know?"

She's mentioned it before. "I can send you some if I see any. I'll go back through them."

"That's sweet of you, honey. Thank you."

"Actually, the reason I'm calling is that I found a photo of me when I was a little girl. I was maybe four or five in the photo, and I'm standing with another girl I don't recognize. She's much younger than I was, probably only about one, with bright, almost-white, blonde hair."

She clicks her tongue, thinking. "Hmm. I don't know who that would be. Maybe one of your grandma's friends' grandbabies or something. Your mom would probably remember better than I could."

"Can I send you a picture of it, just in case? Maybe it'll jog your memory."

"Well, sure, honey. I can take a look."

"I'm going to send it here in just a few minutes, okay? You can call me back if she looks familiar."

"If I can figure out where my glasses are..." she mumbles, more to herself than anything. "Okay, honey. Talk soon."

I end the call and snap a photo of the picture before sending it to Aunt Lydia.

CHAPTER TWELVE

CORINNE WILDE - PRESENT DAY

Taylor is in the shower later, and I'm working on unpacking some of the boxes in the living room when my phone rings.

I set down the photo album I'm holding and hurry across the room, expecting Aunt Lydia to be calling me back.

Instead, it's a number I don't recognize.

"Hello?"

"Hello, may I speak to Corinne Wilde, please?"

"Speaking." What is it about that introduction that always makes my shoulders tense?

"Ma'am, this is Alison with Franklin Connections on a recorded line. I'm calling because we received your request to move your installation up?"

"Oh." Relief bubbles in my stomach. "Yes. Right."

"We're not able to get you in today, but it does look

like we might have time to have one of our technicians out there tomorrow. The only problem is that they'd be squeezing you in if one of their appointments finishes up early, so we wouldn't be able to give you an arrival window. We'd need someone over the age of eighteen to be available all day. Is that something you're interested in?"

"Um, yes. That would be okay. That's amazing, actually. Thank you."

"You're welcome. We do charge an eighty-dollar service fee for priority service, on top of the ninety-nine-dollar fee for your installation. We require you to pay the priority fee up front. Will you authorize me to charge the card on file with us?"

I swallow. I don't have eighty extra dollars, not really. My accounts are basically drained after the divorce. What's in there has to last us until I turn in my next manuscript to my editor.

I glance toward the bathroom as I hear the shower shut off and think of Taylor. She doesn't even have a working computer right now, but she still needs Wi-Fi for her phone.

It's the only chance I have of making her happy here. Of convincing her to stay.

I'll have to make it work.

"Yes, of course. That's fine."

"Excellent. You'll receive an email confirmation of your payment and instructions for your installation appointment tomorrow. As a reminder, your technician can arrive any time between eight and five, and your appointment is scheduled to take up to an hour. You'll get a text when your tech is on the way. Do you have any other questions for me at this time?"

"Nope, that was it. Thank you."

I end the call just as Taylor steps out into the hallway. She looks over at me. "Were you talking to me?"

"No." I lock my phone. "That was the internet company. They'll be out here tomorrow to get us up and running."

Her eyes light up, and that's all it takes for me to know it's all worth it. "Really?"

"Mm-hmm."

"It's about time." She turns away from me, disappearing into her bedroom.

I sigh. I know I should say something about her attitude, but there's a sense of helplessness that set in the moment I signed the divorce papers. A realization that she could leave me, if she wanted to. That she's only a few months away from leaving me anyway. I just want her to feel at home here, whatever it takes.

My phone vibrates in my hand, and I glance down.

"Aunt Lydia."

Her voice is soft in my ear. "Hey, honey. Sorry, I had to run to town, but I just had a chance to look at your picture."

"And? Do you recognize the little girl?"

She sighs. "I do. I recognize both of 'em, but, honey, it's not you in that photo. It's your mom."

"What?" We look just alike, if so. "Are you sure?"

"Couldn't be more positive. And that little girl..." She pauses. "It's your aunt Violet."

Impossible.

"What?"

"Your mom's sister."

"My mom doesn't have a sister."

"Vi was just a baby when she disappeared. Your grandma didn't talk about her much after... It was too hard. Especially with your grandpa having passed just a few weeks earlier. It was a lot for Hazel's heart to carry all at once. But Violet existed. I should say I'm surprised your mom didn't tell you about her, but I guess I'm not. They were so young."

I pause, processing. "You're telling me I have an aunt who...disappeared? Died? What?"

"Well, far as I know, we never got answers. She was only one, I think—maybe two—when she disappeared. So right around when that picture was taken. The police came in and did a whole investigation. I was stationed in Arizona then, but I took leave and came home a few months after it happened. Your great-aunt Marie came into town, too. Your grandmother was a mess, as you can imagine. It shook the whole family, you know? And, well, they questioned a bunch of the people in town and all your family's acquaintances, but nothing ever came of it."

"And they just, what, gave up on her?" Something cold slithers through my stomach.

"Well, not so much gave up on her as lost hope. It was too hard on your grandma to talk about. Too hard on all of us. Doesn't mean we didn't miss her, or think about her, but...she was gone. Wasn't anything any of us could do about it once the police gave up. Case turned cold, or whatever they call it. They seemed to think she'd fallen into the creek, and if that was the case, there was no telling where she ended up."

I shiver as if I'm the one in the icy cold water. I'm not sure what to make of this story. It feels impossible that this entire person was once part of our family, and I've never even heard her name.

"I, um..." I clear my throat. "What do *you* think happened to her?"

She's quiet for a while. Almost too long. But eventually, her answer comes. "If I had to say, I guess I agree with the police. Those woods are perfect for exploring, but that doesn't mean they aren't dangerous. It would be easy for a child to get lost, to slip and fall into the water or into a small ravine. I think she and your mother were out there playing and she fell."

"Do you think Mom remembers it?"

She sniffles. "Now? No. But then...it's possible she knew what happened without realizing what it meant. She was just a baby, too. So young. Your grandparents were always comfortable with the woods—they let those girls play outside all day, every day—but that doesn't mean they were safe. Your grandma told me the police asked your mom about it, of course. Like your grandmother did, but she claimed not to know. If she was around when she fell or slipped, or whatever it was, I'm sure she was terrified she'd be in trouble."

I press my lips together. The fact that such an unspeakable horror is just a casual part of our family's history makes me feel ill.

"Is that all you needed, honey? The weather's about to come on, and I want to see how it's looking for tomorrow."

"Oh. Um, yeah. That was it," I tell her. "Thanks. I'll, uh, talk to you later, okay?"

"Anytime you want," she promises, then ends the call.

I drop my phone on the couch, staring blankly in horror at all that I just learned. It feels impossible. This place seems colder now. Those woods—the woods where they let me play as a child without a word of warning or, seemingly, a care about what might've happened to me—no longer feel like a place of solace. The trees here witnessed what happened. The dirt, the water. They know.

The earth here knows the truth, but we never will.

I want to call Mom, to ask her about it and why she never bothered to tell me, but what would I even say?

I know you aren't talking to me because I skipped your wedding and got divorced instead, but what about your dead sister? Why didn't you think I should know about her?

Doesn't she ever wonder about her? Does she miss her on her birthday? Does the day she went missing haunt her each year? And, if any of that is true, how did she manage to hide it from me so completely? Why would she?

Anger and sadness wash over me like waves, competing with the settled, older, and wiser devastation and fury that have been there for months already. It doesn't matter. None of it matters anymore—what happened here, what Mom is hiding from me.

Eventually, she'll come around. For now, I have to protect my daughter. Taylor deserves all of me. She deserves for me to make Foxglove the magical refuge I know it can be.

I have to forget about what happened here and focus on the future.

When I open my eyes, the house is dark. It takes a few seconds for me to orient myself and remember where I am and why. Foxglove has a distinct scent—damp, floral, and earthy—that brings me back to reality before anything else.

I sit up on the couch, my shoulders and neck stiff. I can't get my bedroom set up quickly enough. I didn't think it was worth it to bring my mattress back into the living room again for just myself, but another night on the couch might just be the death of me.

I rub my eyes, checking the time. It's nearly two in the morning. I roll the predicament around in my mind. Should I try to go back to sleep or make my way into the bedroom and move my things around to make space for the mattress on the floor? I definitely don't have time to put my bed frame together, which is what I should've done in the first place, but it's currently buried behind boxes.

With a stretch, I stand.

Then...freeze.

Slowly, oh so slowly, I turn my head toward the sound I just heard.

It's the sound of the doorknob. Across the living room, someone is turning the knob at the front door, rattling the metal handle. *Is that what woke me up in the first place?*

With the lock freshly changed, there's no chance anyone has the key.

Unless I didn't lock it after dinner.

My throat constricts as I recall the evening, trying to decide my best course of action. Phone in hand, I take a cautious step toward the door. I could call 911 right now, but it would be half an hour before they'd get to me. I grab an iron fire poker from the stand next to the stone fireplace. It's old, but heavy. Its handle is ornate, with loops and swirls that settle into my palm easily, giving me a good grip.

I lift it as I move closer to the door, then, all at once, I flip on the porch light.

My breathing catches as I wait to see what they'll do. They know they're caught. That this home isn't empty anymore.

Seconds later, the doorknob rattles again. Whoever it is, they aren't leaving.

CHAPTER THIRTEEN

SARAH WILDE - 1655

The wind outside rattles the house and its windows, whistling under the eaves above. The storm rages, shaking the trees surrounding Foxglove so terribly they sound fearful themselves, whispering warnings of what's to come.

But perhaps that's not about the storm at all.

Here in the belly of Foxglove, all is still, but I can feel in my bones that all is not well. All is not right. I place my hand against the stones of the hidden door, pressing it there to keep myself from doing something that might make this worse somehow.

I'm taut as a wire as I listen, my body aching with the need to go. To do. To save.

I wish to believe my instincts have deceived me, but there is no mistaking that sound. The tread of boot, of firm leather sole, upon the wood of the floor above my head, drawing nearer. I remember the sound well from my days as a young girl, the time my mother descended the stairs of the oak to save me from this very passage when the air became too tight around my lungs.

Except these shoes have not come to do any saving.

His boot comes into view on the stairs, following the light from her candle.

My Anna is just on the other side of this wall, just two arm reaches away, but I cannot get to her. She doesn't know I am here, but then again...neither does he.

My Anna. My little lamb. Quiet and gentle as she has always been as she plays with her dolls in the cellar, her safe place from the storms. Oblivious to the monster descending.

If I had not gone to the meadow to collect herbs before the rain, she would be with me, and this man would not have found her. This monster would not have found her.

Here in my hiding place, I weigh my options.

His footsteps draw nearer as his figure comes into view, and I watch her pause her play, her face turning away from me and toward the stairs. A wicked smile grows across his terrible face.

No.

"Mama?"

My heart becomes a wild boar, ramming and fighting against the cage of ribs under my skin. My temples pound and my hands shake.

I wait to see what he'll do. One breath. Then another.

"Your mama is not here to help ya now, child." His voice is low and thick, dripping with malice and likely the foulest of breath. "I'm here to bring ya a message."

She stands for the man, trembling but respectful of her elder. I curse the day I ever taught her manners as my darling girl shakes before him in a way I feel deep in my womb, her first home and safest place. How I wish I could tuck her back there, safe and sound and with me always.

"The Lord has seen your evil ways, Anna Wilde." He wags a dirty, beefy finger at her, and I want to tear it off with nothing but my teeth. "Your father was killed riding horseback, and your mother has taken up with the devil. Taken you with her."

"S-s-sir?" Her voice is so small. *She* is so small. Just shy of thirteen and still a baby in every way that matters. She hasn't grown like her sister did, like I myself did. She doesn't yet know the dangers of the world.

I'm trapped with very few options. If I reveal myself, I will have to kill him. My mother's warning rings in my head, and I know Foxglove will accept nothing less.

"Don't play dumb with me, girl. I watched you in the meadow just last week, with your tokens and devil's weeds."

At once, the blood drains from my limbs, though it's not his words I'm afraid of. His kind is familiar to me. He's but an image in a looking glass that reminds me of so many others. Men who fear what they do not understand. Godless, terrible men who only care for power and how they can wield it. Men who name themselves as righteous in church each week, though their hearts are black as night. No, I do not fear his tongue or the vile words he uses. I fear his hands only and what they might do to my daughter.

My sweet girl trembles, her voice as feeble as a candle in the strongest wind. "Sir, I wouldn't. I-I'm afraid you are mistaken. In the meadow, I only gathered herbs like my mother taught me—"

"Herbs?" He looks at her through hardened eyes, as if he's never heard the word. He does not wish to know the truth, only to punish. "It was only herbs, was it? And was it only herbs your mother gave to my daughter, then? I expect you'll want me to believe that just as well. Lies spill easily from the lips of witches."

My jaw tightens as I realize who this man is, and just how I helped his daughter. How I tried. But by the time she came to me, she was too sick. The bloodletting he'd subjected her to had weakened her body too much.

But Anna knows nothing of that. I have taught Mary the things I know. How to pull fever from the blood and how to quiet the womb when she aches. I showed her valerian root and where to find it in the woods, showed her its uses. I have taught her to heal, never to harm, but dear Anna knows neither yet.

Her only tasks have been to fetch the plants and herbs I need for my tinctures and salves. She knows that I use them, but she does not yet know what for.

This man cares not what she knows. I see it in his

eyes. For nothing, for picking flowers and playing in the meadow, they will string her from the gallows tree, should they have their way.

I hear my mother's voice in my ear, and I am but a child again, needing her so desperately in this moment. From the second William passed, I have known a day like this might come. I know what the men in the village must think of me, out here alone and happy to be. I know how they must hate me for it.

He takes a step nearer to Anna, and I hear his weight shift, the leather of his boots straining. Something in my chest ignites like the flame of her candle. I can smell him now, that's how close he is to me.

I can smell the sweat and smoke and horse that clings to his skin.

"I do not know what you mean, sir. Mama and I are not witches." Her little voice is so strong, so brave, and I can't stand here another moment. I bend down, my fingers grazing the cool, damp earth until I find a stone large enough to do what I need. I toss it with all my might, down the passage and into the darkness. The stone clangs against the walls, this way and that, and the man turns. His head lifts as he hears it.

With his back to me, I see my chance. I push against the secret door, and it releases with a sound that feels like a breath, as if Foxglove is breathing with me in this moment.

When he turns back to Anna, he does not see me. Not right away. I am hidden in the shadows of the cellar, in the darkness. I step forward slowly, my body moving with the shadows cast by the candle on the ground.

He lurches back as if I'm a snake, and he is but a horse. I rather like that comparison, though I suspect most horses are much smarter than he.

"What the devil is this? You rise from the shadows like the witch that you are."

I step forward, unafraid. "I come to my daughter's rescue, like the *mother* I am. Standing between my blood and the wolf."

Anna moves to stand next to me, and I take her hand, holding her close against my side. His dark eyes flick down to her and back up to me, and his lips curl with something dark and dangerous. Something that has been carried in the expressions of men since the beginning of time. Something women have always known to fear.

"And what's to stop that wolf from killing you both in the name of God?" he asks, his rank breath on my face. "Ridding this village of the witches you are."

"You know nothing of which you speak."

"Don't I?" he asks, but I see it then, a flicker of fear that wasn't there before. My body knows what it is, though, that part of him—of men like him—that can't allow for a woman who does not flinch. "You are a midwife, a trafficker of potions and unnatural remedies. Remedies men don't have names for. I've heard whispers of you throughout the village. I know what you are, and I know what you have done."

His words are cruel, but they don't shock me.

"I am not a witch, but a woman. A healer. I have buried this village's babes in the earth while their mothers cried out over their bloody bedsheets. I have returned home to work our fields and harvest food to feed my own daughters, and my hands have been raw from both labors. I have sat at sick beds and birth beds, holding hands and whispering prayers. I have washed blood from my skirt and the skirts of others, and prepared soup for weary souls. I have done all of this because it is what my mother taught me and her mother before her. If that is what you call the work of a witch, then you should know there are witches all across this land from Windsor to Hartford. A witch is sure to have brought you into this world, and your family must be mighty grateful for it."

I pause, studying his haggard face. "Call me a witch if you must, but I tried to save your daughter," I whisper, a plea to whatever humanity might still exist in him. "I tried."

He lifts his hand, his palm coming down over my cheek before I see it coming. Anna whimpers, burying her face against my back. I glance down, squeezing my eyes closed until my tears dry, then look back at him, my cheek burning as hot as the fire in our hearth.

"You are a witch, and you'll die like a witch," he says, lips curled up with pleasure.

"And you," I say, taking a step toward him, "are a coward who creeps into a woman's home under the cover of darkness. You are not wanted here, nor are you welcome."

He lifts his hand as if to slap me again, but the secret door behind me is caught by a sudden wind.

THUD.

It slams shut with a powerful gust that blows from me toward him—a gust so strong it pushes me forward.

"Black magic..." he mutters, stumbling backward, eyes wide.

I know what will come of my refusal to argue, to explain that it was merely the wind, but I can't. To protect Anna, I will let him believe whatever he must.

His boots are already retreating toward the stairs when he speaks again. "Your magic won't save you, witch. Nor your child. They will come for you. They will burn your house to ash and your name will be but smoke in their mouths, a whispered warning to those tempted to do devil's magic. You've lain with the devil, and now we shall banish you to hell."

I don't answer him, because I have no answer to offer. No amount of pleading will save me now. I have made my choice, and I will not beg for understanding, for he has none to give. He flees up the stairs and the door above us slams shut. I hear him sliding the old cedar chest on top of it, and I know he thinks he has us trapped down here, but he knows not of the ways Foxglove will provide for us, the secret passages we can take that will set us free.

At last, Anna wraps both arms around my waist, gripping my skirt so tightly her little fingers turn white.

As I hold her, I am struck by the undeniable fact. She

is old enough to prepare for a husband, for the life she will have after I am gone. I must start telling her things. I must get her ready.

I press her face to my chest, stroking her silky hair. "Hush now, my darling. He is gone, and he will not be back tonight. We are not broken. He will not break us."

She cries against me, wetting my dress, and I don't dare stop her. Not tonight. Weeping in the way she is, releasing so much all at once, is a sort of prayer from your soul to the earth.

I do not know what the morning light will bring, or if I'll be given even another fortnight with these hearts that walk around outside my body. I do not know if I made the right choice, if I should've said or done more. If I should've killed him.

All I know is that I faced the darkness tonight. For it is he who is the devil, not I. And I would do it for her again, any number of times.

Foxglove will protect us as she always has, and I will protect my daughters.

Let them come if they must.

We aren't going anywhere.

CHAPTER FOURTEEN

CORINNE WILDE - PRESENT DAY

After the rattling of the doorknob starts, I hear my name. "Corinne?"

My stomach does a little flip. *What the hell?*

It's impossible and yet...

I whip the door open in a blur and stare into a face I shouldn't be seeing. "Lewis?" I hiss his name, and it feels like a curse and a blessing all at once. "What are you doing here?"

His eyes scan my face, then my body, before surveying the room behind me. "Are you all right? What's going on?"

"What are you talking about?" Am I still dreaming somehow? What is this?

He tries to step inside the cabin, but I'm not moving. I refuse, keeping him in the doorway. This is my home. My space. The only thing in the world, thanks to our divorce decree, that is just mine.

"Why did you change the lock?"

"Why do you still have a key?" I demand right back.

"We had one in the junk drawer in the kitchen. I forgot about it until I got your text. Are you guys okay? Where's Taylor?"

"My text?" My brows knit together as I replay my evening. Taylor and I made Alfredo and ate it while watching *Pride and Prejudice* on DVD. Then we played a game of Uno before reading until it was time for bed. "What text? I didn't text you."

He scrutinizes me, as if I've lost my mind, then steps back, pulling his phone from his pocket. Within seconds, I'm staring at a text that definitely didn't come from me, except that...it did. It's from my number, both according to the contact name and our earlier texts in the same conversation.

> Can you come to Foxglove?
> Emergency here. We need you.

I shake my head, switching my attention from the message to the phone in my hand. I open my text messages, trying to prove I didn't send it, but there it is.

The same message greets me. The last text message sent from my phone, around noon yesterday.

"I didn't send this." I rack my brain for possible explanations, but then it hits me all at once. The only explanation that makes any sense. *I'm going to kill her.* "Jesus, it must've been Greta. She was here and she was worried about us being out here alone with the storm on the way. But I'm fine. There's no emergency. You really shouldn't have come."

His eyes are wild as he watches me, like he can't believe what I'm saying. Like he thinks I might be lying. Does he really believe I would do that? I'm not a monster. He rests his hand on the doorframe next to his head.

"Well, I did come, though. I came all this way. I'd like to see Taylor. Please."

At least he says please, but that doesn't make any of this easier. He can't stay here. I'm not ready.

"You can't. It will just make this harder. Please, Lewis. You have to... Wait a sec." My brain is still catching up. "Why didn't you just call me?"

He scoffs, staring at me in disbelief, then turns his phone back around. Moments later, I'm staring at his call log.

It's nothing but calls to me.

"What is this?" My entire world feels like a dream sequence right now.

"I've literally been calling you all day long, Corinne. You didn't answer. Not once. Now, it's after midnight, and I'm exhausted. I bailed out of a meeting. I haven't eaten. I know you don't have to, but please just... Come on. Let me stay. At least for the night. I'll check on Taylor, get some rest, and then I'll be gone and out of your hair. I promise."

I'm barely listening to what he's saying, barely comprehending as I stare at his call log. It's not... This isn't real. It can't be. My phone didn't ring a single time. Service is spotty here, but missing every single one of these calls from him today would've been impossible. With a shaking hand, I open my phone and dial his number.

The phone screen goes black, and I wait, but within seconds, it ends. No voicemail message. Nothing. On a hunch, I search for my settings, then the page that lists my blocked contacts.

Sure enough, there it is. Right at the top.

"I can't believe she would do this. Greta must've texted you from my phone and then blocked it so I couldn't tell you not to come." I huff a breath. I love my best friend, but sometimes her protectiveness can be overbearing. She had to have known this wasn't what I wanted. I try not to feel angry, but it's hard. She was acting out of love, but it doesn't feel like love right now.

He swats his arm, then gestures into the house with an exasperated smile. "It's late, and the mosquitoes are going to eat me alive. Can I come in until we figure this out? Please?"

When I look up, his blue eyes lock with mine, and there's that stomach flip again. As if my body still hasn't gotten the memo we aren't supposed to love this man anymore.

With a hesitant step back, I release a heavy breath. "Yeah. Yeah, of course."

CHAPTER FIFTEEN

CORINNE WILDE - PRESENT DAY

There isn't really anything to discuss.

Lewis is in my house with me again. He's here, he came because he still cares, because underneath it all he is still Lewis, and I am still me, and there's no part of me that feels strong enough to send him away.

The next morning, I'm awake early despite being exhausted. I couldn't sleep with Lewis in the house. It was as if every cell in my body was acutely aware he's here. That he's just feet away. That this is really happening.

And then there's the text and the blocking of his number. The second I left Lewis on the couch, I uncovered my mattress and made space for it on my bedroom floor. Then I texted Greta to ask for an explanation and unblocked Lewis's number to be safe. I won't be angry with her, no matter her reason. I know she was doing it to help, and that she genuinely thought she was protecting me or keeping us safe somehow, but it's not okay. She can't manipulate this process and our emotions this way.

Greta isn't married and therefore hasn't been divorced. For so long, we've just been Lewis and Corinne, and she doesn't understand how complicated this is now. We're still just us in her eyes, still her friends. Her family. Even if she has taken my side, she doesn't hate Lewis, and I'd never ask her to.

After herself, I know she trusts him the most with me, and I have to admit that I do, too.

As the morning sun floods the kitchen, I stare into the fridge. I've always loved to cook. I love knowing that there's a clear place to start and end with each recipe. That it becomes a simple thing to check off a to-do list. I love that it allows me to be creative and experiment without the risk being too great. There are few recipes I haven't been able to save. But lately, I'm cooking more than usual and enjoying it less than I ever have.

These days, each meal feels like a test. Like a burned panini or soupy stroganoff would be enough reason for Taylor to decide to leave me for good. After all, the person she looks up to most in the world already has.

I weigh the breakfast options, ignoring the obvious one. Lewis's favorite breakfast is an omelet with hash browns, but I can't bring myself to make them. Doing so could cause him to think I want him here, and I don't. It's too hard to have him in this house, and as much as I might be glad to see him, it will only make it harder when he inevitably has to leave.

Because he does.

Because we are divorced.

Because he left me.

We left each other.

We changed our minds about all the plans we made, and we walked away. We aren't meant to know each other anymore.

Him being here right now, him running to us, driving so far to see us, doesn't change anything. It doesn't mean anything.

Fifteen minutes later, the scent of freshly baked blueberry muffins fills the house. It's no one's favorite, but it's a safe option that everyone will enjoy. For now, that has to be enough.

The smell must rouse Lewis from sleep, because a few minutes later when I turn around from the sink where I've been mixing up the sweet tea, he's sitting up on the couch. His brown hair is messy, blue eyes red and glassy, face swollen.

He's so beautiful—so familiar and safe—I have to look away.

I clear my throat. "Sorry if I woke you."

His voice is gravelly from sleep. "Guess we're even, assuming I woke you last night."

I smile a bit to myself, but he can't see it as I slip the pitcher of tea into the fridge. "I'm making breakfast. I wasn't sure if you were planning to stay. Not that you have to. Really, I'm sorry you drove all this way. You must've been... I'm just, I'm going to talk to Greta about this. She meant well, but it wasn't okay, and I'm sorry."

"Are you sure it was—"

"Dad?" Taylor's voice carries down the hall. She's heard us. My heart sinks.

What am I going to tell her? How am I going to explain this?

Moments later, her door swings open and she runs down the hall. Her blonde hair is tied back in a messy French braid as she appears, looking from me to him. Her smile widens—a stab in my chest—and she rushes around the couch, launching into his arms and nearly knocking him over.

He pulls up from the couch, trying to keep from being strangled by her love.

"Hey, Bug." He kisses her cheek and ruffles her hair as she releases him, and I'm hit with a pang of nostalgia, of missing what was and hating what is. How did we get here?

"What's going on? What are you doing here?" Her eyes are wide as she stares at him, like she can hardly believe it.

Briefly, I've considered that Taylor might've been the one to text Lewis, but it was Greta who had my phone when she was shining the flashlight as I changed the lock, and Greta who mentioned calling Lewis to come. Taylor wouldn't have done this. Not when she's technically free to leave whenever she wants. All signs point to a meddling best friend, and unless she tells me otherwise, she's my culprit. She has to be.

"He's not staying," I warn her.

"What? Why?" she asks, but she's only looking at him.

"I..." Lewis's eyes linger on her for a moment before he looks at me. We are supposed to be a united front here. This is a decision we made together, but somehow, I feel as if I'm standing on a shore somewhere, watching the two of them sail away, neither one sad to see me go. Throughout this divorce, I continue to feel like I'm losing things. People. Myself.

I don't budge, standing across the room behind the kitchen island, gripping onto the corner for dear life.

Eventually, Lewis turns his gaze back to Taylor. "Your mom's right. I was in the area and needed a place to sleep. She was kind enough to let me crash. I've gotta get back home, though."

"But...no. Come on, you can stay for the day," Taylor says. "You have to. You're all the way here, and who knows when we'll see you again."

"In the fall," I tell her.

"Please, Dad," she begs, ignoring me.

Lewis looks at me again, asking the silent question, but does it even matter? I already know I've lost. When it comes to those two, I always do.

"Okay, just for the day," he says, then adds, "but only if it's okay with your mom."

My smile is stiff and strange, and my lips twitch,

muscles straining until I look away. "How could I say no now?"

After breakfast, Lewis clears the table. I meet him at the sink, where he's apparently planning to wash the dishes. I can't remember the last time he did that.

"You don't need to wash our dishes."

"I don't mind." He shrugs. "You never told me why you changed the lock." His eyes narrow on mine again, and my stomach betrays me like always.

I look away. "I just wanted to make sure we were safe."

"I never liked the idea of the two of you being out here alone in the woods."

"We didn't have much choice, did we?"

"Now, don't say that like it's my fault. I would've sold the house, you know that. It would be enough for us to split and—"

I put a hand up. "I can't do this again." My voice is calm and cordial, but he seems to sense I've drawn a line in the sand. I've spent months in negotiations explaining why I can't let Taylor's childhood home be sold, why one of us should keep it. Lewis had nowhere else to go, and I have Foxglove. This was the only path that made sense.

My phone buzzes, distracting me.

"It's Greta." I put the phone to my ear as Lewis shuts off the water. "Hey."

"Hey, so um, got your text. What are you talking about, crazy pants? I didn't text Lewis."

"You didn't?" I swallow. "From my phone?"

"Um, no. Why would I?"

"You mentioned having him come here, after..." I pause, hoping she remembers our conversation. "I told you no, but I thought you might've texted him anyway because you were worried." My eyes flick to Lewis. "Because of the storm."

"Babe, I asked you and you said no. I wouldn't just... text him without permission. Come on."

My blood runs cold as I look at Taylor, sitting across the room, nose in a book. "You swear it?"

"Swear. Is he there right now? Seriously? Are you freaking out? Do you need me to come?"

"No. We're good. I have to go, okay? I'll call you later."

"Is everything okay?"

"We're fine," I promise her.

Once the call has ended, I look at Lewis. "So Greta says she wasn't the one who texted you."

"Do you think she's lying?" His brows rise.

"She doesn't lie to me."

He bobs his head with a slow nod. "Why did you think it was her?"

"I told you. Because she was here yesterday, and she mentioned—" I cut myself off, trying to decide how to tell him the truth. Do I even owe him the truth? About any of this? It's not his problem anymore. "It doesn't matter. She was mostly worried about the storm coming in tonight."

"Who texted Dad?" Taylor asks, suddenly interested in the conversation. "Was it before the police got here?"

Lewis balks. "The police?"

Moths flutter through my veins. "It's nothing—" I try to say, but Taylor is already telling him everything, laying bare my every flaw.

"Someone broke in and ruined all of my stuff. And then Mom had to change the lock so they couldn't come back. The police were here and everything, and we found all this trash like someone has been living here. It was, like, straight out of a horror movie. And"—she takes a deep breath, as if the worst is yet to come—"we still don't have internet."

Lewis looks back and forth from her to me in a state of shock. Finally, he lands, *rather firmly*, on me. "Someone broke in, and you had to call the police, and you didn't think you might want to let me know?"

Something in his tone switches something in mine. "It's not your concern anymore."

"It's my concern as long as my daughter is involved. If she's in danger—"

"She's not in danger." I run a hand along my face, my voice powerless. "She's fine. We don't even know that anyone broke in."

"But someone damaged her things."

"Water. Water damaged her things. The police told

me to change the lock to be on the safe side, which I did. We're fine, Lewis."

"It doesn't look like it."

"The house has been empty. There are bound to be road bumps. I'm a big girl. Her parent. An equal part of this, don't forget. I can handle things just as well as you can."

His eyes shift between mine, reading me. "Taylor, could you go to your room for a minute?"

"What? Why?" she argues. "What did I do?"

"I need to talk to your mom."

"There's nothing left to talk about," I say, but Taylor is already getting up. If it had been me, she would've fought much harder.

The second she's gone, Lewis's voice softens, both in tone and volume. "Maybe she should come stay with me for a while."

The sentence is a punch to the gut after everything I went through to ensure she would be with me this summer. "What? No. Absolutely not. She's fine. We're fine."

He puts his hands up. He knows, of course, he doesn't have a leg to stand on here. It's already been agreed upon that she'll be with me until school starts back. At which point, if she'd like to go to school here, she can. And if she wants to return to her old school, I'll either have to buy a house in that district, or she'll stay with her father for the term and visit me during holidays.

The latter isn't an option, obviously. If it comes to it,

I'll do whatever it takes to have an address that allows her to stay with me.

"I'm not saying you aren't. I just know you've got a lot on your plate." He looks around at the mess of boxes yet to be unpacked. "Let her come with me for a week, give yourself time to settle in, and then I'll bring her back."

"Absolutely not. She's old enough to help."

"Right. Just how every teenager dreams of spending their summer." He turns back to the sink, flipping on the water, but I grab the faucet, pulling it to the opposite side and flicking it back off.

"I don't need you to do the dishes. We've had breakfast. I think it's time for you to go."

"Are you really going to do this? We agreed to be civil. I'm trying to help."

"I'm being civil."

"Let her come with me."

"I've already given you an answer."

"You aren't even thinking about what she wants."

"You think she wants to come back with you?"

He hesitates, but we both know the answer. Does it make me a bad mother, a selfish mother, to fight to keep her where she doesn't want to be? Is that what I'm doing right now? Pushing her? Making her miserable?

My thoughts, though, are drowned out by Taylor's voice, the answer to all of my questions, though she doesn't realize it. From down the hall, there's an enthusiastic scream. "Yes, Mom! Please let me go with Dad!"

CHAPTER SIXTEEN

ANNA WILDE - 1695

The knock comes too late in the day, just before the sun disappears behind the lowest part of the trees. It's a knock that worries me—three hard raps at the wood. Too rigid to be a friend, too brazen for a peddler. Besides, no one comes to Foxglove without cause. Not for many years.

At first, I don't move. I just sit straight as a stick at the table, my palm wrapped around my mug of tea, steam rising to fill the air in front of my eyes.

I lift my hand and place it on the gem I wear around my neck, rubbing my fingers across the cool stone. Long ago, I learned to wait when the knocks come. Not every visitor who arrives at Foxglove comes in kindness.

The knock comes again, more urgent, and I blink my eyes, looking for signs of a torch or any movement outside the window.

Slowly, as quiet as a mouse, I rise from my seat. My

joints scream in protest, and I wonder if I still have willow bark in the cupboard. At the door, I'm slow to open it, but as I do, I find my guest still waiting.

She's young, no more than five and thirty, and at first glance her face reminds me of my dear Mary. I'm struck by how badly I miss her, how badly I miss our mama. Her dark hair clings damp to her brow, though I can't recall it raining, and her cloak is far too thin for the season.

Her eyes speak of secrets, her expression of fears. Something is wrong, and I know it without her having to say a word. In the distance, the trees seem to know it, too. I feel them leaning in, listening.

"Are you Anna Wilde?" the woman asks me. Her hands are wrapped tightly around the shoulders of a girl —and a girl she is, barely more than a child.

The girl keeps her eyes down, not meeting mine, and I want to tip her face up, ask her the meaning of this. Ask her why she looks as empty as a mug that's never been refilled.

Her expression is vacant. Hollow. Haunted. I know that look. I wore it myself after Mama was taken from us. And then again after the cough took my sister from me last winter.

"Please," she repeats, and my eyes find hers again, looking away from the child. "They said... I asked, and they said if there was anyone who could help, it was you. It was Anna Wilde." She repeats my name as if it's an incantation, low and slow. "Please, Mistress...."

Still, I don't speak. Not yet. Our family has been tricked by their type before, and I won't make the same mistakes again.

The woman thrusts her daughter forward, so I can get a better look at her in the firelight from the hearth. "It's my daughter who needs your help. She's just a child."

I survey the girl. She flinches under my gaze as quickly as if I've slapped her and, for the first time, I notice the way she's clutching her cloak tighter over her belly.

My joints ache, but it's no longer from my own pain. I'm feeling hers. I understand now that I don't have a choice. I never did.

With a quick nod, I step aside, glancing over the woman's shoulder toward the village to be sure they haven't been followed. "Get inside."

The woman's breath sounds more like a prayer as she pushes the girl forward and through the door. I latch it behind them, whispering a prayer of my own, asking the earth to shield us, and for it to look away.

Silence fills Foxglove as heavily as rain as I move across the parlor to the kitchen, picking up my candle from the table on the way.

I set the candle upon the wooden counter and take two mugs down from the shelf. As I turn, the hem of my shawl brushes the candle, sending it tumbling to the counter with a sharp crash.

I scoop it up, but not before the wax has spilled a line

as white as bone, and the flame has scorched a dark spot the size of my finger. I scrape away the wax with my fingernail, hands trembling, then pause and draw in a breath. My finger—wrinkled and swollen at the joints with age—passes over the blackened scorch mark.

I can't fix it.

This moment and this memory will remain with Foxglove long after I am gone. I close my eyes, grounding myself the way my mother taught me to when my worries get the best of me.

By the fire, I take the copper kettle and fill their mugs with tea.

"Chamomile," I say, though I'm not sure if the name means anything to them. Not everyone cares to know what works and why, the way I do. I add honey from the fresh comb I collected in the garden, and one would think it were manna straight from God himself, the way they drink it down.

I wonder—but don't dare ask—how far they must've come. How fast they must've run. I wonder if anyone is looking for them.

"The man lives in our village," the woman says when her mug is empty. "He has a wife, Mistress. A family. But it wasn't my Sophia who caused him to stray, you have my word."

I don't need her word, but I don't say as much. I want to tell her that I would help her regardless, that she is a child and he is a man. That there would be no excuse.

But these types of things aren't said by decent people, I have learned. So, I remain quiet.

"He visited our farm while my husband was away. We thought he was a good man when we invited him inside." She puts her hand out, taking her daughter's. "We were very wrong. I tried to stop him. I begged him to take me instead, to leave her be. She was... She was promised to another man, and now she's ruined. We'd already paid her dowry, and we haven't got anything left. She'll be penniless, as will we. Unless..." She looks at the girl, whose stony eyes remain fixed straight ahead, at nothing and everything all at once. "I've had eight children myself, Mistress. I know the signs."

Something twists deep inside of me. Ancient pain. Fear that feels even older. I think of my daughters, long since grown and gone.

"Does anyone in town know? You said they sent you to me. Who?"

"No one knows, ma'am. I assure you, I would never tell a soul. I asked for help with my sleeping. Told the ones I asked that I've been waking hot as a flame. They were friends, not enemies, but I couldn't take any chances." She shakes her head, pinning me with an angry glare. "They'll blame her, you know. Say she tempted him, that she tricked him somehow. Or worse, still—they'll claim it's devil's work. That she lay with the devil himself. They'll kill her, Mistress. There's still plenty of men who remember the trials, who are just aching to sink their teeth into the witches again. Like they..." She bows her head. "Forgive me, but just like they did your mother."

My eyes go sharp. I feel them and refuse to soften them. Does she think I've forgotten the trials that took my mother away from me? All on the accusations of a man who meant to harm me? Does she suspect I've forgotten how they tried to burn down Foxglove with us inside, how my mother let them take her to save me? I will never forget that day, nor will I forget that evil man, though I heard he died before the rope went around Mama's neck.

She quiets, looking ashamed.

They left her body hanging in a dirty shift while Mary and I watched from the tree line. We were just girls then, despite the baby growing in my sister's womb, hidden beneath layers of cloth. We were too young to run —and had nowhere to go should we have tried—but too old to forget the way her face looked as she went still.

After, we buried her alone next to the oak tree, next to our gran. Next to the others. And with her death, I vowed to never use the knowledge she'd given me, to never help this town that took her from me ever again.

Whether or not she meant it, this woman has just reminded me of why. "I'm afraid I can't help you. That work died right along with my mother."

"They will kill her," the woman reminds me, angry.

"Perhaps." My voice sounds cold to my own ears. "Perhaps not." I stand, moving away from the fire. "There are others who—"

"No." The woman slices through my words with her own, dripping with venom. "There aren't. Not anymore. The ones who survived moved away. Or they married or joined the church. Do you know how far we had to travel to see you? Do you have any idea what we've done? They said you—"

"They misspoke."

She bites her lip, and I can see that she's fighting back a rage as hot as the fire itself. The room is still, silent. The only sound comes from the fire crackling in the hearth, reminding us it's there. Alive. Right here with us.

"You should leave," I tell them. "The woods aren't safe after dark." The world isn't either, but I don't say as much.

The mother doesn't move except to look at her daughter, and when she does, the girl finally looks up. But it's not her mother's face she looks into, it's mine. Her eyes are so dull and deep, like the river stones I used to skip with Mary. She looks lost in there. Drowning.

"Where can I go?" she asks me, her voice small. "Where can I go that he'll never find me again?"

That does it. Her words, the innocence in them, crack something open inside my chest that I've kept bound up with rope and silence for as long as I can remember. I feel it unwinding, unfolding. In her eyes, I see myself. Alone. Afraid. Marked by Mama's death. Condemned for surviving.

Slowly, I turn away from her. I don't speak, just act. I find the cupboard and open the false back. Inside, I take down the old bundles and vials no one has touched in what feels like a lifetime.

I open cloths Mama wrapped in twine. Inside, I find some of her favorites. Sage, pennyroyal, and ginger in one. Rosemary, turmeric, mint, and tansy in another. In a third, valerian and thyme.

All forbidden.

All remembered.

The linens are stiff with age, and the herbs crumble beneath my touch as I slowly run my fingers over each of her ingredients, thinking of my mother. These items were her life's work. It meant so much to her to learn and to help, and in the end, it cost her everything.

I close my eyes, tracing the edge of one of the cloths with my fingers. When I turn back around, the woman is watching me. She doesn't want to look afraid, but I see the fear in her eyes.

The girl still doesn't look afraid. She doesn't look as if she feels much of anything, and deep inside my chest I understand why. If I can help her, I must.

Yesterday, I was merely an old woman, prepared to take our secrets to my grave. Now, I'm no longer certain these secrets should be forgotten.

My daughters should know the truth. Of Foxglove and of my mother. Of the secrets that run in their blood and what it has cost us.

But first...

"This is not without risk. And pain. There will be fever. You will think you are dying." I wait for the girl to nod, and when she does, I look at her mother. "She'll need to rest. And she'll need to stay here, so I can help her through it."

Her mother's voice is soft and raspy. "Will she survive?"

I nod once. There is no other option. This house cannot withstand another death in my lifetime. I refuse to see it happen, and I tell Foxglove as much.

The old house hears me, even if nothing changes in the air. "I'll start the broth and get clean linens. Settle in. It's going to be a long few days."

The woman lunges for me, and I lurch back. She takes my hand, gripping it tight. "Bless you, Mistress."

My smile is stiff, and I can't thank her. I don't say a word, in fact. I take the girl's hand and direct her to the chair nearer to the fire. Her skin is cold as ice.

She and her mother sit together, whispering softly to each other as her mother strokes her hair and kisses her temple. I wonder if she's thinking of when the girl was very young, of when she told her stories of sunshine and happiness and promised her the world would bring her nothing but. It's all I can think of, the days when I told those same tales to my own girls.

Why do we lie to our daughters?

Perhaps because the truth is too brutal to bear.

I stoke the fire all night, keeping it going as I boil the water and grind the herbs. My hands are tired and unpracticed, but I remember everything Mama and Mary taught me, and I work in a way I hope would have made them both proud.

I remember watching Mama work, sitting at her feet as she stirred, ground, and boiled this or that. It's strange how long it's been since I've thought of those days, and how easily they slipped back into my memory.

I thought I'd buried this part of myself along with my mother. I thought it was gone and that I'd never miss it, but Foxglove hasn't forgotten.

She doesn't forget.

My hands may grow old, and my body may give out, but the knowledge passed between mother and daughter within these walls lives on. It will never leave, and I must make sure of it.

When it is time, I pour the tincture into a small glass and whisper my mother's name softly into the night. Wherever she is—within these walls or somewhere far away—I want her to know she's with me. That her wisdom will live on.

Nothing changes as I pass the drink to the girl. The flames don't flicker or hiss. The windows don't rattle. The walls stay just as they've always been. As they will always be.

Even so, somehow, the room is warmer.

CHAPTER SEVENTEEN

CORINNE WILDE - PRESENT DAY

Taylor appears at the end of the hallway again, a bright smile on her face. "I'm going with you," she announces. "Can we stop by the Apple Store?"

Lewis holds up a hand to her. "Now, hang on. Your mom and I were just talking—"

"You aren't going anywhere," I tell her. "You're staying with me just like we agreed you would."

"*I* never agreed," she says firmly. "Neither of you asked me."

"We asked you so many times," I argue. "How can you say that? We made sure this was all right with you."

"You said we were going to stay in a cabin you owned. You didn't tell me it was a shack with no internet."

"That'll be fixed later today," I offer.

She sighs, her shoulders dropping in defeat. "I hate it

here, Mom. It's dusty and old. And none of my friends are here. There's nothing to do."

"That's not true. There's so much to explore here, you'll see. Once the house is unpacked, I'll show you. You're going to love it here, honey. I know it isn't what you're used to, and I know it's not your home, but Foxglove is so special." When I can see she's not buying into it, I add, "And if you want people to hang out with, you could always go into town. Make more friends there."

She scrunches up her nose, her glare burning me. "Gross. I'm not, like, a child. I already have friends. This is so stupid. I don't want to live in the forest like a woodland creature. I thought this would be, like, a cute little lake house moment, not...this." Her gaze meets Lewis's, and she steps forward, begging. "Come on, Dad. I was supposed to spend the summer with my real friends. The ones I already have. Just because you guys hate each other now, you don't have to ruin my whole life."

"We don't hate each other," I say quickly.

At the same time, Lewis says, "Well, let's not be dramatic."

We exchange a glance, and, finally, I add, "I know this is tough on you, Tay, but what if your friends came here for a weekend or something? You could camp out in the woods, build a fire in the yard. I'd even let you invite some boys over for a few hours, if their parents say it's okay."

Lewis gives me a look, but I ignore him, too preoccupied by the horrified expression on Taylor's face. "I don't want to invite people here, Mom. I don't want anyone to know I'm here, living like freaking Laura Ingalls or something. It's not a good look. This is not a vacation spot, okay? None of my friends want to come, like, build a fire and roast s'mores. We aren't seven."

I huff out a breath. This would've been a lot easier if she *were* seven.

Lewis steps in, a hand raised to calm her down. "Bug, listen, as much as I would love for you to come with me, your mom's right. You need to stay here and get settled in. Help unpack. I'll order you a new computer tonight and have it sent to you this week, okay?"

I want to argue. To say I'll take care of the computer, but we both know I can't afford to, so I don't say anything at all. I just watch my daughter stand there, hating us both.

A knock on the door interrupts our conversation and we look around, confused.

"Expecting someone?" Lewis asks.

"The internet company, but they were supposed to text first." I check my phone before hurrying across the room to open the door, grateful for the interruption.

Conrad stands at the door, a casserole dish in his hands. He looks almost shocked that I answered.

"Um. Sorry if I'm interrupting. I just... Here." He shoves the casserole dish at me awkwardly. "They aren't homemade, but I'm not supposed to tell you that." He scratches the back of his neck. "I, uh, I wanted to make sure everything was okay after yesterday. The police came by to check on, er, well, you know. Everything."

"Thank you," I tell him, glancing into the side of the clear casserole dish to see a pile of assorted cookies. "You really didn't have to do this."

"Think of it as our welcome, um, *back* to the neighborhood gift."

"Our?" I ask him. "You're...married?"

"I am." He smiles and twirls the simple, silver ring around his finger. "Ten years in a few months." His eyes dart toward Taylor, then Lewis, waiting for an introduction.

"Sorry. This is Lewis, my hus—ex-husband." Fire burns my insides at the slip-up. "And this is Taylor. Our daughter. Guys, this is Conrad. He lives nearby and has been keeping an eye on the house for Mom."

Lewis steps closer to me, almost too close, holding out a hand to shake Conrad's. "Nice of you to drop by with these."

"Oh, it's no problem. Especially since Corinne let me borrow some apples yesterday."

"Apples?" Lewis asks, looking at me.

"Hedge apples," I correct. "For the spiders. It's a long story. Anyway, thank you again, Conrad. For these and for stopping by. It's kind of you to check on us."

"Well, force of habit, I guess. I used to walk over here every morning, just to check on things. Get my steps in." He pats his stomach, the slight pudge there. "I'm glad you're both okay." His eyes shift between us again, and when he lands on Lewis, they dash uncomfortably back to me. "I won't keep ya. But you let me know if you need anything, okay? My number's written down there." He gestures toward the casserole dish, and I notice a name—Mulligan—and a phone number.

With that, he steps backward and walks off the porch.

Once the door is shut, I move past Lewis and place the cookies on the counter.

Lewis follows behind me. "Who was that?"

"You heard him. It's the neighbor."

"I don't like the two of you out here alone, and certainly not with a strange man lurking around."

"Lurking?" I scoff, staring at him. "You don't get to tell me what to do anymore, remember? It's what you wanted."

"Oh my god, you guys," Taylor groans, disappearing back down the hall. A few moments later, her door slams shut.

Lewis's eyes narrow at me, hurt. We can't be together for more than five minutes without screwing something up. Without fighting. "I'm not trying to tell you what to do." He takes a step closer slowly, and I feel my breath deep in my stomach as our eyes lock. "And I don't care what any divorce decree says, I still care about you. I don't want to see you hurt."

I shouldn't care what he says. I shouldn't believe him.

"Taylor needs us both," he clarifies, dropping eye contact, and just like that, the moment is over.

Gently, I reach out and touch his arm. It lasts only seconds, but a bolt of lightning dashes through my muscles regardless. "I will take care of her. You know that."

"I know. Of course I do. I just...I really hate this." He doesn't have to clarify which part of this he means for me to agree.

"We're going to be okay. All of us." I desperately want to believe that.

He puffs out a sigh, eyes squeezed shut. When he opens them, he's going to ask me something, I can read it on his face. "Can I just...could I stay here for another night or two? Please. It would make me feel a lot better. Just to make sure the two of you are safe."

I press my lips together, ready to fight it every way I can. The longer he stays, the more it hurts.

"Please," he begs, seeing he's got a foot in the door. "Corinne, listen, I promise I'll go when you ask me to, but I'm asking you...not to ask. Just for another night. Let me stay. Let me see her. I'll...I could take her to the Apple Store today, replace her laptop, and give you time to work on the house, have a moment to yourself. I swear I'll bring her back by dinnertime, and we can have dinner together as a family. Like old times."

I sigh. I was always the one who had to set the boundaries. The one who had to be the bad guy, even in this divorce apparently. "It isn't like old times anymore."

"Yeah, but we get to make our own rules," he says.

"Please, Mom." Taylor appears in the hallway again,

not trying to hide that she's been listening. She walks toward the island, hands clasped together. "Please. I need a new laptop. Please, I promise it'll be fine."

"The closest Apple Store is going to be a few hours away," I tell them both. "And the storm's supposed to get really bad tonight. You shouldn't be out in it."

"That gives you several hours to work on the house. I promise we'll be home before the storm hits. And hey, when we get back, I can help if you want," Lewis offers.

I bite the inside of my lip, staring at them both. I'm outnumbered here, like usual. Besides, I do trust Lewis when he says he'll bring her home. I just hope it isn't a mistake.

"I want her back by dinner. Well before the storm."

"Promise." Taylor squeals, bouncing up on her toes before she disappears to her room. "Oh my god, thank you!"

Lewis smiles at me, and it's familiar and painful. A knife to the heart. Like old times.

CHAPTER EIGHTEEN

CORINNE WILDE - PRESENT DAY

Whether or not I like it, having Lewis and Taylor gone for the day makes me more productive than ever.

In a way I really hate, it does feel like old times. When she was little, Lewis and I would rotate weekends to take her out and go on adventures. Every other weekend, one of us would take Taylor and spend the whole Saturday doing something fun with her. We'd go to city museums or parks or the zoo.

The other parent got the day to do whatever they wanted—relax, catch up on work or house stuff, nap, or even go on adventures themselves. I usually picked a book and spent the whole day reading, while Lewis would either go out with his friends or spend the day napping in his recliner.

During the wild toddler and childhood years, it was our way of keeping each other sane.

Now, with the house quiet and all to myself, I feel it

again. The immediate peace that comes with being alone. I used to feel so guilty about it, like it meant I was a bad mom or didn't love my child enough, but I know now that being alone is how I recharge. My body and my mental health require it to keep me at my best.

With the house empty, I'm able to get every single box unpacked, the minimal decor we brought hung up, and the remaining furniture placed where I want it. The internet technician arrives around three, and it takes every bit of an hour to get it set up, but once he does, I can't resist the urge to sit down on the couch and check social media. By which I mean...*Lewis's*... social media.

It's the first time I've done it since the day the divorce was final, and I can't help wondering if it's changed. If he's now a completely different person online. I open Instagram, but to my surprise—and relief—the last picture he posted is still the one of Taylor and him at Christmas.

I don't know what I expected—a photo of him and his new girlfriend? A photo of him on a tropical vacation? It's only been a few days, and yet it feels like a lifetime. He feels a lifetime away.

I close the app and return to the bedroom to get my laptop. With everything put away and the house quiet, I should really attempt to get a chapter or two written. My agent will be expecting my latest manuscript to be turned in next month, and I'm really struggling to make it happen.

Before I've typed the first word, my phone buzzes with an incoming call. It's Greta.

"Hey, just checking back in to see how things are going. Did enemy number one leave?"

I smile to myself. Somehow, I needed that reminder. That he is the enemy. That even if I love him and know he can't actually be an enemy for Taylor's sake, I have to treat him like one where my heart is concerned. Nothing has changed.

"He took Taylor to get a new laptop."

"Well, isn't he just Dad of the Year."

"It's fine, honestly. She needed one, and I can't afford it right now. It's better this way. Besides, it gave me a chance to finish unpacking the house."

"You're all settled in now, then?"

"I think so. The internet guy just left, and everything's put away. I'm starting to feel okay again."

"I'm glad. Well, listen, I just got to a showing and had a few minutes, so I wanted to check in. You call if you need anything, okay?"

"Always. Love you."

We end the call, and I return to the couch, opening my latest manuscript.

When the door opens later, I'm in a haze of my story and have completely lost track of time. Taylor appears, keys and new laptop in hand. She looks around, eyes wide.

"Wow, Mom. It looks great in here."

She's in a good mood, then.

I close my laptop as Lewis appears, carrying an armful of bags from different stores.

"Did you have a nice time?"

"The best. Dad took me shopping for clothes, too. Since so many of mine got ruined."

I glance toward the bags. "You mean they got...wet?"

She turns back to Lewis, taking the bags and disappearing to her room.

His hands go up in surrender toward me once she's gone. "I know you're probably going to say she didn't need them, but I just bought a few things for the summer. The Apple Store didn't take long enough, and after eating lunch we still had time to kill. If it helps, we went by the bookstore too, and she picked you both out a few books."

"You shouldn't buy things for me."

His smile is patronizing. "That wasn't in the divorce handbook." He comes to sit down on the couch next to me. "We agreed to be friendly. Friends gift things to each other. It's a thanks...for letting me see her. For letting me stay here."

"Just for the night," I remind him. "And only because it'd be irresponsible to drive during the storm. Tomorrow, you have to go."

It takes several seconds, but eventually, he agrees. "Yeah, you're right. Tomorrow. But tonight..." He glances over the back of the couch. "Why don't you go and take a bath? I can get supper going."

I sniff myself, and he laughs.

"You smell fine. I'm just trying to be nice."

"Oh, good. 'Fine' was what I was going for." My brows rise without warning. "Did you say you're going to cook?"

He chuckles under his breath at my surprise. The husband I once had could—and frequently did—burn toast. "I'm having to learn."

I place my laptop on the couch and stand. In the kitchen, I search through the fridge. "We have stuff to make taco bowls, meatloaf, or...stuffed pepper soup."

"Taco bowls are her favorite," he says from where he's standing near the stove.

I grab the pound of ground beef. "Taco bowls it is, then."

"I'll see if she wants to help," he says. My face must be skeptical, because he laughs. "Taylor! Come help with dinner, Bug!"

She appears at the end of the hallway a few moments later, eyes glued to her phone. "Internet's working?"

"The technician was here earlier," I confirm.

"Finally. I have to call Heather." Without another word, she disappears back down the hall. I can't fight my smug grin as I look at Lewis. Did he really expect that she'd help willingly? Taylor hates to cook, like her father.

"Don't worry about it." He opens a cabinet with a

shrug, unfazed. "I can handle dinner. You go take your bath. Relax."

My throat is dry as I watch him pull out a cutting board. This all feels so strange, like a trap, but I'm trying to trust him. To find our new normal. "Knives are in the drawer next to the sink."

He spins around, opening the drawer with a quick wave of his hand. "I'll find everything. Don't worry."

An hour later, my skin is wrinkled and red from my bath, and I'm three chapters deeper into the book I've been reading—the dystopian one about the teenager who saves the world. It's not generally my genre, but I need escapism lately and I'm finding it helpful.

The spicy scent of tacos fills the air outside the bathroom, and I make my way down the hall, running my fingers through my wet hair. He was right, I needed this more than I realized.

The food is waiting on the island, already in serving dishes, but Lewis is on the couch, one leg crossed over the other as he does a crossword puzzle on his phone.

"You didn't burn the house down."

He startles, glancing over his shoulder at me like he didn't hear me coming. "For once, no," he says with a soft laugh. "No fires." He holds his hands up so I can see them. "All my fingers are still intact. I managed to make it all on my own."

"Look at you, growing up."

"Didn't think I had it in me, did ya?"

His words hit me with a pang of sadness. We were supposed to grow up together. Grow old together. "I always suspected you did," I say simply.

He clears his throat, standing up and crossing into the kitchen. "I waited for you before calling Taylor, but I'll go and tell her dinner is done."

I pull three bowls from the cabinet while he heads down the hall, and when he comes back, we make ours side by side. After a few moments of silence, he asks, "Are you...uh, planning any trips anytime soon?"

The question catches me off guard. "No. Why?"

"I just didn't know. With summer and everything. And all your newfound freedom."

"I have deadlines." And solo bills to pay for the first time in nearly three decades.

"I thought I might take Taylor somewhere for fall break, if that's okay with you."

"We'd have to discuss it," I say first, quickly, then after thinking about it, I add, "but I think she'd like that."

He seems relieved when he adds, "And then there's her birthday. I'm assuming you'll want to do something together for that."

"If that's what she wants."

"Would we..." He pauses. "I don't know what the rules are here. Would you want to do a family trip? You could bring whoever you want with us. Greta or..."

There's a clearing of his throat that I feel in my veins. "A boyfriend or whatever."

I stop sprinkling the diced tomatoes into my bowl for a second, wondering what he's telling me. "Okay."

"Yeah? Do you... Are you seeing someone, then?"

I resume making my bowl, simply for something to steady my shaking hands. How are we possibly going to have this conversation? I want to lie. To say, "*Oh yes, I've been dating quite a bit actually. My first time being single since I was sixteen, and I'm making the most of it, dating so many people. Countless people.*" But the truth is... "I don't think I'm ready for that yet."

"Oh."

I suck in a breath. "What about you?"

He draws his lips in, opening the taco sauce. "I...I went on a date with someone Brad set me up with. Just one date. I don't think it'll go anywhere."

I always knew I could count on fucking Brad from accounting to come through with a quick after-divorce date. Can't have Lewis getting lonely. Can't have my side of the bed getting cold.

The knife in my gut twists at the mental image of him sitting across the table from her. Whoever she might be. Did he like her? Did he think she was pretty? Did she like him back? Did they kiss? Or...

Someday, I have no doubt he will remarry, and that woman will become Taylor's stepmother. Someday, I'll have to deal with that, and perhaps even attend a wedding if I'm invited.

"That's nice," I say simply. There's nothing else to say. We said it all on the pages where our signatures have now dried.

"Estelle," he says. "That was her name."

The name, at least, gives me a small reason to smile. "What, is she a nineties talent agent?"

"Cloud of smoke, red lipstick, and everything," he says, immediately catching my *Friends* reference.

And just like that, we're back to normal. Or, at least, whatever our new normal is.

It's always been easy with Lewis, but maybe that's the problem. It became too easy. Too easy to slip into the roommates routine. Too easy to be hateful toward each other over simple things just because we assumed we were rock solid. Because we'd been together for so long, through so much. We didn't think we had to work for it anymore.

Eventually, our rock solid became rock bottom, and instead of fighting for our way back, we washed our hands of it all and walked away.

He moves to the fridge to get a drink, then holds the pitcher of tea out in my direction and, when I nod, pours me a glass. It's easy to allow this to feel normal, but I can't forget that it's not.

Tomorrow, he goes home. Tomorrow, this all ends.

When my phone starts vibrating and I spot Mom's name on the screen, I nearly drop the bowl I'm holding. Lewis turns around quickly.

"You okay?"

"Yeah, it's Mom. Sorry. I need to take this." I back away from the island and down the hall to my bedroom. The last thing I need is for Mom to hear him in the background and assume we're getting back together or something.

In the bedroom with my door shut, I answer.

"Mom?" I don't even know where to start. There's so much I want to ask her now that I have her on the phone—who had access to Foxglove, why she never told me about her sister, and why EJ is screening her calls.

"I hear you have a visitor." Her voice is distant. Cold.

"What?" My blood turns to slush as I hear Lewis talking to Taylor outside the door, telling her it's time to eat.

"Lewis. Is he still there?"

"What are you talking about?"

"He told me he was coming," she says, sounding pleased with herself. "Are you two playing nice?"

This is why she called? Not because I've called her half a dozen times asking her to call me back. Not because she wanted to check in on her daughter after a brutal divorce. Not even because she wanted to check in on her grandchild after she was uprooted from the only home she's ever known. No, it's because her beloved son-in-law is here.

I should've known better.

I've always suspected Mom loves Lewis more than she loves me, but here's the proof in black and white.

"What do you want, Mom?"

"I wanted to see how it's going."

"You wanted to gossip." I suck in a deep breath, then look down at my phone. I can hear her saying something, but I don't know what. If I end this call, there's a good chance I won't hear from her again, but what use is this?

This isn't the phone call I expected or wanted. It's not the phone call or conversation I need.

I end the call, fuming. How dare he do this? How dare he tell her he was coming, give her false hope. I know they're still close. I know they'll still be in communication. That he's been in my mom's life for decades, and they will always be family. I don't want them to hate each other, but I don't want them to *have* each other, either. She's supposed to take my side in this.

It's the bare minimum.

Bitter tears sting my eyes as I prepare for the confrontation.

If he wants to be in my life, and not just Taylor's, he has to keep our private life private. He can't tell my mom everything. Every conversation and every visit. I won't allow it. He knows how complicated our relationship is.

I open the door, ready to confront him, but I'm met with Lewis standing in Taylor's doorway, looking my way, eyes wild.

"Were you eavesdropping?"

"What? No, I—"

"She was all too pleased—"

"Corinne—" He holds up a hand, cutting me off, and then I hear it. The panic in his voice. Something's wrong. Something is very wrong. His voice breaks when he speaks next, pushing the door open farther so I can see into our daughter's room. "Taylor's gone."

CHAPTER NINETEEN

EMMA WILDE - 1731

I hear them before I see them. The horses' hooves on the muddy path, the men's boots heavy on the ground. They are dressed neatly, in Sunday coats despite the warming weather.

From the window, I watch as they descend upon the house, feeling a terrible dread in my stomach. The wind seems to deliver them to me, bringing them slowly from a distance and then all at once. They arrive like a murder of crows, dark and important. The man in the front carries a paper in one hand, hubris in the other.

I step out onto my porch before they get the chance to call for me, hands folded tight behind my apron.

I remember the stories my gran told me about her mother, about how the men came for her, too. Men just like these before me. I don't dare let them see the way my hands shake beneath the cloth.

Inside, the girls are watching from atop wooden

stools at the parlor window. Though they are quiet as shadows, I can feel their presence without looking, without even hearing a creak of the floor underfoot.

They radiate nervous energy, like field mice caught in a storm.

"Evening, Mrs. Wilde," says the first man, his hat pressed carefully against his chest as if he's here to mourn something not yet dead.

Up close, I recognize him as Mr. Clemens, a local shop owner. When I do not respond or bid him well, he goes on. "We're here on account of concern from the village. Real concern. For you and your daughters."

"Are you now? I don't recall sending for any concern, real or otherwise."

That seems to silence him for a moment, but then he just gives me that smile that men often give you when they mean to talk over you. When they think you're just a foolish woman who says foolish woman things. "Be that as it may, Mrs. Wilde, we've convened a special meeting on your behalf."

"Very kind of you, but unnecessary, you can be assured."

He's growing irritated with me now, as his men become restless. "We've spoken with Reverend Hawkins, and he's in agreement. As is the town council." He braces himself, his feet shuffling about like a turkey. "It's not proper, nor is it safe, for a woman—a widow—to hold land alone. Now, we're only looking out for you."

"Your concern is very decent, Mr. Clemens, but I

assure you, you need not worry. Foxglove's stood without a man on its deed as long as it has stood, more than my seven and twenty years of living. More than my gran's. It'll stand for a few more, God willing."

He squeezes the paper in his hand, balling his fingers into a fist at his side. "You must have a husband, Mrs. Wilde. Or male kin to see to your wellbeing. It's only right."

Now it is my turn to smile, for I have been warned about these men and their rules all my life.

My eyes scan the crowd, the others there prepared to tell me what is fit and right and proper for my own life. Among them are farmers and shopkeepers, nearly ten of them—though one is just a boy who has not grown into the hair on his chin. They watch me with wild expressions, nodding and clucking their agreement like the hens in the coop.

Their greedy eyes take in Foxglove, then me, and I see the fire of which I've heard tales. The hatred.

"I have a brother," I say. "Many of you know Henry. And my late husband, James. But their names have never been on the deed. Will never. Foxglove is and has been mine from the moment my mother was placed into her grave."

"Henry is a good man," Mr. Clemens says. "But he is not taking responsibility for you and your daughters in your time of grief."

"I didn't ask him to—"

"That's just it." He cuts me off. "It's not about

asking, Mrs. Wilde. You and your daughters being here alone...it isn't right."

"Ain't lawful in some counties neither," calls a man from the back, hand in the air. Around him, the other men mumble in agreement.

Mr. Clemens puts up a hand to quiet the crowd. "You're putting your daughters at great risk, and we know that is not what anyone wants. Not you. Not us. You're leaving them out here alone, unprotected. No husband to look out for you. No *proper* name on the land."

"Forgive me, Mr. Clemens, but your concern is starting to sound more like a threat." I take a step toward the edge of the porch, and the men retreat like a wave pulling back to sea, fear in their eyes. It's the most powerful I've felt in my life, save for the moments I brought my daughters into this world.

"No, ma'am." He bows his head but meets my eyes again in a way that tells me he doesn't plan to budge. "We just want things done the decent way."

"My name will have to be decent enough," I tell them, my voice firm. My next step takes me off the porch, so the hem of my dress drags through the mud and puddles left by this morning's rain. "For it is the only name that will ever claim this land."

"But you're a woman." He says the word as if it is a curse.

"And?"

"A woman can't own land. Can't protect herself and her family."

"And yet I have."

Another man from the back of the crowd speaks up, and I recognize his voice without looking for his face. Daniel Blackwell—a man who reeks of soured milk and old whiskey, with a face that looks like an apple rotting beneath its tree. Unbelievable as it is, his temper is worse than his breath. "You're barking mad, woman. Be reasonable. You'll only draw trouble if you mean to keep this place on your own forever. It's already got folks whispering."

"Better they whisper about me than some of you," I say. "The village needs something to worry themselves over or else they'll be bored, don't you think?"

He snarls his upper lip, revealing brown teeth. "Ain't it bad enough your line has been tainted by that no-good witch blood?"

His words burn me where I stand, and I feel water from the hem of my skirt brush against my skin through my stockings as I take another step forward. "You know nothing of which you speak."

"I know enough," he says with a snort from that oversized nose of his. "All you Wilde women up here alone. Half of you never marry, and the ones who do bury their men far too often."

A wicked smile grows on my lips then, like mandrake sprouting from the ground. "Yes. Isn't it strange how the men keep dying, yet the women live on?"

That, at least, seems to quiet them. Worry them. They're nothing more than they've always been—fearful little hornets.

Mr. Clemens steps in front of me, keeping the rest of the men back with a wave of his hand. "We're here to help, Mrs. Wilde. Like we said...concern is what brought us and nothing else."

Lies.

"There is a man. A widower, like yourself. John Reardon is decent. He has land of his own, and he'd make an honest husband. We've already spoken to him, and he's willing to take on the burden of your girls. Foxglove could remain in Henry's name, or you and Mr. Reardon could sell it in. Or save it for your sons one day." He looks over his shoulder, then back at me, lowering his voice. "For your daughters' sake, ma'am, I beg you to think on it."

I don't need to think on it. "From the day my James died, I've done nothing but think. The answer is no."

There's a rumble of disagreement, and it surprises me when the youngest boy speaks up. "But surely you don't mean to leave your daughters with nothing, Mistress. Mr. Reardon—"

"They will not be left with nothing, not so long as Foxglove stands." My voice is icy as I stare at them, an odd companion for the fire I feel in my gut, in my palms. "This house will be more than enough for them."

"A house with no husband is—"

"These walls were built by the hands of Wilde

women." I'm shaking now, my voice scarcely escaping my bared teeth. "The well was dug with our sweat and bloody fingers, the land cared for by our souls. No man had a hand in building this place, and none will claim it. Not as long as Wilde blood flows through our veins."

"It's unnatural," someone shouts from the back, though I can't tell to whom the voice belongs. It doesn't seem to matter. They have but one brain between them all.

I take my time, looking over the faces of each one of them. I want to remember their eyes. "Unnatural? Is that what you think?"

Their heads bob.

I take another quick step toward them, and again, the men move back as one, like water crashing against a rock in a stream. As if I am stone, commanding their direction. "What's unnatural is thinking the moment you were born a man, God placed the world in a box and handed you the keys for safekeeping. You are not needed to protect—not me nor my girls—and as long as I live, I vow it. Gentlemen, you will own neither Foxglove nor this land. Your keys may have gotten you inside a lot of doors, but they are no good here."

Mr. Clemens stares at me a long while, the deep wrinkles in his face folding, shadows darkening like bruises. "We'll take it to the court then, see what Judge Roberts has to say about it."

I can't deny the fear that flicks through me, but I don't let him see it. "You do that." Without daring to turn my back on them, I step up onto the porch. "I do hope you brought your lanterns tonight, sirs. It will be night soon, after all, and these woods aren't safe after dark. Even for men."

They all stand still and steady for several moments, like they don't know what to do. I can almost hear their thoughts, see them sagging like rocks in the pockets of their usually thoughtless minds.

The wind picks up as if she's trying to carry them away as quickly as she brought them, and their horses begin to stir, whinnying nervously. The animals can sense the incoming storm. Same way I can.

The men take the nervous air as their cue to leave. They turn, backs stiff as boards with pride and discomfort, as they mutter to each other and mount their horses. The last of the men to leave is the boy, who looks over his shoulder just once at me, his face ashen.

I don't leave the porch until the final image of them vanishes through the trees. I whisper my thanks to Foxglove for keeping me safe, and my hopes that they'll stay gone. Funny things happen when you speak your hopes out loud, my gran used to say.

Inside Foxglove's walls, the girls rush to my side. I draw them close to comfort them, their small, frightened faces shattering my calm. Rose is barely twelve, Lyddie not even nine. They do not yet know the dangers this world holds, but they will all too soon.

Their small fingers cling to my skirts like roots, so tight I fear they may never let go.

"What did those men want, Mama?" Rose whispers. "Will they make us leave Foxglove?"

I kneel down next to her, taking both cheeks in my hands. "My darling, Foxglove has stood too long under the feet of Wilde women to ever fall to man's paper. They will try, as others have, but do not fear. They shall not succeed."

Lyddie squeezes against me, her voice trembling. "What will happen if they come back?"

I lift my arms and drag the girls in closer to me, holding them tight and wishing I could make everything right again. Wishing it were as simple as it was when they were very young and a kiss could mend all wounds.

I glance out the window, at the trees and shadows surrounding our land, dark and buzzing with ancient secrets we may never understand.

"This land knows our name, my darlings. It knows our blood and our intentions. It was never theirs to claim nor covet. Foxglove is ours, and she will protect us. We are safe here, do you understand?"

They nod against my skin, and I kiss their heads.

That night, as they sleep beside the hearth and the storm rages on outside, I rise and make my way to the kitchen, retrieving a knife from its box. The handle is made of a beautiful blue stone, and it fits perfectly in my palm. It was a gift from James during our last Christmas together, meant for cutting and preparing the herbs I collect.

Until this moment, I haven't found the strength to

use it, but now, rage bubbles over like a pot of boiling water as I carry it back to the fire, to the hearth that has warmed this house and fed this blood for centuries.

I run my hand across the stone mantel, knowing the work this will take, knowing it might break the blade, but I have to do it.

I whisper apologies to Foxglove as I begin to carve each letter, taking my time. It will take weeks—months, perhaps—but I will make it happen.

Each night, after the girls are asleep, I set to work again. Just me, the knife, and the stone.

And in the end, when I am finished and the knife's blade is dull, I step back to admire my work. In the stone mantel, the very heart of our dear Foxglove, I have carved one word.

I run my finger across each letter.

W-I-L-D-E.

WILDE.

For she is ours, and we will always be hers.

CHAPTER TWENTY

CORINNE WILDE - PRESENT DAY

I shove past him into Taylor's room. "What do you mean she's gone? I just heard you talking." But even as I say it, I know I'm wrong. I heard *him* talking. I heard *him* calling her name, telling her dinner was ready. Asking if she was ready to eat. I never heard her answer.

...did I?

I shove the covers back on her bed. Her phone is missing, too. Her purse.

Darting past him, I rush into the bathroom, through the open door.

"I've checked there. She's gone. We need to..." He spins in a circle, lost. "We need to do something."

"Brilliant," I bite out. "Great idea." Of course he's useless right now, as he ever is. Our daughter is missing, and his idea is to do...something.

I hurry to the window in her bedroom. "How did

she get out? You were in the kitchen, so not the door. It had to be the window, right?"

He doesn't answer, just stares at nothing in horror. My heart seizes as I run to the front door, dialing her number on the way. Of course he missed her. He probably had his back turned, and she snuck right past. She didn't even need to use the window.

Her phone rings on speakerphone as I rush outside.

"Taylor!" I shout, darting off the porch until I stop short in the driveway, processing. *Shoot, shoot, shoot.* I spin around to find Lewis standing behind me, my blood cold. His eyes meet mine, and I don't have to say it, but I do. "She took my car."

His face is pale, even in the porch light, as we stare at the driveway, at the spot where my car should be. Where it was hours ago when they got home.

The air is warmer now, the humidity dampening my skin. The storm is close.

I try to call her one more time as I dash down the driveway, hoping to see taillights. Hoping we've caught her just in time.

Why would she leave?

I spin back. "What did you do?"

He looks at me as if I've slapped him. "Why do you assume I've done anything?"

"You took her out, and now she's gone."

"I was the one who realized she was missing!" He waves a hand in the air toward the driveway. "If this was my brilliant plan, don't you think I would've kept that a secret until you noticed on your own?"

"You must've said something." I turn back away again, trembling with rage as my call goes to voicemail once more.

"Yeah, well, it always was my fault, wasn't it?"

I roll my eyes. "Please don't make this about yourself right now. The storm's on its way here, and it's supposed to be bad. We need to find her. This isn't about us."

He backs away, hands up. "Forget it. I'm going to try to call her. Maybe she'll answer me."

"I'm going to town. I'll look for her. You stay here in case she comes back. I need your keys."

He turns away from me, walking inside slowly as I wait on the porch, running through ideas in my head—possibilities, questions. When he returns, he holds out his keys. "Do you think it's smart to follow her? She's almost eighteen. We should give her some leash—"

"*Leash* is a privilege you don't get when you sneak out." I don't look back at him as I get into his car and drive toward town. Nearly a mile up the road, I spot taillights and slam on my brakes. They're heading down a small, gravel road. A driveway perhaps.

It's a risk. In America, people get shot for turning down the wrong driveway. I've heard worse stories on the news. But I have to do it. I dial her number again, leaving another voicemail as I turn onto the road, following the car.

"Taylor, honey. Please call me back. What's going on? Where did you go? You're old enough to go on your own, but you need to tell us where you're going and who you'll be with. We've talked about this. It isn't safe. We need to know where to find you in case anything..." I catch myself before I say something terrible, speak a jinx into the universe. "Just call me back, okay?"

The wind has picked up, blowing the trees wildly in my headlights, and I can feel the shift in the air even from inside the car.

I can smell the storm coming.

I drive slowly down the gravel road, and finally, a small, white house comes into view. The car in front of me stops, and my throat goes tight. With my headlights locked on it, I now see that this is not my car at all. The color that looked black earlier is now clearly a dark green. I'm here alone in the woods at a house I don't recognize.

My heart gallops in my chest, and I slam the car into reverse, ramming the gas as the person in the car in front of me opens their door. My heart races, throat tight as he steps out.

Go. Go. Go.

Then...Conrad.

My breathing catches, and I hit the brakes, squinting.

I spot the man's head, his face turned back to me from the car in front, eyes narrow as he tries to figure out who I am and what I'm doing. I slam on my brakes again and jam the car into park, opening my door.

"Sorry." My hand is up. I must look like a feral animal. I can't breathe. "It's...sorry, it's me. Corinne from next door. I didn't realize it was you. I'm...I'm looking for Taylor. My daughter. I thought you might've been her. The taillights and everything. I just. I don't know where she is, and you were here and... Sorry. I, um, have you seen her, by any chance?"

He takes half a step closer to see me better. "Corinne? You said your daughter?"

"She's missing. Er, well, she took the car and snuck out. We're just trying to make sure she's okay."

He presses his lips together, looking around. "I can't say I've seen her. Did you check in town?"

My chest deflates. "That's where I was heading when I saw your taillights."

Behind him, the door to the little house opens and an old woman steps outside. She's wearing a long, blue-and-white nightgown, her white hair loose around her shoulders. She looks frail. Sick.

"What's going on?" Her voice is soft on the wind, so low I almost miss it.

"Girl from next door is missing," Conrad informs her.

The woman doesn't say anything as her head turns toward the woods, in the direction of our cabin.

"I'm going to go," I say. "Will you please keep an eye out for her?"

"Sure thing," Conrad says. "She'll turn up. Ain't

many places to go in a town like this. Let me get these groceries inside, and then I'll drive around and help you look. I'll let you know if I see her."

"Thank you," I breathe out, my voice cracking. "Thank you."

CHAPTER TWENTY-ONE

CORINNE WILDE - PRESENT DAY

Two hours later, there's still no sign of Taylor, and I haven't heard from Conrad.

When I get back to Foxglove, Lewis is pacing on the porch. He looks up frantically when I round the last patch of trees, and he sees his car come into view.

I watch in real time as he processes that it's me, not her. His face falls, shoulders slump, and it crushes me because it means he hasn't found her either.

As I exit the car, he rushes toward me. "Anything?"

"I didn't find her." I swallow, licking my lips. "I think it's time we called the police."

He pauses. "I'm not sure."

"I'm not really asking your permission." In fact, I'm already dialing.

He puts his hand on my phone, stopping me. "Don't I get a say in this? She's nearly eighteen. If we handle this the wrong way, she might hate us."

"If we handle this the wrong way, she might end up dead, Lewis. These woods aren't safe. Especially not at night. Especially not for a young girl." The words catch in my throat, and I realize too much about what happened to my mom's sister is playing in my head here. She disappeared and was never heard from again. Maybe I'm overreacting, but she won't answer our calls, and we can't find her. I'm not waiting until it's too late.

I look at him finally, wondering whether he'll agree or leave me alone in this decision too, but eventually, he nods and pulls his hand back.

"I'll try her one more time, but if she doesn't answer, I'm calling the police. Period."

"Agreed." He touches my arm as I tap her name in my call log, waiting.

Seconds pass, but she doesn't answer. I meet Lewis's eyes, warning him of my next step without saying a word. Just as I'm preparing to call the police, deciding what I'll say, the phone rings.

I answer in one breath. "Taylor?"

"God. What do you want, Mom?"

Her voice stalls my heart. "E-excuse me?"

"Why are you blowing up my phone?"

"Where are you? I was about to call the police. I've been all over town looking for you. Everyone is looking for you." My voice is breathy and scared. I can't feel my fingers or toes.

"What the heck? I'm fine."

"I asked where you are. The storm's almost here. It's not safe for you to be driving."

"You can't just disappear like this," Lewis chimes in, leaning over my shoulder to see the phone screen.

"I'm out. I went out."

"Not an answer. You need to tell us where you are. You can't just take my car without asking."

"I didn't take it. I borrowed it. I'll bring it back when you two stop fighting."

We exchange a look of confusion. I'm not sure I heard her right. "But...we weren't fighting," I tell her.

"All you ever do is fight anymore. Over the house, over me. It's miserable. I'm sick of it."

"Honey, what are you talking about? No one was arguing tonight. We made dinner. We were planning to eat together. You need to come home so we can talk about this." It feels so out of left field. I have no idea where any of this is coming from.

Did Lewis say something to cause this after all? Did something happen while I was taking my bath? Or maybe while they were out today? Did he tell her I'm always picking fights? Did he complain about me enough to make Taylor leave?

I side-eye my ex-husband, wondering why I ever thought I could trust him again after all of this. He comes back around for one day, and Taylor disappears. I'm not naïve enough to think that's a coincidence.

"I'm not coming home," she says firmly. "Not tonight."

"Taylor, Bug, listen—"
But she doesn't listen. Not to either one of us.
Instead, she hangs up.

CHAPTER TWENTY-TWO

EMMA WILDE - 1733

I have learned that knocks arriving after nightfall seldom bring kindness. That is why, when I hear a rap at my door this night, my heart stumbles and falls like a newborn foal.

It is neither friendly nor patient, the kind of knock that might come from the neighbors or a passing traveler in need of bread or warmth. No, this feels different down to my bones.

I set the mortar down on the table with cautious hands. My palms are stained green from the rue I've been grinding this evening, and the distinct, spicy scent of rosemary still clings to my dress.

I wipe my hands on my apron, the skin itchy and inflamed from handling nettle earlier.

The knock comes again before I reach the door—angry and demanding.

Carefully, I open it and stare into a familiar face.

"John." My voice is as stiff as an unused muscle, dripping with politeness and kindness I do not feel. I squeeze my eyes shut, shaking my head as I correct myself—out of fear only, not manners. I hate the way the fear tastes, the way the smell fills my nostrils, seeping out of my skin. "Mr. Reardon. What can I do for you this evening?"

The man stands tall in the doorway, so tall he has to crouch down slightly. He holds a hat in one hand, the other shoved into the pocket of his trousers. Behind him, clouds gather in the sky, gray and filled with warning.

A warning is no longer needed. The storm has arrived.

His face is flushed, and I suspect it's more from drink than anger, but I could be mistaken. He's out of breath and reeks of sweat. There's no question he walked here from the village, likely with his thoughts festering like a rotting wound.

"You know why I'm here," he says, his voice deep and slow.

"I'm afraid I do not." I clasp my hands together in front of me.

"No doubt you've had time to think. Plenty and then some. And what have you decided?"

I'm careful to keep my voice steady as I answer. "I've already given you an answer."

"Yes, you said no. It was obvious you needed more time to think."

Rain begins to pour, quieting the earth around us, drowning out our noise. It smacks the roof, a chorus of pelting and pattering so loud I pray the girls won't hear us.

"Sir, I am sorry. My answer remains unchanged. I cannot marry you. I will not."

He steps closer to me, but I refuse to move back. He will not be my stone, and I shall not be his water. He will not move me.

"Those daughters need a father, and you need a husband. There's no denying it, Mrs. Wilde. Now, I'm trying to be reasonable."

"We do not need anything other than what we have. This land is more than enough."

"People have died over less," he mutters, so low I almost don't hear him.

"Foxglove will protect us. My daughters and I are safe here, though we thank you for your concern."

"Protect you." His lip curls with a laugh. "You think the land can do anything to protect you from men? You and your kin, you've always been different. Mad. All the talk of herbs and roots and healing. You think we don't know what you do up here in this house all alone? You think I don't know what you are?"

"I am a woman," I say. "A mother. Nothing more."

"You think you're better than all of us. Tainted goods with a dead husband and two daughters who will end up beggars because their mother can't see past her own stupid pride."

I inhale deeply, breathing in the smell of the storm. It's heavy, like a warning. "I never claimed to be better, sir. Only free. I do not wish anyone any harm. I only want to live in peace with my daughters, here on our land."

He nods slowly then, thinking. "Your daughter, then. The oldest must be coming into her womanhood. I'm willing to marry her, and I'll allow you to remain on this land as long as you live."

Bitter fury rises in me, ready to explode. He'll *allow* me to live on the land I own? Lightning tears through the sky, alighting our faces through the window, mirroring the crack of rage I feel. "That is very kind of you, sir. But I'm afraid the answer is still no."

He lunges forward without warning, mad as a hornet. I jerk back, but my heel catches on my skirt as he grabs my arm. I twist away from his grip and rush across the room, searching for anything I can find to defend myself.

He grabs my skirt as I reach the table. He throws me forward onto it, scattering my herbs and vials to every corner of the room. The mortar is just out of reach, but I grab the first thing I can—the blue-handled herb knife James gave me, the one I used to carve our name into the heart of Foxglove. I roll over against the table as he fumbles with my skirts, and I know just what he means to do.

The knife is slick in my palm, still covered with plant oil. I slash at him once, but his grip doesn't loosen. He spits at me, and I feel it warm and hot on my chin. I swipe again, this time for his face, and the blade catches his cheek.

He curses and covers the wound with both hands. I rush past him, hurrying for the door to lead him away from where the girls are sleeping soundly in their beds. He grabs me just before I make it and slings me across the room.

My shoulder slams into the hearth, and the knife clatters from my hand. My breathing stops as I reach for it, begging—pleading—for my fingers to find it again.

I watch in utter horror as it slides across the floor, striking a place where a knot in the wood has bowed the plank. In a mere second, the knife vanishes between the floorboards, out of sight and unreachable.

My heart thuds in my ears as I curse under my breath, turning to fight with my bare hands, but his own hands are already around my neck. He holds my body down, my cheek pressed against the cold stone. Above me, the fire crackles, and if I could just lift my hand, I could grab a log and burn him. If I were half the witch they claim I am, I could move the flame to his skin with just my words, but I can't.

He lowers his face next to mine, gloating with his foul breath. "You think no man can own you, eh? I warned you of the dangers of being out here alone. How about I show 'em to you now?"

I struggle against his strength, my mind only on the girls. They're sleeping peacefully, and I owe a great degree of thanks to the storm for that. The land is protecting them from the horrors unfolding in their home. But what next? If he kills me, what will come of them? What will he do to my babies? Marry Rose, perhaps, but what of Lyddie? She is too young to marry. Too young to be alone.

And then, as if I conjured her simply by thought—

"Mama?"

It's her voice filling the air. My Lyddie.

I was wrong.

The storm didn't protect her, though it has kept her sister in peaceful dreams. Our noises must have woken her from sleep.

I don't want her to see me like this. I don't want her to know of these monsters just yet. I turn my eyes to her, choking, barely able to get the sound from my throat. *"Lyddie—run—get your sister and go—"*

John swats at her without looking behind him, knocking her to the ground. I fight harder, using every ounce of my strength to remove his hands from neck.

He will kill them both if he gets the chance. If I don't stop him.

The words swell in my chest with a deep sense of knowing, but as my vision fades, I see movement behind John again.

Lyddie is back. Perhaps she never left. She didn't run.

My sweet angel, my lamb, barely ten winters on this earth, stands just behind John on the wood floor. She's barefoot, her hair tangled from sleep, her nightgown dusting the floor. She looks between us. Takes in the sight of the man holding her mother down, at the panic that must be on my face. Without a word or hesitation, she moves.

She takes the fire poker resting on the chair. My eyes lock on her small hands wrapped around the ornate handle, at how perfectly it fits in her palm.

He doesn't see her coming. Doesn't hear her. Doesn't feel her the way I do, even when my vision fades in and out, even when I can no longer hear anything. I feel her moving, know where she is.

She raises the iron poker high above her head, and with one single stroke, she brings it down over his head with more fury than should fit inside her tiny body. She grunts from the force of it, all the breath leaving her little lungs.

Foxglove is filled with the sickening sound of iron against flesh. Against bone.

He shouts—loud, strong—and it startles her. She teeters, stepping back and away from him. For a moment, I'm certain she's going to drop the fire poker and run. For a moment, I hope she will.

His eyes search the air for help that isn't here. The sounds escaping his dry lips become a cry, one that dies in his throat when he stills.

She swings again. He groans, and his groan turns to a gurgle. He stands to his feet, hand to his head as he staggers, turns, and rushes toward her.

Without a drop of fear, she lifts the poker into the air, pointed at him, and when he lunges, I watch as the black iron slices through his neck, silencing him at once.

He drops to the ground in a heap. Firelight casts dancing shadows across his form as I try to catch my breath. My neck burns under my own touch, my skin raw from the wood and stone underneath me as I struggled against him.

I gasp for breath as Lyddie runs to me, her little body shaking as she releases the heavy sobs she'd fought desperately to hold in. I gather her in my arms, rocking her against me. I can't find my voice, can't speak, though I don't know which words I would choose even if I could.

Outside, the storm rages on. Rain smacks the roof like stones, and thunder booms over Foxglove, drowning out all else.

The land tried to warn me today when I felt the storm in my bones, but I ignored it. I wasn't listening hard enough. Lyddie, though, she must've heard. She must've known. This moment, as unfair as it is, was meant for her.

Not her sister. Not me.

My brave, wild daughter answered the call when she felt it, and she saved us. I don't know if I'll ever forgive myself for not being the one to do it.

We remain there, unmoving, for quite some time. When the storm is over, the ground will be soft enough to hide what we've done. The earth will protect our secrets once again.

CHAPTER TWENTY-THREE

CORINNE WILDE - PRESENT DAY

A raindrop hits my cheek, bringing me back to reality. Lewis takes hold of my arm gently, ushering me toward the door. "Let's get inside. The storm is coming."

Of course it is.

The wind picks up, whipping my hair in every direction as we move inside.

"Why would she do this?" I mutter, shutting the door and enclosing us in silence. Of course, nothing is silent here. Not really. The rain patters on the roof, and the wind howls through the cracks in the stone walls.

"She's a teenager," he says, his voice soft and exasperated. As if that's explanation enough. And...I suppose it should be. Maybe I'm expecting perfection from a young woman being raised by two imperfect people.

I look up slowly to find his eyes on me. "We were supposed to do this together." The vulnerability in my voice swells to fill the space between us, the cabin itself.

We were supposed to be a united front. We were supposed to come to bed after a particularly bad day and find solace in each other—to remember that even on the worst days, at least we had each other. And now...we just don't.

"We are doing it together," he says, his hand reaching for mine. Slowly, ever so slowly, our fingers intertwine, and the smile he offers breaks my heart. "Even if we aren't together, I'm still on your team."

"Not in her eyes." Gently, I release his fingers. "I just want her home. She doesn't know anyone here. Where could she possibly be?" Tears sting my eyes as I stare at him, begging him for an answer. Any answer.

"I'm sure she's just driving around. Being a kid."

"How can you be okay right now?"

His face wrinkles, and he looks away, almost smug. But then I realize I've misread him. I hear it in his voice. "You think I'm okay? Corinne, I haven't been okay for months. You think I can live in that house—the house that still smells like you and is dripping with memories of the past twenty-five years—and be okay? But I am, because that's what you want. You needed that house to still be there, for Taylor, and so I have to live in a tomb."

I can't tell if he's angry or hurt, and that scares me. I used to be able to read him so well. "I never thought..."

"I don't think any of us are okay," he says when I don't finish my lingering sentence. "So, if she needs a little space, I say we give it to her."

"We're her parents. We're supposed to keep her safe."

There is a part of me—a sane, rational part—that hears what he's saying. I know Taylor is almost an adult. I know she's going through a lot. But there's this other part that says she is in a new place where she doesn't know anyone, with a terrible storm rolling in, and that she left without warning.

Everything in me is screaming, warning me that something about this isn't right. That I need to get her home so I can better understand what happened today to make her leave.

I move past Lewis on my way to Taylor's bedroom and swing open the door. There on the bed is her new laptop. I open it and type in her password. The same as her old one. That's one of the rules we have—she has access to whatever technology she wants, with the understanding that I will know her passwords and be able to look through her devices anytime I need to.

Parenting in the tech age is not for the faint of heart.

When she was younger, I looked more often. Searched through her things to keep out all the bad. The danger. I was a dragon, guarding the tower I kept her safely inside. But lately, with all the distractions, I've failed. I don't remember the last time I checked on her social media and apps.

What if she's met someone? A predator? What if he convinced her to run away? What if she's meeting him?

I'm leaping to conclusions, I understand, but this is just so unlike the daughter I know. She might have been more difficult than usual lately, but I thought it was because of the divorce. I just accepted that was why.

What if...

What if I was wrong?

I wish more than anything that I could call Mom right now, ask her advice, but I know it wouldn't help. If she even answered the call, the chances of her offering anything helpful right now is slim.

I open Taylor's social media accounts, searching through her recent messages. There aren't many. She's required to keep her accounts private, which means the few messages she has are from people I know. My heart slows slightly.

Maybe I'm overreacting after all.

I open her iMessages, scrolling through her texts there. Lots of complaints to her friends about me. My face burns as I hurry through them, wishing Lewis wasn't standing behind me, reading confirmation that he made the right choice in leaving. If this is what my own daughter thinks of me—what must he?

"What are you looking for?" he asks, touching my back.

"Anyone she might've talked to." I turn around to face him. "Did she mention anything weird today? A new boy, maybe? Or...was she acting differently?"

"She was...quiet, maybe. But not really acting weird."

I shuffle the questions around in my mind, trying to decide what to ask. She left with him, and things were fine. And now she's gone. She came home and didn't say a word. What happened while they were out? Something must have.

"Did the two of you argue? Did she complain about me?"

He hesitates, but eventually says, "She asked about coming home, but we both know it's only because I brought it up." My stomach crashes like ocean waves somewhere deep inside my core. "I shut it down quickly. She was just...complaining to complain."

And she'll have even more reason to complain if I become the bad guy in this situation. I'm walking a fine line, trying to keep her safe and not make her hate me. I don't know what the right move is.

My eyes light up. "Would she have driven home? To...your house?"

The space between his brows wrinkles as he contemplates the possibility. "It's a long drive all on her own. Especially in this storm."

"Maybe you should go home. Just in case."

"I'm not leaving you here without a vehicle." His eyes search mine. "Come with me?"

"No." I cross my arms. "No. Someone has to stay here in case she comes back."

"Well, we don't know that she went home. Unless we get proof she's there, I'm not leaving you."

I purse my lips, thinking. "Fine. I'll call Greta. Have her go by the house and wait to see if Taylor shows up." My eyes flick up to meet his. "Maybe you should call my mom in case she goes there. She seems to answer your calls more than mine."

He studies me. "What are you talking about? I haven't spoken to your mom."

"Don't lie to me right now." I wave my hand at him. "I know you told her you were here. I don't even have time to be mad about it at the moment. I'll yell at you later."

His head cocks slightly to the side. "What are you talking about? I didn't tell her I was here. I'm not lying. I haven't spoken to your mom in months."

My heart sinks as I stare at him. Is it possible he's telling the truth? Then, all at once, it hits me. I know what's happened. I know the one person who might try to poison my daughter against me.

"Of course. She must've been talking to Taylor."

CHAPTER TWENTY-FOUR

CORINNE WILDE - PRESENT DAY

We snap into action. Lewis calls Taylor, and I try Mom. When neither of us get answers, I call Greta. I leave her a panicked voicemail, begging her to call me back.

Mom wouldn't hurt Taylor, of course. She's not a monster. But if the drive to Lewis's house is too far, the longer drive to my mom's is out of the question for Taylor to make on her own. Especially in this weather. If Mom can talk her out of it, or if Greta can instead, I need them to.

A few minutes later, Greta calls back.

"Sorry, I was in the shower. What's wrong?"

I swallow. "I need a favor. Taylor is missing."

"What?" Her voice is softer than I expected. Flatter. She must have someone over. She's trying not to overreact.

"She took my car, and we can't get ahold of her. Er, well, we spoke once and she said she'd come home when we stop fighting, but that's the thing... Today has been a good day. There were no signs she was going to do this."

"Okay, babe, breathe. It's going to be okay. What can I do?"

"Could you try to call her, maybe? Tell her to come home. Or go by our house and make sure she doesn't show up there?" I catch myself calling it *our house*, but I don't correct it. It's the least of my concerns.

"Sure thing. I'll do both. Anything else?"

"I think she might be talking to my mom. If there's any chance you can swing by her house and just make sure she's not there, we'd really appreciate it. I know it's out of your way." I look at the time. "We don't really know what time she left or how long she's been on the road." She and Lewis got back to the cabin nearly four hours ago. "She wouldn't have had time to make it there yet, but soon. By the time you get there, maybe."

"Consider it done. If she's here or at your mom's, I will find her and get her home, okay?"

With that, we end the call, and now there's nothing to do but wait. The cabin's air seems full of something charged. Carbonation. Fire, maybe.

Lightning cracks outside and thunder booms, the world around us as turbulent as I feel inside.

Please let us find her. Please bring her home. I don't know whom my prayer is going to—the universe, Grandma, or Foxglove itself. I just hope someone is listening.

CHAPTER TWENTY-FIVE

JOSEPHINE WILDE - 1765

I've always loved night best of all. I love the way the cabin glows amber from the fire's light. I love the fuzzy feeling over a warm, full belly, and the quiet peace of a good day ending.

Tonight, the smoke curls up from the hearth and the scent of rosemary fills the air from the kitchen where my aunt Rose works at the table.

I love watching her work, love helping even more. On this night, the table is covered in herbs—some I recognize, a few I don't.

Behind the herbs, she has lined up a row of vials, each one decorated with a scrap of paper and a description, so we'll remember their uses.

For a full night's sleep
To ease the belly
To calm a cough

For pain
To extract venom
For the nerves
For rash
To stop the bleeding
To bring down a fever
To heal wounds

I've always found the labels to be strange. Mama and Aunt Rose know most of the tinctures by scent, but they say it may not be either of them who needs each one in the end.

Desperately, I hope they don't mean they think I'll never learn their tricks and secrets. I want to know how to tell a poisonous plant from a safe one on sight, even when the blooms look just the same, as they can. And how to make the perfect remedy for every ailment.

My fingers wrap around my chipped mug as I rock back and forth in my chair. My mother sits in her chair across the room, peeling potatoes for our next meal.

"Have you let him kiss you yet?" Her voice surprises me, interrupting my thoughts, and when I look over, her eyes are on the fire, not me.

My cheeks flush as I look back at my aunt, who is pretending not to have heard the question.

I don't answer right away.

My sister, Elizabeth, and cousins, Rachel and Serena, are already grown. They're married and happy. I am the baby, and therefore, the one left behind. The final daughter to be married off.

"That means yes," she mutters. Her tone is not unkind, but it is pointed. I worry I'll find disappointment as I meet her sharp eyes. She brushes a bit of her silver-threaded hair back from her face. "And the two of you have been to the meadow."

"He wanted to see the orchard," I admit. "It was only a walk. Aunt Rose stayed with us, of course."

"Of course," Mama says. When she says my name, it sounds heavier than it ever has. "Josephine, I want you to be careful with that boy."

I sit taller in my seat. "Yes, ma'am."

She digs in the basket for a new potato. "You love him?"

Heat hits my stomach, pulling somewhere deep. "I don't know. I think I might."

Her smile is tired, and it worries me. "That's how it starts, you know."

"Why do you look so sad? I should think you would want me to marry. Mr. Langley is from a decent family. He is kind to me."

Mama stops her search for a potato, focusing her attention on me. "Oh, he's quite all right, my darling. But this means it's time we had a conversation that comes with age."

I watch her carefully. Beth has hinted at such things, but I've been kept the baby. Kept in the dark. I wish to know everything that comes with being a woman. A wife.

"This will be the most important thing I ever say to you, my love. Do you understand?"

"I'm listening."

"Wilde women have more responsibilities than most, and if you're going to start courting, it's time you learned about them. When it is time to marry, I hope that you'll find a man who loves you and is good to you. Some men aren't."

"Most men aren't," Aunt Rose chimes in under her breath.

Mama doesn't flinch. "Even the best men have bad moments. Even the best men keep secrets and break promises."

"That's terrible." I lower my hands to my lap, thinking of Elliot and how I'd feel if he ever broke a promise. I want to think he's different.

"You, too, will have secrets, my dear. And yours will mean much more than his." She adjusts in her seat. "I'm speaking of Foxglove."

I blink. "The cellar."

"Among other things, yes. The hidden doors. The hollow walls. The tunnels beneath the floor. The set of stairs hidden behind the broom cupboard." She eyes me like she always has when I've been caught doing something wrong. "Don't think I don't know you've found most of her secrets by now." There's a deep breath before she adds, "The dark places we go when we need to vanish are just for us to know. The places they built for us."

"They?"

Her gaze falls toward the hearth, then travels up to the word carved into the stone: WILDE.

Our name. Our home.

"Our mothers. And theirs. The women who bore our name and who knew what it meant to be hunted, to be silenced, to be owned. Long before you or I existed, they carved this house into the land with their bare hands, their tears, and their blood. And from that moment, she has protected us. All she asks is that we keep her secrets. The *daughters*—not the sons—keep her secrets."

Slowly she stands, and I know by the look on her face that her joints are hurting tonight. *Willow bark.* The remedy for her pain comes to me at once, a whisper of a lesson I learned long ago.

She crosses the room and pulls open a drawer near the cupboard. Carefully, she sifts through the contents before pulling something out.

When she returns to me, she reveals a piece of old linen. Her eyes lock on mine, and I feel fear like I've never felt.

"You will think you are the exception. That you can outsmart Foxglove, that you can share her secrets, and there will not be consequences. You will be like many others before you, and you will be wrong." She unwraps the linen, and I gasp at the lock of dark hair. There's also a brass ring and a rusted metal brooch.

"What is this?" I ask, my voice catching in my throat. Whatever it is, it feels like I'm at the bottom of a river, like I can't reach the surface.

"These belonged to the men they loved. The ones they tried to break the rules for." She places it in my hand. "Your grandmother gave it to Rose when she came of age. It's a reminder—a warning—passed down from mother to daughter. Women before you broke the rules for the men they loved, and they paid the consequences."

I stare at the items, afraid to touch them.

"What happened to them?" I can't bear to think of my family being killers.

"Different things," Mama says. Her voice is flat. Not cruel, but not sad. "Now, don't go looking at me like that." She knows what I'm thinking even if I can't bring the words to my lips. Heat blooms in my cheeks. "It's not always us. The stories I've heard...there was a grandfather who got trampled by a horse, another who fell in the creek and never returned. By that same token, a man who threatened a Wilde woman many years ago, who learned her secrets by accident, grew very ill and died in his sleep just weeks later. It is a blessing and a curse, you see, but what matters is that *it is*. You must treat the rule as law, as sovereign. Foxglove does not wish to be known by men. That is the pact she made with the Wilde women who love her. That is what she demands in exchange for all she gives us."

I can't hide my disappointment, and I don't care to try. "But what will I tell my husband? What did you tell Papa?"

"You can tell him you love him. That's all they need. You can share your bed, your life, your table with him. But Foxglove and her secrets belong to you and you alone." She puts a hand over my heart.

"I don't want to lie to the man I love." I feel like a child as cool tears spring to my eyes.

When Mama looks at me, I see no judgment, just calm. She is solemn and steady as she takes the cloth back and returns it to the drawer. Slowly, she pads across the floor and back to her chair. We sit in heavy silence as she sets to work on the potatoes again.

"You are not alone in your feelings, my darling. Generations of Wilde women have shared your sentiments, many of whom fought it and handled it in their own ways. But the result is the same. If you keep her secrets, this cabin will love you. She will keep your daughters safe from the weather and from the wolves. She will give you something to return to whenever you feel lost, and warmth for your tired bones when the world is too cold. She demands very little from us, but loyalty is not optional. Neither is secrecy. I don't tell you this to be cruel, but to prepare you."

Again, the silence stretches long before she adds, softer than before, "One day, you will understand the need for secrets. Even the men we love can become men we don't recognize. Our ancestors understood what you have not learned."

I nod, but she's wrong. She has to be. I will prove it. Elliot and I will be different. Mama gives me a smile that looks wary to the bone, one filled with grief and worry, but she need not worry.

Elliot isn't like the others. The men of whom she speaks. He will keep our secrets.

Later, in bed, it takes me a long while to fall asleep, but when I do, I dream of the women who walked these floors before me. My mother and grandmothers, the ones I know of and the ones I never will. The women who moved through the shadows of Foxglove, hidden and safe, who led their daughters through tunnels, carried them in silence from unnamed danger.

The women who trusted the wrong people.

They were secret keepers. All of them.

Tonight, the secrets rest with me, and I vow—to myself and to Foxglove—to learn from their mistakes.

CHAPTER TWENTY-SIX

CORINNE WILDE - PRESENT DAY

In the kitchen, Lewis puts on a kettle of water as I pace. He finds a bag of chamomile tea in the drawer without me needing to ask.

"Maybe we should call the police. They should be patrolling the highway," I say. "Watching for her car, just in case."

He takes a moment to respond. "I don't want them to pull her over. It would scare her."

"We have to do something."

"We *are* doing something." His voice is soft as he watches me with concern. "We're calling everyone we know, and we're waiting to hear from her."

"I don't do...waiting."

The corners of his lips quiver, fighting a smile. "I'm aware."

"I'm just scared."

He crosses the space between us, gathering me in his

arms without warning. Somehow, it's the last thing I want and everything I need all at once. I rest my head on his shoulder, breathing in the warm, salty scent of him. The scent of my home.

The home that once was.

I step back quickly. It's too much. This is all too much.

"Are you okay? Did I—"

"I need to go back into town," I tell him. I just need to get out of this house.

"I'll come with you."

"No. No. You stay here."

I take a step toward the door as my phone vibrates. I jump, pulling it from my pocket to check the screen, praying it's her.

It's not, but Greta's name is a welcome distraction.

"It's Greta." I read the text message. "She made it to Mom's. Said the entire house is empty. All of her lights are off, and no one answered the door. They must be out. She's heading to our hou—*your* house—next."

The anxiety under my skin is like a thousand tiny spiders preventing me from standing still. I shove my phone back into my pocket and race toward the door, whipping it open. I just need to do something.

I stop when I see the man standing at the door.

Two men.

Conrad and a man I don't recognize. He's stockier than Conrad, but around the same age. They're both close to my mom's age or older, if I had to guess. They're clad in raincoats, positively drenched from the storm. My eyes dart between them as I take in the sight.

"Did you find her?" I ask.

Conrad doesn't move. "You need to come with me."

The blood drains from my face, and I feel Lewis beside me. His hand brushes my arm, his voice the steady rock I need to keep me from tipping over. "What's wrong?"

I can't move. My feet are made of stone.

The men exchange glances, and I don't care who this stranger is. I just want to know what's going on.

"We found a car in the woods," Conrad tells me, his eyes drilling into mine, setting the truth in a safe place in my mind. "It might be Taylor."

CHAPTER TWENTY-SEVEN

CORINNE WILDE - PRESENT DAY

Somehow we end up in Conrad's car. I don't recall the walk to the car or the moment he started it up. I don't recall if they've said anything since we left. All I know is that the moment my mind finds its footing again, I'm in the back seat, my hands clasped together in my lap. Lewis's arms are around me as I stare out the windshield, raindrops pelting the glass like pennies.

I don't know how far we're going or how bad of shape the car is in. How bad the wreck might have been.

Why didn't they check the car instead of coming to get us? What if she's hurt? What if she needs us? What if they could've helped her?

"She's going to be okay." Lewis's voice is close to my ear, his message just for me as he rubs small circles along my spine.

"Was she in the car?" I ask, speaking up. "Was she hurt?"

The other man—the stranger I still don't know—is the one who answers. "There was no one in the car when we stopped. It was empty, but it didn't look like it had crashed. More like someone had pulled over and gotten out."

This phrase sends my brain into new spirals. *How? Why? She wouldn't have just stopped.*

My phone vibrates, drawing me from my thoughts, and Lewis leans away from me, removing his hand from my back and giving me space to pull it out.

My heart skips as I read the name.

"Mom?" I put the phone to my ear, and Conrad turns down the heat so it's easier for me to hear her.

"I have Taylor."

I'm flying and falling and crashing all in a second, my face burning hot. "What?"

"She just showed up at the house. She can stay as long as she wants, but she's safe."

"What are you talking about? She's...there?"

"She says she was tired of the two of you fighting. She's been saying it. You just don't listen."

I can't answer. Can't argue. Lewis leans closer, trying to understand what's happening. "She's there, though? And you're...where? Home?"

"I've already told you that."

"Greta said you weren't home. She was just there."

"What? Who was here? Greta? We've been home all evening."

"I don't..." I can't think. Can't breathe. It's as if my reality has been placed into a blender and puréed.

"She's there?" Lewis asks as I feel the car slowing down. "She's with your mom?"

I nod, but I'm not sure what the truth is. "Can I talk to her?"

"She's just gotten here and is in the bathroom, but I can have her call you back. If you want my advice, though, you should give her space. Both of you."

"So it's not her car?" Conrad asks. "The one up here?"

"What kind of car was it?" Lewis asks, and I realize we should've asked that already.

"Who is that talking?" Mom asks.

Conrad looks at the man, who looks back at me. "A Lexus, I think. Looked black."

My hand trembles without warning, and for just a moment, everything stops. Time doesn't exist. It's just me and the sound of my breathing, the pulsing of my heart.

"It's just up here." Conrad turns down a gravel road as my eyes find Lewis's in the dark.

Neither of us drive a Lexus, but we both know who does, and I see it all over his face. The realization, followed by the questions.

Because this isn't possible either.

My stomach aches. "Mom, can I call you back?"

Before she can answer, I hang up, leaning forward to

get a better look at the car just up ahead, pulled off to the side of the gravel road.

"What the..." Lewis, trying to see as well as I am, is pressed up next to me. Just as confused.

But it's real. It's her.

Greta.

CHAPTER TWENTY-EIGHT

HESTER WILDE - 1787

From my earliest moments, I have understood my home is both a blessing and a curse. My father, Elliot, died before I was brought into the world, and my mother never fully healed from his loss.

My mother was a kind but broken woman. One I never actually got to know. Oh, she was here, all right. She called Foxglove home until the day she died, but she didn't leave the bed most days. It was my mother's cousin who raised me—Rachel. Who fed me and my mother along with her own daughters, who made sure I knew how to mend my dresses and prepare a meal.

Long before the sadness took my mother from me, I knew the price of Foxglove's secrets and just how heavy her weight can be.

Because of all I've lost, because the rules have been hammered into my bones from the time I took my first step, the moment I bring Jonah to live at Foxglove, my hackles are raised, and my world flips on its head.

I do not feel safe here, though I should. I feel in danger of my own tongue, of whatever cruel fate it might condemn him to, this man I love.

I'm thinking of this as I stare at him sitting next to me, our legs brushing on the sofa as the fire crackles in front of us, warming us on this chilly night. Snow covers the ground outside of Foxglove—has for many a night now—and the chill has set into my bones.

He has this way of looking at me—through me—as if he can see everything inside of me, my brain and my thoughts. My heart and my fears. That's how he's looking at me now, innocent and kind as ever as he watches me in the firelight.

And it's because of this, because he makes me let my guard down so, my own heart betrays me. Love and Foxglove do not mix, and I know this. I just wish I didn't.

He touches a hand to my growing stomach, to the babe inside my womb. "Just think of what our little lad will get up to in this place. In the meadow catching frogs and sword fighting with his shadow."

"She'll be a little girl," I tell him, the words slipping out without thought. That's all it takes, and I know this. I *have* known this.

He leans away from me, a peculiar look on his face. "How could you know?" He smiles up at me so brightly it hurts, trusts me so much it hurts.

I swallow hard. "I didn't mean anything by it. My family always have girls first, that's all."

"We may break the spell, then," he says with a wink, and the word seeps into me like water into soil.

My lips are tight as I force a smile. "Perhaps."

My mother's warnings, the images of her wasting away in her bed flash into my mind like lightning. Like thunder.

No man must ever know Foxglove's secrets.

I swore to myself I would never make her mistakes, that I would never fall in love, never let my guard down. And yet here I am, so painfully in love it drips off of me like sweat. And for the first time, I understand why she broke the rules and told my father. I understand the feeling of wanting to be so close to someone you think about cracking your ribs open and sliding them inside of you.

"A little girl will be all right," he promises, kissing my cheek. "A daughter to tend to the house and keep us fed. A girl with her mother's eyes."

"And your smile," I agree.

"And then more. The bigger the better, I say. Eight or nine, likely. As many girls as you desire, but we'll need a boy or two to pass along my charm, as well as our name and this house." He crosses his hands together behind his head, leaning back in his seat. "I'm willing to try as many times as is necessary, so long as you don't mind."

My breath goes steely. "Oh. Foxglove will stay with our daughters." We haven't spoken about this, though we should have. I've been so petrified about telling him the wrong things that I haven't told him any of the right ones.

He leans his head to the side, curiosity glimmering in his dark eyes. "What on earth do you mean?"

I hesitate to answer. Not for fear of him—Jonah would never lay a harsh hand on me—but for fear of how to answer. I feel as if I'm walking on the tightest rope and a fall in either direction will destroy everything.

"Foxglove belongs to the Wilde women. It will pass from my name to our daughters', should the Lord bless us with them."

His jaw hangs open as he stares at me, bewildered. "Darling, you are my wife. Foxglove is as much mine as it is yours. And it will be our sons'."

"Foxglove is not the same as other houses. Other homes. It belongs to daughters only. That's the way it has always been and how it must stay."

The warmth of his expression dries up like a puddle in the afternoon sun. "You must know no gentleman would ever agree to such an arrangement. What will they think of me?"

"I should think it doesn't concern any 'they' of which you speak. Your concern should be with your wife." I take his hand and place it on my stomach again. "With your daughter. We should've spoken about this already, and for that I apologize. But I'm afraid I can't budge on this, and I'd ask you not to press the issue. For both our sakes."

He pulls his hand back from me, but not roughly so. "You're a madwoman, and I love you. We'll discuss this more tomorrow. Once you're not so tired."

"I am not tired." Panic seizes my lungs as I realize what I've done. How could I have been so foolish? How have I let this happen? "I beg you to let this go, Jonah. Foxglove is your home as long as I am breathing, but it will be mine until it is your daughter's. And her daughter's after that. Our sons may stay, and their families, too. We've always been able to make room. But Foxglove belongs to the Wilde women. Please just say you understand."

His eyes dance between mine. "You speak of this house as if it is a breathing entity, not a pile of stones."

The moment the words leave his mouth, the breath deflates from my lungs. Something sparks in the darkest depths of his eyes, an understanding that brings me pure terror. For it is not only understanding I see—it is something far more dangerous. Something hungry rests there, a monster that I have awoken. It stretches its back and yawns at me, ready.

"You know, my father warned me of the whispers he's heard about your family, but I chose not to believe it because I loved you. *Love* you. But you must tell me, Hester, and you must tell me now. Is this magic you speak of? With the house? With our daughter? Is what they say about the Wildes true?"

My breath is like frozen fog, so cold in my chest I can't quite catch it. *Magic.* The word feels strange.

Wrong. There is no magic in this house, not in the way he means. What we have is different, but no less powerful. It is a love for the land and the way it loves us back.

It is a bond for which we have no name.

My heart races something wild against my ribs as I hold his gaze, trying to make sense of what he's asking. I cannot tell if he understands the weight of this moment, of what he's doing. I do not know where Foxglove draws the line, but I know I must lie and lie well.

"Don't be patronizing," I say, stroking his shoulder. "The only magic that exists in this house is this babe growing strong in my belly."

His smile is soft, but the hunger hasn't faded. The beast in his gaze is still wide awake. "You would tell me, wouldn't you? If there was something to know?"

I nod, pulling my lip into my mouth. "'Course I would."

He looks away from me then, toward the hearth, but the panic is already spreading through my bones and flesh. My body knows what my heart doesn't want to accept.

It is already too late. Even without my saying a word, Foxglove's secrets—my secrets—have entered his mind. I let him into my heart and this house, and I fear doing so has sentenced him to an early grave, just like my pa.

The conversation dies in uneasy silence, both of us lost in our own thoughts. Later in bed, we say good night with a quiet kiss, and as he lies sleeping peacefully beside me, I tell myself everything will be okay. That he doesn't know anything, not really. That I did what I was supposed to do.

But the next day, he's different. And the next. A week goes by, and I know something has changed at the very core of our marriage. Jonah is distant. He stays out late into the night, and when he returns, it's often he's been drinking.

His eyes are hazy when they meet mine, and I still see the beast there, lurking and waiting, no longer asleep, no longer tired. His voice becomes cautious, ready for something I do not understand.

I keep waiting—for what I do not know. For him to ask again, to push for answers that will take his life. But he doesn't. He just smiles that Jonah smile and tells me good night.

Weeks pass and nothing happens. We settle into a normal that is not quite our own, but not quite new.

This morning, when he needs to go into the village, he kisses my cheek, and I stroke Jewell's mane while he saddles her up. I wave goodbye to them without much care. My worries have started to wane.

When two days pass with him still gone, fear returns with a vengeance, gnawing away in my stomach. I remember the stories passed down from mother to daughter, of men arriving, of accusations and torches.

I worry they will come for me. That he will tell them what he suspects, and they will believe him because he is a man, and I am but a stupid woman.

Then there is a knock.

When I open the door, it is a man from the village who awaits me, with a face I barely recognize. He does not carry a torch, nor is he traveling with a horde of men. He is alone, and he wears a grim expression on his wrinkled face.

"Mrs. Wilde." He pulls his hat off his head and places it over his heart, his voice trembling slightly. He doesn't need to utter another sound, for I know in an instant what words will come. "I hate to bring this news to ya, on a Sunday no less. Your husband, Jonah, well they found him late last night, ma'am. Dead."

My fingers turn to ice as I squeeze them against my skirt. I can't summon a single word.

"They don't know what happened. He was in the woods, just outside of the village."

The earth beneath my feet seems to swing this way and that, and I take a small step away from him, grabbing onto the door to keep from falling over. In front of me the man is still talking, but for the life of me, I can't understand what he's saying. His words blur together, silenced by the blood rushing in my ears, as loud as a raging rapid.

I find my senses again as his words come back into focus.

"The reverend said it looked like the animals had gotten to him before he was found. He was..." He ducks his head. "Forgive me, Mistress, but he was torn apart. I can let his family know, if you need. His father is a good friend."

I think I nod, but I can't be sure. My legs below me are as liquid as broth, and the walls are holding their breath, closing in.

Eventually, the man leaves, though I don't recall sending him away. When night falls, I sit in Foxglove's kitchen, drinking my tea with trembling hands.

The world feels terribly lonely, terribly silent. In my belly, my daughter moves, as if to tell me I'm not alone. Someday I will tell her why she is wrong. Why life as a Wilde woman will always be lonely.

I don't sleep for two more days, except for fits of exhaustion here and there. I sit and I drink my tea, thinking of my mother, wondering if her pain felt this sharp.

I watch the fire as it dances, casting shadows that look strangely like women, and I imagine they are the women long gone from this place—women who knew better than to trust. Women who lived, loved, and lost in the belly of this house—a mother's womb meant to protect and hold us. Though for some, the grip could be too tight.

Someday I will smile again. For my daughter, if no one else. I won't waste away like my mother, I promise myself that.

But for now, silent tears fall down my cheeks, and I don't dare dry them. These tears feel sacred, necessary. I cry for my mother, and for myself, and for a home I will never be allowed to share.

CHAPTER TWENTY-NINE

CORINNE WILDE - PRESENT DAY

As soon as Lewis steps out of the car, I leap from my seat, rushing forward ahead of the men. I reach Greta's car in what feels like a vacuum.

All things, all time, all sound have ceased to exist.

I run my hand along the door, breath shaky. It's definitely hers. Even through the rain-covered window, I can see the David Rose air freshener hanging from the rearview mirror.

Very uninterested in that opinion.

I pull at the handle, surprised to find it unlocked. Rain smacks into me, drenching my hair and clothes as I lean inside the car, searching for her phone or any sign she's been here recently.

Come on.
Come on.
Come on.

I pull back out. "She's not here," I say, though it's

obvious. "The keys are gone." I look at Conrad. "This is our friend's car. She wasn't supposed to be here." I shield my eyes from the rain, searching through the dark for answers that feel impossible. "She shouldn't be here."

"Maybe she was coming to help," Lewis guesses.

"Even if she was, she was supposed to be at Mom's house, like, minutes ago. She wouldn't have had time to make it here. We're too far away, especially with the rain. This doesn't make any sense."

"We need to look for her. Make sure she's okay. Maybe she had car trouble and tried to walk to find you. The storm may have knocked cell service out. We'll walk this way and look for her," the man with Conrad says, nodding his head farther into the woods. "You guys go that way. Oh. What's her name? So we can yell for her."

"Greta," I tell them, moving to the opposite side of the car. With serious looks, the two men move away into the woods, and I hear them calling for her.

I shout her name, but it's drowned out by the sound of the storm. If she's out there, she'll have no way of knowing I'm calling for her. Is she hurt? Is she hiding? Did I...misunderstand somehow?

I think back over our conversation. Did she ever tell me outright that she was at home? I can't remember. I can't remember anything. She wouldn't lie to me. She wouldn't. I know her. Something else happened. Something I'm not understanding.

She was...she was showing a house. And then...she was home taking a shower.

Thoughts swirl in my head like a wind tunnel, as unstable as the storm raging around me. I open my text messages, reading over the last one I received from her.

> Checked your mom's. No lights on, and no one answered the door. Garage doors are closed and doesn't look like anyone's home. I'm heading to Lewis's now. Keep you posted. Hang tight.

There's no way to misunderstand that. And there's no possible way she was just at my mom's and is here now.

It doesn't make sense and yet...

I stare down at my phone again, finding her name in my call log. As it rings, I beg her to pick up—beg for some sort of sign or signal, an answer.

Ahead of me, Lewis disappears into the tree line, his face shielded with both hands.

After several rings, it's clear she's not going to pick up. I curse under my breath and lower the phone from my ear. Just then, it connects. I rush to raise the phone again.

"Hello? Hello? Greta, can you hear me?" I plug my opposite ear. "Greta? We found your car. In the woods. I can't hear anything. Where are you?"

There's no answer.

I switch the phone to my other ear. "Are you okay? It's storming out here. I'm worried. Where are you? You're really scaring me."

I think I can vaguely hear soft breathing on the other line, but it's hard to tell. Either way, she doesn't answer. "Greta? Can you hear me? Please say something."

"Corinne!" Lewis shouts, and when I look over, he's disappeared farther into the woods somewhere.

I've lost him. I'm standing alone in the dark, the rain pouring down around me.

My heart climbs into my throat as I end the call. I hurry forward, past the car and into the trees. "Lewis?"

"Corinne!"

I can hear the panic. The fear. He's close. "Lewis!"

"Corinne!" he shouts again, still hidden somewhere ahead in the darkness.

"Where are you?" I bellow, brushing water from my face and blowing it from my lips as quickly as it falls. I'm practically drowning.

"Here!" His voice is close.

I don't think, I move.

I dart in the direction the sound is coming from.

"Keep talking! I'm coming!" I run, and I race, and I pray that he's okay. That this is all some misunderstanding.

And then, all at once, I trip. Over a root or a rock, I'm not sure. My hands slam into the muddy ground, my face next. I taste the mud, and it feels as if there's sand in my mouth.

I sit up as I feel Lewis grab my arms. "Are you okay?"

I scrub the mud from my face, spitting it from my teeth. "What happened? What did I..." As I turn over, as the dirt clears from my eyes, I see. I don't finish the question, as it's already been answered for me.

Through the rain, I'm looking at what I tripped over.

Or rather *whom* I tripped over.

Through the rain, I'm staring at my husband's muddy form as he kneels next to my best friend's body.

CHAPTER THIRTY

CORINNE WILDE - PRESENT DAY

Cool, wet leaves cake my hands and arms as I turn around on my knees to get a closer look at her.

Is she okay? Nothing about this makes any sense.

I just spoke to her. She was home. She was…showering. Then driving. I suspected she had someone at her house. A date. She was vibrant. She was fine.

And now? She's lying on her side in the cold rain, in woods where she has no reason to be.

Lewis squeezes my shoulder gently, his wild eyes full of fear as lightning flashes in the sky. "Are you okay? Are you hurt?"

"I'm fine." I shove his hands away, turning her onto her back. "What happened?"

"We shouldn't move her."

I'm not listening. "Is she…" My hands search her face, and I place my head against her chest, listening for a heartbeat.

"She's alive," he says.

A wave of relief washes through my body, white-hot. He's right. Her chest is rising and falling with slow, steady breaths.

I run a hand over her tenderly, searching for injuries, my fingers shaking as I wait to feel blood. There's no sign of any.

"It doesn't make sense. It's like she's sleeping. She's not hurt."

"The injuries could be internal." Lewis's response is quiet, but it seems to reverberate through the woods. My eyes fall to her stomach, imagining a black-and-purple bruise spreading across her stomach the way I've seen on the medical shows Taylor loves.

Gently, I lift her shirt, just enough to ease my fears.

We hear footsteps and heavy breaths, and my heart ricochets in my chest. I can't leave her. There is no time to think, to process. I can't hide, even if I wanted to, so I wait. I sit still as a stone, silent, as I watch.

A figure appears through the rain, then another. I release a breath of relief.

"You found her?" Conrad asks, dropping down next to us. "What happened?"

"We don't know," I say. "She's unconscious."

"We need to get her up," Conrad says, his hands hovering over her body as if he's afraid to touch her. "Get her to the hospital."

He looks over at the other man, who nods.

In agreement, we each grab hold of her. Lewis and I

take an arm, a shoulder. Conrad's friend slides his arms under her back, bearing the brunt of her weight, and Conrad keeps her legs from dragging the ground.

"Careful," I warn as we take hold and lift. The second she leaves the ground, her eyes flutter, as if awakening from a long sleep. "Greta?"

We pick up speed, hurrying through the forest. The slick mud makes it impossible to stay steady. She turns her head and rests it on my chest, and I hold her tighter against me, wanting to protect her from the rain smacking her face.

"It's going to be okay," I promise.

Her eyes open as we reach Conrad's car, and she jolts, screaming. She flails, trying to escape our grasp.

"It's me. It's me. It's me," I rush out, one hand up to defend myself from her swings.

It takes a second for her eyes to find focus on me. "*Corinne?*"

Lewis pulls the car door open, using his foot to push it back farther, and we slide her inside. I sit down next to her and shut the door. She wipes the rain from her face, eyes searching and scanning in a panic.

"What are you..." She jerks her head this way and that. "Where are we?"

I turn toward the window as Lewis opens the door on the other side, sliding onto the seat. Conrad and his friend are next. Once we're all safely inside the car, all eyes are trained on Greta.

"We're in the woods outside of Foxglove. We...we found you out there."

Her eyes find mine without urgency, still dazed and afraid. When they land on me again, a sort of calmness washes over her expression. "What's happening?"

"You're okay," I tell her, desperately hoping it's true. "Do you remember what happened?"

She squeezes one eye shut, looking around, but doesn't answer. "Do you remember coming here? We spoke on the phone. You were supposed to be looking for Taylor. I don't understand why you're here. Or how."

She opens her mouth slowly, eyes lost and dizzy. "I...I don't remember. I was at the cabin. At Foxglove visiting you..."

She's lost an entire day's worth of memories. "She needs to go to the hospital," I say, not breaking eye contact with her. "We need to go. Now."

"No. No. I'm okay," she argues. Because of course she does. She wouldn't be Greta if she wasn't stubborn and pigheaded, even when she can't remember where she is or why. "Really, I'm okay. I just...I need to sit down."

"You are sitting down. You've been sitting down," Lewis argues with her. "What are you doing here, anyway?"

She gives him a stern look, and I'm grateful, at least, that she still has her fire. "What the hell are you talking about? Foxglove? I've been here."

"No. You left yesterday." I touch her cheek. "It's okay. It's okay."

She looks at me with confusion swimming in her eyes. "What are you talking about?"

"You left Foxglove to go back to work, remember? We've spoken. You did showings, and you were supposed to be looking for Taylor. You said you stopped by my mom's house."

She looks between us. "That's impossible. I don't remember anything past leaving the cabin. I was..." She pauses. "I'm sorry. I don't really remember that. The last thing I remember is hugging you in the yard. And then... I was driving and someone was..." She pauses again, thinking. I can practically see her scraping the cobwebs from the hazy memory. "Someone was standing in the road. They flagged me down."

"Who?" I lean into her, like she is a soft song I'm trying to hear better. "Who was it?"

She pauses, rubbing her neck. "I... I don't remember. I'm sorry. I... Maybe I'm imagining all of it. It feels hazy."

"Your phone." I want to prove my story to her. I need her to remember. "I'll show you." I reach for her pockets. "It wasn't in the car, so it has to be..." But as I check her damp jeans, I realize it isn't there either. "What the..."

That's when I remember someone else answered her phone before. When I called, there was only breathing, but someone *did* pick up.

"Someone stole it." Her words are almost a question as she looks at me with an expression of perfectly mixed fear and confusion. She lifts her hand to her neck again, massaging it. I brush her hair back, examining her neck in the light from the dashboard in the front of the car.

I slap Lewis's arm, and he and Greta both startle. "Look at this."

He leans over as Greta turns her neck for him to see. "What's wrong?" she asks, eyeing us both.

"A bruise." Lewis touches his finger to the bruise there on her pale flesh.

"It's sore," she agrees, rubbing it again.

"It's not a bruise." I pull my phone out and turn on the flashlight. Greta squeezes one eye shut, blinded. Lewis leans toward me again, looking. "It's a needle mark. Someone injected her with something."

Greta tenses against me. "What?" Her voice shoots octaves higher, out of breath.

"It's going to be okay," I promise her. Promise myself. My mind is working overtime, hunting for an answer to this mystery, the missing piece to this puzzle, but I keep turning up empty.

"Someone has your phone," I say, thinking aloud. "If we can figure out who it is, that'll be a start. It'll lead to answers. It has to." I tap her name on my screen and hold my breath, waiting.

When the line connects, I hear it again—the breathing, but nothing else.

"Who is this?" I demand, my voice low and shaky. "Who are you?"

CHAPTER THIRTY-ONE

HANNAH WILDE - 1814

The night air is heavier than usual, the sort of stillness that presses against your ribs, suffocating and thick with anticipation. With dread.

On tiptoe, I slip through the narrow hall toward the girls' room, a gnawing panic in my throat. Foxglove is too quiet, even for this hour, and each step on the wood floor makes a soft thud, drawing an arrow right to me.

Every so often, the walls creak and groan under the pressure of the wind outside, but it's not enough to mask the sounds of my movements.

The silence around me shreds my nerves. I listen for the intruder I saw coming up the road moments ago—horse beneath him, lantern in one hand. His arrival at such a late hour can only mean he's come for me.

I reach the doorway and draw in a deep breath, holding it as I prepare myself. Moonlight filters through the window, casting harsh shadows and pale-blue light across the room.

My eyes fall to Millicent first, to the sight of her tiny body tangled in bedsheets. Her face is sweet and peaceful, the sort of peace she doesn't know when she's awake. Beside her, Katherine sleeps like a windstorm. Her body is twisted, lying sideways, hair wild on her mattress, mouth dropped open.

My divergent daughters. Olive oil and river water.

I step forward, my heart breaking as I do. They should be safe in their beds, safe in their home. Just eight and four, they are still too young to understand what is happening tonight, why I must wake them.

I crouch down next to Katherine's bed and place a careful hand over her mouth. Like she's been struck, her eyes shoot open. She stares at me in the darkness, and for what feels like a lifetime, I freeze. I can't summon a breath as I pray she won't scream.

"Shhh..." I whisper, shaking my head urgently. The sound that escapes my lips is more air than voice. He could be anywhere now. At our windows, at the door. My eyes flick up to the window on the wall just briefly, looking for him as if he's a ghost.

Her petrified breaths warm my palm, fast and worried, and I wish then I could take her fear away, let it seep into my skin and carry it with me. Feel it for the both of us.

Slowly, I lift a finger to my lips, nodding with hope

she'll understand what I'm asking. I need her to be silent. Quiet as the butterflies she loves so much.

When she nods back to me, I slowly pull my hand away from her mouth one finger at a time, the world standing still around us.

Her little eyes are wide with confusion, but when I lift a finger to my lips again, she nods, entirely trusting and obedient. She waits to see what I will do next, to understand why I've woken her. The blind trust our babies have in us is painful sometimes, the purest form of love that we have not earned.

I hold up a trembling finger, telling her to wait without saying a word, then move to Millicent's bed. When I pull back her blanket, she stirs, and the smell of sweat and urine hits my nose. I scoop her up into my arms as a pang of guilt strikes me in the center of my chest.

She's had another accident.

They happen more often now, since their father passed last spring. A bad cold took him from us in just a handful of days, and neither of the girls have been the same since.

Katherine has grieved in her own way, but it's Millicent who has taken it the hardest. The grief and fear have piled up inside her in ways that devastate me. She is fearful of everything. Meek. She worries so much for such a little girl. Doesn't run or play like she used to.

I wish my mother were around to advise me, to tell me what to do, but the only way I speak to her now is when I visit her grave. Mama would know how to fix this; she always did. Without her here to guide me, all I can do is keep my girls safe, and tonight, that is my only job.

I reach for Katherine's hand, still waiting in her bed.

No. I freeze when I hear footsteps on the porch.

The next sound feels as if it's right next to my ear.

KNOCK. KNOCK. KNOCK.

Slow, like that. Drawn out, like he's a wolf encircling us in the woods. The girls watch me with wild but tired eyes, trusting that I will make this all right. They know nothing yet of monsters or evils, but they know the fear in my breath.

Another knock comes quicker, then another—*angrier*—and I can't help the way I quake at the sound, as if he's knocking right on my flesh.

"Hannah!"

I wince. The devil knows my name, but I don't yet know his. The knot of dread in my stomach twists deeper, warning me of what's to come. Warning me we aren't safe here. Not for a moment longer.

His voice seeps through the cracks of the door again, low and teasing, like smoke. "I know you're in there, woman." His words are jagged and slurred through the thin wood of the door, proof of the whiskey swimming in his veins like a current.

I swallow, steeling myself. I place a hand on Katherine's back, nudging her from the bed and nodding toward the wall, mouthing the word "go."

She just stares at me, not understanding.

I can't blame her. She doesn't know, and shouldn't need to.

She's too young.

She fears the monsters lurking in the shadows, but I haven't had the heart to tell her about the monsters that will someday pass her in the village with a tip of a hat and a kind word, the monsters she won't see coming. How do I explain that they are so much worse than anything hiding under her bed?

She presses her little lips together with a look that says she's ready, that she trusts me. Bravery fits my daughter, sits on her features well, and that breaks something deep within me.

She doesn't make a sound as she tiptoes forward. Millicent wiggles in my arms, rubbing her eye with the back of her hand. She doesn't speak, nor cry. She just watches. Just waits.

I desperately wish my George were here. He would protect us.

I am not ready for this. Not on my own.

Still, I move, my hands trembling fiercely as I nudge the head of Katherine's bed aside just a finger's length or so. The metal feet groan against the wood floor, and I wince, my mouth going dry.

I push against the boards and hear the familiar click. The wall opens, revealing the narrow, hidden passageway. When Mama showed me this place—and the others—she said it was put here long before I was born, before even she or my gran came along, which seems an awfully long time, if you ask me. She said it was left by someone who knew there would be nights like this one. Nights when the storms and wind raging outside were preferable to the monster awaiting us inside the walls of Foxglove.

They gave us hiding places and passages in which to move like shadows, to disappear whenever we might need to. Somehow, they predicted this night, and I'm eternally grateful for it.

I push Katherine forward into the passage, holding Millicent close to my chest, her tiny body limp and heavy in my arms. She's nearly too big for me to carry her anymore, but I don't dare ask her to walk.

Behind us, the door at the front of the house slams open.

"Hannah Wilde!" His voice roars like a beast, full of rage. Katherine looks up at me, and I shake my head, nudging her again. I push the hidden door closed behind us and take her hand. The air in the passageway is thick with dust, and very narrow. My skin scratches against the grooves of the cold stones as I straighten us on our path.

We move in silence, my focus only on getting away, on finding safety. The girls stay close to me, Katherine's hand in mine, Millicent's arms around my neck. They don't speak or ask questions, their instincts warning them to keep silent. To trust me.

I hear him stumbling through the house, yelling my name and slamming doors. It sounds as if he's breaking everything in his path. Knocking over my precious things, *irreplaceable* things, in his drunken rage.

Foxglove creaks under his weight, telling me where he is, keeping me alert to his movements. There are times when he feels very close to us, when his footsteps stop with just the thin wall between us, and—when we're deeper into the passage—just above our heads.

He paces and curses, saying things not meant for little ears, but all his anger means is he hasn't found us.

I move steadily, not rushing for fear I might trip and fall, but my breath is coming heavier. My arm burns with Millicent's weight, palm sweaty from Katherine's tight grip. My chest aches. Still, we move. I lead them through the winding path, connecting one to the next until the scent of fresh air meets my nose.

I see the old spiral staircase, and I know we've reached the oak tree. From above, a small crack of light can be seen, peeking around the iron door.

We could stay down here, I know, and I weigh the possibility heavily, but in the end, it feels as if it's too much of a risk. He may never leave Foxglove, may wait for our return, and if that's the case, we must run under the cover of night.

I set Millicent down finally, my arm screaming for relief from her weight, and sink to my knees so I'm nearer to them.

I pull them in close so they can hear me whisper. "We're going to climb these stairs, my darlings. And when we get to the top, we're going to run." I kiss their tiny hands. "I want you to promise me, no matter what happens, no matter if I fall or...no matter if I can't come with you any longer, I want you to promise me that you will run into the woods and you will keep running until you reach the orchard. And once you get there, you will hide, and you won't come out." I squeeze my eyes closed, wondering to what fate I'm sentencing them.

If he catches me, if they run alone—hide alone—who might find them?

If they make it to the orchard safely and survive the night, who will come looking for them? Who will save them?

Their cousins might come someday, but how long will they last all on their own?

Will they die without me?

Will someone hurt them?

Tears sting my eyes, burning my throat, and I force the thought away. I won't let that happen. I refuse.

"We promise," Katherine whispers.

Millicent just nods.

Protect them, I beg Foxglove, rising to my feet. *If anything my mother ever told me is true about you, protect them. Protect us.*

At the top of the stairs, I push open the door and peek out at the night sky.

The moon shines bright, lighting our path. It's the same moon that has looked down upon so many mothers, grandmothers, and sisters before me. The same moon that will shine on generations of daughters after me.

For their sake, we have to make it through this. With their strength, we will.

The wind cools my sweat-soaked skin as I slip out of our hiding place. A rock sits in my stomach as I look around, watching like a doe in a meadow.

When it feels safe to do so, I rush to close the door and cover it with stones and leaves once again, protecting our secret. Then, I wave for the girls to follow. Their faces are pale and streaked with tears I had not seen fall. I want to comfort them, but I can't. Not yet.

We need to run, and now.

I inhale deeply, filling my lungs with the cool night air. With a quick glance back at Foxglove, I pull them forward, my bare toes digging into the damp ground.

Without a word, we move, rushing forward just like we planned. We don't stop when we hit the tree line, or when we pass the creek. We don't stop at the fallen log or the rock that looks like a bear.

We run as hard and as fast as our legs will carry us.

And, in the end, Foxglove keeps her word. We arrive at the orchard safe and sound.

CHAPTER THIRTY-TWO

CORINNE WILDE - PRESENT DAY

The moment the question leaves my lips, the stranger on the other end hangs up without giving an answer. Conrad starts the car and backs us out of the flooding road. Lewis, Greta, and I share worried looks. I have no idea what to make of this. Of any of it.

Why would someone hurt Greta? Why was she back here in the first place? I feel as if I'm in a dream I can't wake up from. And still, Taylor is missing.

Taylor.

I've been so distracted I momentarily forgot our daughter ran away from us.

"I'm going to call Taylor and tell her to stay with Mom," I say. "I may not want her there, but at least she's safe far away from here until we figure out what's going on."

"Taylor's with your mom?" Greta asks. "I thought

you said I was supposed to be looking for her. That she was missing."

"We just found out where she is," Lewis fills in as I dial.

She doesn't answer—no surprise—so I leave her a voicemail. "Taylor, honey, it's Mom. Listen, I don't want you to worry, but I need you to go ahead and stay at your grandma's tonight, okay? I'll explain later, but just stay where you are. Where it's..." I stop myself from saying *safe*, not wanting to worry her. "The storm is getting bad. You're better off there right now. Okay, we'll, um...we'll talk in the morning, okay? I love you."

I end the call just as I feel the car lurch. Conrad slows the car to a stop without warning.

"What's..." I don't finish the question. Don't need to. I can clearly see what's wrong. Up ahead, a fallen tree lies across the road.

Conrad and the man lean forward in their seats, getting a better look. They turn back toward us almost in unison.

"We'll have to turn around," Conrad says. "This is the only way into town tonight."

"What? No. She has to go to the hospital." I gently squeeze Greta's arm.

"I don't disagree, but unless someone in here has a plane I don't know about, there's no way. We can't move the tree on our own, especially not in the middle of this storm."

"Then, we'll get out and walk," I argue.

Conrad shakes his head. "The storm's too bad. The roads are already starting to flood, and we haven't even made it to the worst parts."

I glance out my window with a sinking feeling in my gut. Dark water covers most of the road. There's no denying he's right.

"About half a mile up, the road floods for quite a ways every time it rains," he goes on. The storm is so loud he's having to shout to be heard. "If it's already this bad here, it'll be worse there."

"We could try," Lewis says, but he doesn't sound convinced.

"It's not safe," his friend says. "You can call an ambulance if you want, but whether or not they'll be able to make it through is questionable until the storm clears and the water drains. For now, we'll get home and get the wound on her neck cleaned up. Get a better look at it and ride out the storm."

"There has to be another way," I argue, trying to think of one. He's right, however. This is the only road into town, but I can't give up.

"Look, he's right. Let's just go back to Foxglove. I'm really okay," Greta tells me, putting a hand on my shoulder. "It's not worth dying over. We'll find a way into town once the storm has passed."

"You have no idea if you're okay. You don't even know what day it is." My words are biting, but she takes them in stride.

"Either way, we don't have a choice."

"She's right." Conrad backs the car up, turning us around.

"Hey, who are you guys anyway?" she asks Conrad and the stranger. "Why do I recognize you?"

"You met him," I remind her. "At the house after Taylor's stuff was ruined. You saw Conrad then. Our neighbor."

"That's right," Conrad says. "And this is my husband, Benji."

"Husband?" The word smacks me in the chest. "I thought...what about the woman at your house earlier?"

Conrad glances back at me. "My mom. I was delivering her groceries before the storm. Benji is my husband and a nurse. He can take care of her, at least until we can get more help."

Relief floods my chest so quickly it takes me by surprise. "A nurse."

"Partially retired." Benji smiles at me. "Also a baker, but he only ever brags about the nurse part. I'm not sure whether to be offended." I remember the cookies then. "It's nice to finally meet you."

Before I can respond, my phone rings. "Taylor." I put the phone to my ear quickly. "Hello?"

"Mom, what are you talking about? I'm not driving all the way to Grandma Billie's."

My veins freeze, then turn to slush. "What?"

"It's way too far. I'm not driving there alone."

"You..." My head spins. "You're not already there?"

"What? No. I'm...I'm in town. I was supposed to be

meeting Madison, but her mom made her turn around when the storm got bad."

"You're... Jesus, I don't understand, Taylor. You're in town? Right now?"

"What's the big deal?"

"The tree," Lewis reminds me.

The tree is the last thing on my scrambled mind, but he's right. "You won't be able to get home, honey. Listen...there's a tree in the middle of the road." I lower the phone, talking to Conrad and Benji. "Is there a hotel in town? Our daughter is stuck there."

"No hotel, but there's an old bed and breakfast on the square," Benji tells us. "Aranka's a friend of ours. I can call her and ask her to get a room ready."

I put a hand on his shoulder. "Thank you." With that, I relay the message to Taylor, telling her to get there and stay safe while we wait out the storm. Then I call Mom.

"You lied to me."

"What are you talking about?" *At least she answered this time.*

"Taylor isn't with you. She's here. In town."

Mom chuckles under her breath. "You're losing it. I don't have time for whatever sort of game you're playing tonight, Corinne. I'm old and tired."

"Cut the crap. Why would you lie to me? Do you have any idea what I've been going through tonight? You're a mother. You have to know how scary this is for me."

"Stop." But now my mom's voice doesn't sound annoyed. She sounds...worried. Her words come slow, measured. "Taylor is right here. I'm...I'm looking at her."

My breathing catches in my throat. "Impossible. Let me talk to her."

"She doesn't want to talk."

"Mom—"

Lewis takes the phone away from me, putting it on speaker. "Billie, it's Lewis. Look, tonight has been weird, and we just want to hear from our daughter. If she's with you, please put her on the phone. We just want to know that she's there."

She sighs. "Well, hang on a second."

Then, after several seconds of excruciating silence, she's there. Impossible, but true. "Dad?"

CHAPTER THIRTY-THREE

CORINNE WILDE - PRESENT DAY

"Taylor, is that you?" I demand, pulling the phone closer to me.

"Um, yes. What do you want?"

"Are you at your grandmother's?"

"Yes. Why?"

"Because..." Where do I even begin? "Because I just spoke to you and you said you were here. In town." I feel like I'm losing my mind. Slowly, Conrad pulls into the driveway and eases up to the cabin. The lights inside are still on, and I hear a strange sort of squeal... "Is someone screaming?"

"What?" Greta sits straighter beside me.

"The tea." Lewis jumps out of the car and rushes inside in a flash.

Moments later, it stops and the pounding in my head ratchets down a notch. I'd forgotten he put tea on before we left.

"Taylor..." I don't even know what to say. I don't know what to do to make sense of this new reality I find myself in. How can she be in two different places? Why would she be lying if she's not? Is this some sort of punishment, the two of them consorting to make me confused? Mom might be angry enough at me, but why would Taylor be?

I guess the answer is obvious, but this feels particularly cruel.

"Okay, honey. Just be safe, okay? I'll call you soon."

Together, Conrad and Lewis help Greta into the house, her arms slung around their shoulders, and Benji directs them to the couch where he begins to look her over. I wet a hand towel with warm water and bring it to him, along with a bottle of rubbing alcohol to clean her wound. "Sorry. I don't have peroxide."

Benji nods. "This'll do just fine."

He wets a dry corner of the towel with alcohol and dabs the bruise on her neck, then uses the water to clean the mud from her face. She winces—it's painful—but she's awake. She's okay.

As he works, I brush leaves from her hair with my fingers.

"What would they have injected her with?" I ask, terrified to know.

"It's impossible to say for certain," Benji tells us, still working. His voice is soft, soothing. I'll bet he has excellent bedside manners as a nurse. "But there are a few injection sites here." He sighs. "Based on her general drowsiness and what I'm looking at, it seems like someone has been keeping her sedated."

Greta yelps when he slides a hand along the side of her head and his fingers tangle in her hair.

"Sorry." He's gentler then, checking around and inside her ears and mouth. "Do you feel dizzy?"

She shakes her head. "Not anymore. Everything's really bright."

"Numb? Can you feel your hands and feet? Wiggle your toes?"

As he assesses her, I realize Lewis disappeared while I was getting towels. I make my way down the hall, searching for him, and when I finally find him, he's in Taylor's room on her bed. Her new laptop is open on his lap.

His eyes flick up to meet mine, then back down.

"What are you doing?"

"Tracking her phone."

My chest tightens. "Oh my god, why didn't we think of that already?" This night has been chaotic, and the feature isn't something we've used in the past, but we should've at least considered it by now. We've never logged on, never had any reason to, but I know it's an option. I move to sit down on the bed next to him, watching as he navigates his way through our phone provider's steps to log in.

His face is stone, unyielding. "No more games. I want to know where she is, and then I'm going to get her."

"The road is blocked."

He doesn't look at me, just keeps working. "If the rain stops, I can take a chainsaw and clear it."

"What if it doesn't stop?"

He doesn't answer. Not right away. Eventually, he puffs out a breath. "What the hell is happening, Corinne? Greta is at home. No, she's here. She was attacked. *Sedated*." It's obvious that word feels as impossible to him as it does to me. "Taylor is missing. No, she's with your mom. Wait, she's not with your mom. This night is like... Jesus, it's like we've stepped into *The Twilight Zone* or something."

"Tell me about it."

He taps the button on the screen. "I just need to know where she is. I feel like I'm losing it. Like we're..."

He stops himself from whatever he was going to say. And then...

I gasp, feeling him tense next to me.

"It's impossible."

He looks over, then up toward the ceiling. "She's... she's here."

CHAPTER THIRTY-FOUR

CORINNE WILDE - PRESENT DAY

According to the screen in front of us, Taylor is here. At Foxglove, or at the very least near it. The house, the meadow, and parts of the woods are encompassed in a green circle. At the top of the screen, there's a warning that our weak Wi-Fi signal may affect the accuracy, thanks to the storm, but this is more hope than we've had all evening.

At once, Lewis closes the laptop, and we dart out of her room. We barrel through the house, shouting her name.

"Taylor!"

"Honey, where are you?"

"Can you hear us?"

"Taylor, this isn't funny!"

"What's going on?" Greta calls from the living room, but I don't have time to answer. I can't. I'm exhausted. My bones hurt. My voice hurts.

As my body grows angrier, it's as if the storm outside responds to it. Thunder quakes and lightning strikes; the rain screams like thousands of tiny pebbles firing at the roof.

As if Mother Nature has awoken at the sound of my rage.

Lewis opens the front door and disappears outside.

I catch sight of him darting past a window, drenched from the storm. In the living room, Benji and Greta are watching us. Conrad is in the kitchen preparing the tea.

"What can we do?" Conrad asks, pausing.

"Just stay here," I mutter before charging down the hall.

I make my way into my bedroom and shove the rug out of the way. My hand shakes as I pull the door up. I glance outside quickly, just once out the window, but I do a double take.

Up ahead, Lewis is facing away, shouting into the storm.

Something flashes in the corner of my vision, toward the meadow. The blood drains from my body for the split second that I think it's Taylor. I'm wrong, but I do see something. I squint, moving closer to the window.

Several feet behind him, I catch sight of movement again.

A person.

Someone else.

My breath catches as they come into view.

Someone in a dark rain jacket is following him.

I hurry to close the cellar, to chase after Lewis and warn him, to scream, but everything in me freezes as I hear it.

A cry. A muffled whimper coming from down below.

CHAPTER THIRTY-FIVE

KATHERINE WILDE - 1844

Outside Foxglove, the storm is angry. Rain smacks the house like lashes from a switch, fierce and unrelenting. It feels as if this might finally be the storm that takes our beloved home from us, levels it so there's no sign Foxglove ever existed. Like the earth has decided to take her back.

Sometimes, I don't think that would be so bad.

The sound is all-consuming. At times, it drowns out all else—my own heartbeat included.

When it calms, even for a second, I hear him. His steps are heavy, as if he owns the earth as well as this house. As well as me.

I can chart his path as the boards creak. He moves from the bedroom to the parlor. Then, always, the slow drag of boots toward the window. He doesn't like storms either, but that's not why he waits by the window. He does it on clear nights, too. As if he's watching for someone. As though someone might be coming.

Each night, I wait as he does, for someone to come. To save me.

No one ever does.

Every night, I listen, and he paces. I breathe, and he lives. I survive down here, while he enjoys himself above me—in the home built by my blood, the house meant for me.

I rot down here, feet bare, skin and dress stained brown from too long in the dirt. The moisture seeps into my body from the soles of my feet, like the sadness, the loneliness, might take root.

To pass the time, I've scratched shapes into the soft dirt with sticks and stones, created games with myself to keep the madness from creeping in.

I've traced my handprint as if to say *I am here,* and scratched stars into the dust, pictures I half remember from books Mama used to read to us by firelight.

As quickly as I draw them, my wild footprints wipe them away during the times when I can't seem to do anything but walk. Like my bones don't realize I'm not free. As though they believe I can move enough to get us out of here.

I can't, though I should be able to. It's Foxglove's purpose, after all. My ancestors prepared for exactly this. They created avenues for me to escape—built tunnels that helped my mother, my sister, and me flee when I was just a young girl. Now, our cellar's walls are lined with whiskey barrels, filled to the brim. Try as I might, I can't budge them an inch.

I've tried to drain them, to break the boards and pry them away. Such efforts only result in bloody fingers and slashed hopes. He wouldn't dare leave tools that might help me.

He doesn't even realize what he's done, placing the barrels down here. Maybe that's what hurts the most. If it weren't for the whiskey, I would be long gone by now.

Though, if it weren't for the whiskey, maybe I'd not have been locked down here in the first place. My husband was not a cruel man when I met him, nor when I married him.

It was not until we lost our first child, still in my womb, that he changed. That he became cruel. After our second child was delivered stillborn, he took to distilling his own whiskey, the pints in the village no longer enough to quell his grief. And when the blood came again, warning of what would be the third loss, he forced me down here.

Perhaps he thinks it is my fault somehow, that I wished for this, but it couldn't be further from the truth.

My face aches from the bruises still healing after our last visit, and the wounds itch relentlessly.

I hate that it heals, strange as it may sound. Like my own body is trying to fix what he broke, erase it as easily as my drawings in the dirt. When he sees me next, I'll be good as new once more, a canvas ready for him to bloody.

When it's late, and he's gone quiet, I shift from where I've been sitting. My dress is soaked and sour with sweat and moisture. With the stench of fear. Of regret.

I creep across the room to the corner where I sleep, hidden from view to give me time to wake before he finds me, should he decide to pay a late-night visit. It's the farthest point from the beam of light that seeps through the slats above, the glowing amber from the hearth. The moonlight that whispers tales of freedom I may never see again.

Each night, I wait for him to sleep, counting the time between footsteps. I wait for the silence to stretch longer and longer still.

Only then do I reach for the loose, sharp stone hidden in the crack of the wall. I pull it out, kneeling next to one of the wooden beams.

There's just one letter left.

As a child, I grew up with our name carved above the fire, a reminder of from whom we came. Of whom I am. Down here, I've missed it. I've needed it, the strength of the women who came before me. The strength of my mother.

I press the edge of the stone into the wood, careful and slow. My hand is steady from years of carving soap with Mama.

I hear her voice down here with me each night as I work—it's the only time she seems to be with me.

Gentle, now. Steady. Not too deep, just enough. Let the shape reveal itself.

And just like she promised when I was a child, the shape does reveal itself eventually, when my arms shake from use, my body nearing sleep.

N.

I lean back, admiring the full thing. WILDE WOMEN.

Not just Wilde any longer. If I ever find freedom again, I vow to take this board and place it somewhere I will see it every day. Somewhere to remind me that I am borne of women who knew of danger, of pain, and weren't afraid to fight it. Women who fought for me.

Each daughter, each woman born, is just proof of generations of women willing to challenge the norms and live bravely. Willing to endure pain and scrutiny for a future she might never see, for daughters who might one day invoke her name when they need to feel brave, too.

I squeeze my eyes closed, whispering my mother's name, the names of the women from the stories she's shared. "Hannah. Hester. Josephine. Elizabeth. Rachel. Serena. Rose. Lyddie." Then my sister's name. "Millicent." My dear Millie, who lives far away. Happy and safe. Who doesn't know of my troubles.

We are the Wilde women, and Foxglove is ours.

And here's the proof—carved into the beam. Our name creates a home for me in this dark corner. The shadows keep it safe until I am.

Until we are.

I am not alone.

As I run my finger across the letters, across days and

days of work, my hand trembles. Not with fear or even exhaustion, but with something familiar. Something deep and old.

I think of what Mama used to say before the sickness swallowed her whole. Before she took her final breath in the room just above my head. Before my world grew infinitely darker.

"Generations of Wilde women have lived here before you, my darlings." She held our hands as she told us of them, Millicent and me. My Millie. "And there'll be generations who come after, God willing. This house is ours. And theirs. And if you ever need help, you just ask the walls, whisper to the shadows. Wilde women live here, Wilde women remain here, and if you believe it, they just might find a way to protect you as they have always protected me."

Her words are stitched into my skin, part of my very being. I repeat them in my head often, when the thunder is too loud, when his temper is the worst. When I feel the most dreadfully alone.

I whisper them under my breath, as if they were a spell.

Wilde women live here.

This is our home, not his. Never his.

Never theirs.

He doesn't know that, but he will. He thinks I am broken. Dirty as the floor I live on. There are times when I believe it, too.

But then I hear them. The whispers of my mother.

Of hers, though I never knew her voice. And when they come to me in those dark moments, I remember.

I remember how the firelight looked in her eyes. How she loved me. I remember how her voice could warm a room, make everything better. I remember the night we ran, how we stayed in the orchard until the bad man was gone. I remember how she held us, that night and others, and told us the blood in our veins runs deep. Strong as the current in the river and wide as the roots of the oldest trees.

It's in those quiet moments I remember that I am a Wilde woman.

And so long as Foxglove stands, I am never alone.

CHAPTER THIRTY-SIX

CORINNE WILDE - PRESENT DAY

Every hair on my body stands at attention at the sound coming from below. Lewis's safety is in the back of my mind, but all I can think about is Taylor. Here in this cabin. Here under these floorboards. Here all this time.

I dart down the stairs, rushing to my baby. Preparing for the worst.

But what I find is...

"Mom?"

My breathing catches at the sight of my mom. She's tied up, a long piece of silver tape across her mouth and ropes wrapped tightly around her arms and waist. Her wrists and ankles are secured with cords and she's lying on her side in the dirt, her graying blonde hair caked with blood.

It's a scene from a horror movie, like the one I imagined the first time I came down here.

"Mom." I hurry across the cellar to her, trying to

decide what to do first. She's thin, sickly so. Probably twenty pounds lighter than the last time I saw her three months ago.

I lift my hand to her mouth. Gently, I take hold of one corner of the tape. She winces, squeezing her eyes shut as I pull it off. Her mouth opens, her lips cracked and bleeding, and I spot something black between her teeth.

Carefully, I pull it out. A sock.

She releases a shaky breath.

"I...I don't understand." I swallow, blinking back tears. "How are you here? I just spoke to you."

A tear falls down her cheek, and when she speaks, her voice is soft. "It wasn't me."

"What are you talking about? It was."

"It was him." She closes her eyes, dropping her head forward. "I'm so sorry."

Him? Him who? I think about every person in this house. Lewis. Conrad. Benji. But no one could have done such a perfect impression of my mom, could they? I think about the two Taylors—the one at Mom's house and the one here in town—my mind racing. What is happening right now?

"It was EJ." His name smacks me in the face. "He was..." She winces again, inhaling through her clenched teeth as I help her sit up. "He was doing it on his computer."

"The voices?"

"He can make it sound like anyone. Me. Taylor.

Greta. He can even copy phone numbers, make it look like anyone is calling you. Honey, we haven't spoken in months. Not since you told me about the divorce. And not because I was mad at you—because he wouldn't let me. I've tried to send you messages, to warn you about his plan, but he always caught me. Stopped me."

"What does he want, Mom?" None of this feels possible, and yet, it's the closest I've felt to answers all night.

"This cabin. He was going to sell it—it and the land—for millions. He'd been coming by here, bringing clients and showing it. He didn't tell me anything except that he was working, but..." Her face is rigid, furious. "It's why he wanted to marry me."

Her voice cracks when she says the sentence, and it's only then I think about how much that truth must sting. "He had a buyer lined up, and after the wedding it would've been half his. He thought he could convince me to sell it. But when you told me about the divorce, he heard us on the phone. Heard me telling you to stay at Foxglove. He tried to change my mind, but I wouldn't. He was furious. *I was furious.* I would've never...never okayed selling Foxglove."

I'm relieved to hear her say it, and glad we agree. Selling this cabin, this piece of our family and our roots, would be akin to selling a child. An appendage.

"But why would he do this? What was the point of pretending to be you? Why did he tie you up?"

"At first, he just wanted you to get back together with

Lewis. If you moved out, he thought he—or, rather, *I*—could convince you to give it back to us. Or sell it. He hoped having Taylor leave tonight would give you and Lewis time together. That it would make you realize how badly your divorce has affected her."

She pauses. "He wanted you to move home, to leave Foxglove, but knew it wouldn't happen if Taylor was happy. So, he started chatting with her on some app. Complained about her not having internet. Teased her about how awful this place was. He wanted her to hate it here, and I think he succeeded. He was supposed to be a college kid. They made plans to meet in town tonight. He told her he drove here, that he could get them a room somewhere close. I tried to stop him. Please believe me, I did everything I could."

I don't doubt that. The evidence is all over her body. My muscles ache with fury. "I check her apps," I whisper, but I know it's a lie. I haven't checked anything recently. "Where is Taylor now? Is she with EJ?"

She starts to answer, but before she can say a word, everything goes dark.

CHAPTER THIRTY-SEVEN

CORINNE WILDE - PRESENT DAY

"What was that? What happened?" Conrad's worried voice echoes from upstairs, talking to Benji.

"Mom?"

"Shhh..." She shushes me, her voice low and shaky. Terrified. This woman who has forever seemed like a pillar of strength to me sounds scared. "You need to leave me. Leave me here, and you need to get out. Go find Taylor. Make sure she's safe."

"I'm not leaving you." I try to help her stand, but she protests, pulling away.

"I'll only slow you down. You need to get Lewis, find Greta, and get out of here. He's not going to stop until he gets what he wants."

Foxglove. The money.

She goes on, "As soon as you're out of here, call the police. I'll be okay."

"Hang on. How did you know Greta's here?"

"She's *here*?" Mom's hand grasps my arm. "She was with me. From the moment she left Foxglove, he kept the two of us in a passage that leads to the meadow. He kept her asleep. Unconscious. She escaped earlier. I told her to get to her car, call the police. I was hoping she made it."

"Has anyone seen Corinne? Did she go out with Lewis?" Above, I hear Conrad's voice.

Lewis.

The man in the raincoat.

"EJ is outside." My throat is full of concrete. I can't breathe.

"He cut the power," Mom whispers. "You need to go now."

"Taylor?" I ask. "Where is she?"

"She should be in town," she says. "He asked her to meet him, but he couldn't go, obviously. He was with us when he pretended to be Greta, saying she wasn't home. He didn't want you to come home to look for her. But then when he realized you were leaving anyway, he used my voice to tell you she was safe. We never had Taylor."

So the Taylor who told me she was in town was the real one. She was waiting to meet a catfish.

"She's safe, but you need to find her. I'm worried he messed with your car. He said he was going to make sure she couldn't get back home tonight. He needed you two to suffer, to want to fix your marriage for Taylor's sake."

"That's why Taylor told me she was gone until we stopped fighting."

"Because it was EJ, yes. He can be anyone he wants,

Corinne. Anyone, anywhere. Phone numbers, voices. I'm so sorry. This is my fault."

Anyone. Anywhere.

I have no idea what's been real lately. But Taylor's phone showed she was nearby, and the real Taylor has her phone. If she couldn't drive here, if her date didn't show up, she might've tried to walk.

The woods. The thought sends chills down my spine. Traveling through the woods in this storm in the dark could be a death sentence. But staying here could be, too.

My mind flashes to Lewis again. To EJ. I don't want to leave Mom, but she's right. I need to warn Lewis. Find Taylor. Get Greta, Conrad, and Benji out of here. I hand Mom my phone, dialing 911.

"Stay here. Get ahold of the police, okay?"

She nods, eyes brimming with tears. "There are tunnels." She juts her head to the left. "After Greta escaped, I crawled through them. I wanted to warn you. I tried..." She sniffles, shaking her head to brush away her tears, no time for them. "Go that way. You'll push on the wall. I'm not sure exactly where. The passage is narrow and small, so watch your head, but you'll come to a set of winding stairs. Take them to the top."

I start to go, but I can't. I can't leave her. "Come with me." I lean over, throwing her arm around my shoulder.

"No. It's too dangerous. He knows about the tunnels, too. He knew about them without me telling him. Maybe he found them when he was here for the listing, I don't know. If he corners you there, you need to be able to run. I won't be selfish and put you in danger."

I set my jaw, thinking. "We'll go through the house, then. I know my way. It's safer."

"The tunnel gets you farther from the house."

"I can't go too far. I need to find Lewis. He's out there with EJ." I pull her forward, no more time for discussion.

"I'll go back through the tunnel, then. You go through the house. That way one of us gets out no matter what happens." She swallows, holding my phone. "As soon as I get service, I'll call the police. You find Lewis."

I grit my teeth. "Fine. Okay." Taking her hand, I squeeze it gently. "Mom, be careful. Promise me."

She throws her arms around me in a quick hug. "I'll meet you out there?"

It sounds like a question, like she's begging the universe to make it happen. Then, with a wave goodbye, she disappears into the shadows.

I climb the stairs carefully and reach the floor above, listening. In the living room, I can hear Conrad, Benji, and Greta scrambling to find flashlights. The breaker box is near the back of the house. I have no idea if the storm is the cause of the power outage or if it's EJ, but if it's him, I have to assume he has a plan.

I just need a better one.

I enter the living room, finding Greta right away. I touch her arm. She jumps, and Benji points his phone's flashlight at me. "Jesus." She puts a hand to her chest. "Where did you go? We couldn't find you."

"It's a long story. Listen, we have to go."

"Go where?" Conrad asks.

"I need to find Lewis. Taylor's in the woods."

"The woods?" Greta's voice goes soft, worried.

"I'll explain everything, we just need to go."

"Why?" Conrad demands. "What's happening?"

CRACK.

The sound comes from somewhere outside. A gunshot.

My stomach roils. Greta screams. My head goes fuzzy.

A man appears in the doorway, his figure outlined by the moonlight. In the commotion, I can't tell if it's Lewis or EJ.

I turn to run, but someone grabs me. Two hands shove me forward, and I can't see anything. "Stop! What are you doing?"

Beams of light from various cell phones scatter through the house, illuminating brief glimpses and flashes of the room and our faces. It's total chaos. I can't tell what's happening.

I'm shoved inside the closet, and the door slams, blanketing me in total darkness.

CHAPTER THIRTY-EIGHT

MARTHA WILDE - 1938

The light is long and golden like straw shining through the trees, casting strange angles and dust that shimmers. My gran, Millicent, used to say that if you look closely, you can see spirits dancing in the woods every evening, keeping us safe. I think of them now, caught in a sunbeam, waving hello.

Keep her safe, I implore them, knowing they'll hear. *Keep them both safe.*

The cabin creaks around us as I walk back into Foxglove, settling as if it's preparing. As if it knows what's coming.

Upstairs in the loft, Ruth's breaths are coming faster and sharper, more primal. She breathes through the pain like she's done before, in that way that comes naturally to us all, the way our bones just seem to know.

Even from the kitchen, I can hear her. There's a low rhythm to the groans. Wind picking up before a bad rain.

It's music—the sound of holding on and letting go all at once. The sound of body-breaking pain and elating anticipation. Birth always sounds the same, no matter how many times you hear it.

Hazel plays by the hearth. She's only seven, but even in a tiny body, she's both serious and clever. She has the scene set—a neat row of the little wooden dolls I carved for her last Christmas. She's given them all careers, unconcerned that they're women, and I admire that small act of rebellion already starting.

They are preachers and teachers, nurses and waitresses.

"This one's Ruth, like Mama," she says. "And Martha, like you. That one's Tabitha, but she doesn't care for it."

"I think it's a lovely name, Tabitha," I say in my most tender voice, playing along. I'm grateful for the distraction, truth be told, as I wipe down the already clean table.

I must keep moving as the evening wears on. There are too many memories that live in stillness. Too many worries.

Hazel looks up at me then, her eyes dark as night like her mother's, like mine.

"Gran, is it true Foxglove's haunted?"

The question throws me, making me pause. I turn toward her, hand on my hip. "Haunted? Where on earth did you hear a thing like that?"

She gives me a deep frown. "Agnes said her father says

she can't come to Foxglove to play. She says he told her it's haunted here. It's not true, is it?"

I chuckle, crossing the room to kneel beside her. "You know, there are some people in this world who can't sleep unless they've got something to worry about. Something to be afraid of. It sounds to me like Agnes's father is just looking for something to help him sleep."

She gives me a crooked smile, missing both front teeth. "What do you mean?"

"Well..." I lift her onto my lap, smoothing her skirt. "If you've got a name for your fear, something you can point at and stay clear from, it makes you feel safer, in a way. A ghost's just one name for something you don't understand."

Her eyes narrow, and she looks away, thinking. Then she finds me again. "So...is that a yes? Or a no?"

A laugh bubbles out of me without warning. She's never been one to let me get away with nuance. "It's neither." I bump my nose against hers, then pull back, rubbing her leg. What can I tell her, really? "Here's what I know. This house has held a lot of women. A lot of love, yes, but a lot of pain, too. Maybe the walls remember it all. The good and the bad. Maybe that's all a ghost is. A place that remembers."

Hazel is quiet, and I can see her mind processing, wheels turning. She looks at the wall, as if trying to see straight through it. "Are we strange? Agnes said her father says we're strange."

My smile softens, an ember of rage in my chest. I

brush a lock of hair back from her brow, weighing my words carefully on my tongue before I speak. "*Strange* isn't always a bad thing to be, I'll have you know."

"But I don't want to be strange."

"They say we're strange 'cause we don't sit quietly when we're told to do just that. Wilde women have never listened to their rules, never had to. Foxglove gave us permission to be free. To learn. And because of that, we know things, remember things, they'd rather us forget."

She mulls that over. "I know a lot of things."

I chuckle and pull her to my chest, resting her head there. "You do, Hazel girl, and don't you ever let anyone make you feel less than because of it. The world doesn't take kindly to women who make their own way in it. And..." I sigh. "I suppose, they see a name like ours, a name like Wilde and...well, they must reckon it means we're just what we are."

She sighs, like the weight of the world is on her shoulders. "Wilde?" She says it like it's heavy, and I guess it might feel that way sometimes.

I turn her head toward me, kissing her forehead. "Yes. Wild. And strong. Stubborn. Not easy to hurt or kill. Not easy to own. And some people—small-minded, simple people—they're afraid of what they can't own. What they can't put a name to."

She nods, like she's filing what I've said away for later. Then she lifts her hand and runs it through the ends of my silver hair. "I like being a Wilde."

Pride swells through me. "I do too, darling."

Above us, Ruth cries out, and it's different this time. Loud, lined with panic.

I'm on my feet in a second. "It's time. She's ready."

Hazel means to follow me, dolls forgotten on the floor. "Can I help?"

I nearly tell her no. It would be easy enough to, but I stop myself. "Bring clean cloths to the washstand for me, could you? Then stand by the stairs. When I call you, you can come. Until then, keep quiet and pray."

She snaps into action, running down the hall, and I can't help smiling. We all have jobs to do tonight.

The stairs creak under my weight as I climb them. My knees remind me of my age with every step.

The loft smells of sweat and lavender, and I can feel her aching deep in my own bones. Ruth lies curled in on herself, forehead slick with sweat. Her hair sticks to her face, gown clinging to her back and belly.

She realizes I've entered the room and looks over, eyes as wild as an animal. As a mother.

"It hurts..." She groans. Pleads.

"I know it does," I say, crossing the room and taking her hand. I crawl onto the bed with her and stroke her back. "I'm here. You know what to do. Breathe, my love. Just breathe."

She lets out a deep cry from the depths of her gut, her lungs.

"Yes, that's all right, too," I say with a small chuckle, drawing circles deep into her muscles. "Howl if you must."

Outside the window, the sun has nearly disappeared in the sky, casting all of Foxglove in shadows, and I think of the spirits then. I'll bet they're celebrating. Tonight, the trees will whisper, and the flowers in the meadow will dance, just as they have for hundreds of years and hundreds of births before this one, announcing the news.

Another Wilde woman is on her way.

And someday our dear Foxglove—our home—will remember her, too.

CHAPTER THIRTY-NINE

CORINNE WILDE - PRESENT DAY

In the pitch-black of the closet, my breathing is heavy and scattered, like the chaotic footsteps beyond the door. I press my palm to the wall, trying to collect myself, to think, but even the solid wood feels unreliable. Like it might shift. Like it might be all in my head. Like every bit of this might.

The air is thick, and it clings to my lungs. It tastes of mothballs and mold. Dust. Like something forgotten. Abandoned. Dead.

The dark presses in around me, and it's not only the lack of light that scares me, it's the tightness of the space. I feel as if I can't breathe fully, like the walls are closing in. I don't know whether to stay or run, don't know why I'm here, but I know I feel as if I'm drowning in this black.

Outside, I hear Greta and Conrad shouting over each

other, and the banging of doors, the clattering of things hitting the floor.

"What was that?"

"What happened?"

"Someone came in. Did you see them?"

I step back, and my ankle knocks into something hard. It scrapes across the floor with a high-pitched squeal that fills the silence here. I flinch and bend to touch my ankle, to ease the pain. My balance falters, and I'm falling all too quick.

Then—a hand touches me. Long fingers wrap around my forearm, grounding me, keeping me from falling. It's cold.

"Who—"

"Shhhh. It's okay. It's me."

The relief is instant, but incomplete. Even as my heart slows, my skin crawls. Mom's words echo in my ears. He can be anyone. Anywhere.

"Lewis?" I reach out, needing to know.

"A man followed me. He had a gun." His voice is barely more than a whisper. I press my hands to his chest, and I know, in an instant, this is my Lewis.

It's him.

I fall into his arms, and he wraps me up. I can't speak. My mind fractures around his words, around our reality.

"I'm okay," he assures me. "But, look, I don't think you're going to believe me." His words are slower, like he's not sure he's remembering it right. Like he's in a dream, too. "I think it was—"

"EJ," I fill in the blank for him. The name leaves a sharp, bitter taste in my mouth. Like rust.

He inhales sharply against me. "You already knew?"

I want to tell him everything. About what I saw out the window. About Mom. And Taylor. About Greta. But my throat is dry.

It hurts to speak, to know.

"It's a long story. For now, we need to get everyone out of here. We need to get somewhere safe, and we need to find Taylor."

"He cut the power when I saw him. The porch lights, everything. It's too dark to see anything. And I dropped my phone. I don't even remember where. I had it one second, and then it was gone. I'm sorry. It was a blur."

My skin prickles at his words, at the confirmation that EJ is behind our lack of power. Of light.

Outside the closet, the world has gone unnaturally quiet. The kind of quiet that sets your skin on fire and makes your ears ring.

"Why did you shove me in the closet?"

"I was running away from him. I didn't...I didn't think. I just saw you, and I needed to get you somewhere safe. This was the first place I thought of."

Something inside me cracks at the thought that his first instinct was to save me. It probably doesn't mean anything. It's a habit, but still. It's nice. "I don't have my phone either," I admit, remembering.

"What are you talking about? Where is it?"

"I..." To answer that would require me to go much

deeper into this night's story than I'm prepared for. "It'd take too long to explain. It doesn't matter anyway. The guys have their phones. We need to warn them. Get them out of here."

The house is still eerily quiet outside the door, and I suspect they've moved into hiding places too. I hope Greta isn't alone.

"He has a gun, Corinne," he reminds me.

My breathing catches. "I know."

"If we go out there, I might lose you."

"If we don't, we might lose everyone."

"Why is he doing this?"

I wish I could tell him, try to explain something that still doesn't make sense to me, but I can't. There's no time.

"He smiled at me when he saw me," Lewis says, his voice trembling. "Right before he shot, he...he smiled."

His words echo through my mind, warping into something unrecognizable. I see EJ's face, but his mouth is stretched too wide. There are sharp, beastly teeth where his should be.

His eyes are dark, lifeless. Hollow. Something rotting behind them.

A sound creaks outside the door.

A footstep, I think.

Or maybe just the house shifting.

I can't hide any longer. Greta's out there. Conrad. Benji. Taylor is somewhere. None of them know what's coming.

"We have to go," I tell him. "I love you." I don't wait for his response. I shove open the closet door. The hallway stretches out in both directions, seeming longer than usual in the pale moonlight. The darkness seems to swallow everything.

My eyes struggle to adjust, and the walls look... wrong. Warped. Like Foxglove is breathing.

I blink, sure I'm imagining it.

And then—

A scream.

High-pitched and cut off too quickly.

Greta. Her voice pierces my chest like a knife. I don't think. Don't hesitate. I run.

Behind me, Lewis shouts, calling my name—but his voice is distant. Drowned in static. It's as if it's coming from a radio that's been buried underground.

I sprint down the hallway, following the direction of her scream.

CHAPTER FORTY

CORINNE WILDE - PRESENT DAY

The house is empty, the front door standing open. I dart outside with Lewis in tow, running, searching. Rain pelts me, making it impossible to see.

"Greta!" I shout, trying to determine which direction her scream came from.

I hear it again, this time louder.

It's as if it's everywhere, filling the air. *Where is Conrad? Where did they go? Did they leave her?* Their car, along with Lewis's, is still in the driveway. Wherever they are, they're close.

Greta's cries grow fainter. Weaker.

"She's hurt..." I spin in a circle. "It's coming from this way."

"Wait, Corinne! *Wait!*" Lewis lunges for my arm, trying to stop me, but he can't.

As I round the house, someone grabs me.

I yelp, preparing to fight, but Mom's voice is in my

ear. "Shhhhhh." She squeezes her hand over my mouth tighter. "*It's not her.*"

Slowly, finger by finger, she releases her hand, staring at me. Lewis is looking at us both as if he's in a dream. I don't have time to catch him up.

"Billie? What are you doing here?"

"It's not her," Mom says again, looking only at me. She shakes her head slowly. Her fear-filled eyes drill into mine. "Honey, you have to remember what I told you—he can be anyone he wants. Anyone, anywhere, any time. You can't trust your ears right now, only your eyes."

"What is going on?" Lewis whispers, his voice trembling. "What happened to you?" He looks at me. "What is she talking about?"

"It's EJ," I tell him. "Not just tonight, chasing you. All of it has been EJ. He led Taylor away, pretended to be Mom and Greta. He's...he's using AI to mimic people's voices. Taylor's, Mom's, Greta's."

He shakes his head. "No. That's ridiculous. Why would he do that? He doesn't know us."

Mom's eyes meet mine, and there's a warning there that I don't quite understand. As if she doesn't want me to tell him everything. It's as if I can hear her voice inside my head, saying he only needs to know the necessary parts.

But it's ridiculous.

We can trust Lewis. He'd never hurt us.

My mind goes back to the divorce settlement, and all the ways we fought over money and the division of our assets. I would trust this man with my life, but can I trust him with this cabin? With the fortune it's apparently worth?

I swallow, the truth buried so deep within my bones I don't really have to contemplate the question.

It's as if every one of my ancestors, every woman who has ever lived within these woods, whose blood and bones rest beneath the earth here, is screaming at me. Leading me.

"He's not a good person," I finally say. "We have to get everyone out of here. Can you help Mom to the car?"

"What? No. I'm not leaving you."

"You're not. I'm going with you." I glance at Mom. "Did you call the police?"

She gives me a quick nod, eyes darting to Lewis and then back to me. *She doesn't want to mention the tunnels.* "Service isn't great with the storm, but they're coming."

I turn around, facing Lewis. "Do you have your keys?"

He pats his pocket. "Yes."

"Good. You and Mom wait for me in the car. Keep her safe. I'll find the others and meet you there."

Reluctantly, he takes Mom's arm and eases it around his shoulders to steady her as they head for the driveway.

I watch them disappear around the house.

"*Psssst...*"

I look up when I hear the sound, Mom's warning haunting my thoughts. Just because the voice sounds like Greta doesn't mean it—

It is.

I catch sight of her peeking out from the woods, and it sends my heart into a spiral. "Oh, thank God." I rush forward and into her outstretched arms.

"What is going on?" she asks, pulling me into a tight hug. "Why is your mom here? The power went out, and then it was chaos. Someone screamed, and then everyone screamed, and there was pushing and shoving and—Conrad got me out, but I didn't want to leave you. I swear I saw someone in there with a gun."

"I know." I release her and step back. "You're right, and I know." I look behind her, to where Conrad and Benji are waiting. Conrad looks positively shell-shocked, while Benji appears hardened. Ready. "Are you guys okay?"

"The police are on their way," Benji says. "I called them, but with the tree down..."

"I know. It's okay. We called, too. We just need to get to the car and get as far away from here as we can. Can you help Greta?"

Benji gives a resolute nod and takes hold of her. "I've got her."

After a quick check around, we head for Lewis's car where he and Mom are waiting. A light flicks on inside the house, and I flinch.

"Power's back," Conrad mutters.

I don't stop to investigate why. Together, we keep moving.

Is EJ inside? Did he turn the power back on? Or was

Lewis wrong? Was it actually the storm that knocked it out to begin with?

As we near the car, I shake water from my hands and wring out the bottom of my shirt, though it does no good. The rain continues to pour.

In the driveway, I open the car door and squeeze in next to Mom in the front seat while Conrad, Benji, and Greta slide into the back.

Once the doors are closed, Lewis locks them.

"Let's go," I say, though I'm not sure where we're going. We're trapped here.

Lewis glances at the house. "The lights are back on. Did you see him?"

"We should go before he sees us," Mom warns.

"Who are we talking about?" Greta asks.

We drive down the gravel road as I tell Greta and the others what I can. That EJ wants the property. That he's been impersonating people in order to get us to leave. That he has a gun, and no one knows his plan.

"At some point, I think he switched from just wanting you to leave to being willing to do whatever it takes to scare you off," Mom says softly, tears in her eyes. "Foxglove is in both our names, Corinne, but I'm the only married one now. If we die, it might go to him. This is all my fault."

I take her hand. "It's not. We're going to make it out of this."

When we reach the tree in the road, Lewis slows

down, coming to a stop just in front of it. "What do we do?"

"We can't just stay here," Mom whispers, terrified. Her eyes flick around the car to every window.

"We can walk," Conrad says. "Going home might've seemed safer before, but now the woods are the best option. We'll stay away from the flooding as much as possible. We can cut through the woods, wait for the police up ahead."

"They should be here soon," Lewis says. "Maybe we're safer in the car."

"He could be anywhere," Greta says. "If he comes up to the car with a gun, we're sitting ducks."

"The woods," Benji says. "The storm will make it hard for him to see. We'll stick together—move together—unless we can't. He can't shoot all of us at once."

His words seem to echo in the car, as if we're standing at the edge of a canyon, waiting to jump. An impasse, deciding what's next. Any decision made here could cost me someone I love. Even *not* choosing could cost everything.

Finally, I nod. "Conrad and Benji are right. We can't just sit here. We'll go through the woods. Stick together. Once we make it to town, you guys can go to the police station. Or, if we can't make it all the way there, we'll find a safe place to wait for them. If we do make it, I'll go downtown to find Taylor."

Lewis shuts off the car. "I'll go with you. We'll find her together."

I don't argue. I'd rather not be alone anyway.

We file out of the car, the decision behind us and only the woods and uncertainty ahead. I'm on high alert, watching for any sign of EJ. My body is tense, braced for the sound of a gunshot.

We set off for the woods, sticking close together as we make our way through the muddy forest. My feet catch on brambles and bushes, and I trip over tree roots as we go.

I pause when I hear something, though no one else seems to.

"What's wrong?" It's Mom who notices I've stopped walking first.

"Did you hear that?"

Heads swivel as everyone looks around. "What was it?" Lewis asks.

"It sounded like..."

"Mom!"

There it is again. The soft sound of her voice, barely carrying over the storm.

"Taylor." I don't hesitate long enough to say anything else. I turn on my heel and run. My feet slip in the mud on my way, but I don't trip.

By some miracle, I don't trip.

I hear them racing behind me, trying to keep up.

"What is it?" Lewis whisper-shouts, breathing heavily. "Did you see her?"

I stop when we reach the tree line, searching for her. I didn't imagine it. I know I didn't imagine it.

"Taylor." Mom whispers her name.

"You heard her, too?"

I look over, but Mom isn't looking at me. Her eyes are trained straight ahead. She lifts her finger, pointing, and I follow the path.

No.

My chest turns to ice as I watch Taylor—completely drenched and muddy from the storm—cross the porch and walk right into Foxglove.

CHAPTER FORTY-ONE

HAZEL WILDE - 1962

When I hear his truck pull up outside, I'm braiding Billie's hair before dinner. It's getting so long I still can't believe it.

I smooth the last stray hairs behind her ear and kiss her head. "Go get cleaned up for dinner before your dad gets inside."

She stands, smooths her hands over the blue dress she's wearing, then dashes off to the bathroom. In the kitchen, I set our small table and fill three bowls with soup. There's a storm coming, and this old cabin gets drafty in the winter as it is. Soup is about the only thing I can stand to make this time of year.

Several minutes pass as Billie and I wait for him to come inside. When it's been too long, I move to the door, forcing a smile and casting a quick glance her way. "I'll be right back."

She nods, but I spot a hint of worry on her delicate features. Even just a few months shy of four years old, she's intuitive and understands more than she should.

Outside, I find Charles still in his truck. I knock gently on the window, and when he looks up, it's as if he's seen a ghost. He leans across the seat, cranking the handle to roll down the window.

"Hi, honey. Everything okay?"

His eyes are glassy, but not from drinking. He hasn't had a drink in months. This is different. It's as if he's not really here. He pats the seat next to him. "Why don't you, uh, get in here for a sec?"

Slowly, I open the door. Dread settles over me as I brace myself for whatever is coming. "What happened?"

He doesn't meet my eyes when he says his next words, and I'm thankful for it—I'm not sure what expression my face must hold as I process the news.

"I'm having a baby."

I chuckle. After we had Billie, I had two miscarriages. My doctor said another pregnancy will kill me. This feels like a cruel joke. "That's not funny."

His eyes find mine, and now I understand the glassiness. "I'm not laughing."

"You..." I suck in a breath, thinking. "You slept with someone else."

He pauses. "Nancy Mulligan."

"When? Why?"

"I don't know."

I'm not sure which of my questions that's supposed to be an answer to. Maybe both. Rage fills my stomach. "You can't have a baby with Nancy Mulligan. You're married to me. Her husband just died last year. She...she already has those two boys."

She already has two, and I can only have one.

He nods but doesn't respond. Eventually, he slips out of the truck. Just before shutting the door, he meets my eyes again. He looks tired, empty. I hardly recognize him. "Probably best not to say anything to anyone for now."

I swallow, batting back tears. By some miracle, I manage to hold them in until he disappears inside the house and have them dried long before I follow him.

The baby comes in the fall. I receive the news over dinner, just after Charles asks me to pass a slice of bread and before he asks for the butter.

A little girl.

A sister for our Billie, and yet, not a single part of me exists within her. She's not mine.

Charles hasn't brought Nancy around to Foxglove. I've been avoiding her in town, ever since I noticed her stomach showing in church. That bump is gone now, but the pain of it will never leave. Even in the happiest moments.

She hasn't spoken to me. Honestly, I'm not sure

what Charles has told her about us, and I don't think I want to know. He hasn't said if they're still seeing each other, and I'm afraid to ask.

Charles always wanted a big family, and I'm afraid if I push, he might leave me for the woman who can give him that—even if that's not why the affair started.

I can hazard a guess as to why it started, too.

I'm not blind. Nancy's been pretty for as long as I can remember. Prettier than me. Prettier than most of the women in town. Bright blonde hair that turns strawberry blonde in the summer. Green eyes.

I expect her daughter to look just like her, but when I see the baby—Violet—all I see is Charles. She has blonde hair like both her parents, but the rest is all him. She's the spitting image of the man I love.

For several months, little Violet comes back and forth between Foxglove and her mother's. He takes her home at night but leaves her with me during the day.

I never planned to take care of the girl, but I can't help falling in love with her. And Billie, *oh*, my girl finally has a playmate, and how could I take that away from her?

I can't. Won't.

Violet shouldn't be punished for her mother's sins.

I feed her and play with her. I teach her things—how to count her fingers and toes, how to clap her hands. It's me she's with the first time she laughs. I hear her sweet giggle before Charles ever has the chance to, and at the end of the day, I decide not to tell him. Maybe I deserve to have some secrets, too.

Even though she's not my blood, I love that little girl. I may not be her mother, but I know I'd do anything for her.

That's why, when she's just over a year old and Charles says she's going to live with us from now on, I don't put up a fuss.

Nancy has her hands full with the boys, after all. And I still don't think anyone knows she's had a baby out of wedlock. Charles hasn't said as much, but I suspect he started bringing her groceries around the time Violet's presence in her womb became undeniable. I suppose it never stopped. We couldn't exactly have her roaming around town with a new baby and no explanation, now could we?

It's better for me, selfish as it is, that no one knows. No one suspects.

The news that little Violet will live with us feels like a reward for all I've been through.

She's better off with me.

Happy with me.

Somehow, we've managed to turn this terrible situation into something good.

It doesn't mean I don't feel dread in my stomach now and again, or that I don't sense I'm being lied to. Deep down, I know having Violet here without consequence is too good to be true.

Still, I guess I thought maybe if I don't ask, I won't have to know.

Because I don't *want* to know.

Not the worst of it. Not the truth of it.

Quite often, truth hurts too much.

When Nancy Mulligan stands on my porch just a few months later, both her eyes are bruised black and blue.

Her pretty face is marked with scars I've never seen before, and her once-beautiful hair hangs in limp, greasy strands. She holds her arm tight against her chest, as if it's hurting, and the closer I look, the easier it is to see the green bruise on her wrist—a bracelet of fingers that once gripped her too hard.

"Is she here?" Her words are soft. Shaky. She looks like she thinks I might strike her.

"Is who here?" We've never acknowledged the child shared by our homes, by my husband, but of course I know whom she means. Try as I might, I can't stop staring at the cuts on her face. "What happened to you?"

She scowls so fast it must hurt because she immediately winces. "Like you don't know."

I stare at her, but I can't bring myself to ask. I can't.

"Is she okay, Hazel? Just tell me that."

"She's..." My voice breaks when I picture the little girl currently sitting on my kitchen floor, fingerpainting with her sister. "She's perfect."

It's not a lie.

She swallows, looking away as tears fill her eyes. "Please let me see her."

"You didn't want to." I repeat the lie Charles told me, though maybe I knew it was a lie even as he said the words. "You didn't want her."

She doesn't bother arguing, and I guess she doesn't need to. Eventually, I look away, stepping back so she can come inside.

She rushes past me, gathering her daughter in her arms in a rush. "Oh, my baby. My baby." She kisses her cheeks. Violet, on the other hand, doesn't seem to know who her mother is. She pushes her away, whining, and it breaks something inside me. Something raw and wild.

"How long has it been since you saw her?"

"Since she stopped nursing." She clears her throat, not forcing herself on her child again, though I can see it's killing her. She sits and watches her as if she's the most fascinating thing in the world. "He locked me in my bedroom after that. And…she was gone."

"Charles wouldn't do that." He wouldn't. My husband isn't a monster. She must've done something. She must've.

She closes her eyes, squeezing them shut. "Is she happy? Is she…is she safe here?"

I study Nancy, looking for a hint of the villain I want her to be. The homewrecker. The woman who abandoned her child. This would all be easier if she is who I've told myself she is. "How long did the affair go on?"

She sniffles, looking down, and from where I am, I'm towering over her as she remains on the floor between our girls.

"It was a mistake," she says finally. "After William died, I was lost. I was drowning. And..." She smiles, but it's bitter. "And Charles was there. He was kind to me at first."

She makes eye contact with me but breaks it in a flash. "I thought he would leave you, and I'm sorry for that. I wanted a family. I wanted my family to be whole again. Charles...he let me believe that would happen."

She sniffles, adjusting her feet against the dirty floor, pulling them under her. "But once Violet came, once she was here, it was different. He was colder. He took her from me and locked me in my bedroom. He said I was hormonal. I was tired. And maybe I was. But I needed help, and he just...he left me. Me and the boys."

She looks away. "And then he started hitting me. Some days, I think he wishes he could kill me. Some days, I think maybe he tries to." She coughs, and the cough turns into a fit.

"My husband has never laid a hand on me." The one time he tried—he'd been drinking, and we argued—I pulled a frying pan out and promised to kill him if he ever tried again. I was a different woman then, younger and bolder, full of fire, but I think he saw in my eyes that I meant it.

"Well, goodie for you," she mutters, holding out her palm to the little girl. Carefully, Violet places her hand into it.

"She loves high-fives," I say.

They look up at me—first Violet, then Nancy—and I see it for the first time.

Their resemblance. It's in the eyes.

"You have to know… I didn't, um, I mean, I had no idea he was… Charles…"

"Lied," Nancy fills in. "Yeah, I'd expect nothing less." She kisses her daughter's head. "So what are you going to do about it?"

My voice quivers. "Wh-what do you mean?"

"I'm not going back home. It's not safe. He'll kill me. I have to take my boys, and we have to run." She licks her lips, squares her shoulders. "I'm asking if you'll let me take her, too. If you'll give me my daughter back."

Her words slam into my sternum, stealing my breath, and tears instantly line my eyes as I look down at my baby. The little girl I thought I'd get to keep. The one who calls me Mama.

"Nancy, I…" I can't. It would be like handing her my heart. Like tearing off an arm and waving goodbye as she walked away with it. "I can't."

"She's my daughter," Nancy says, her voice raspy. Angry. "She was never yours."

"She doesn't know that," I argue. "She is my daughter in every way that matters. In every way that counts. I have raised her. I have loved her."

"Because he stole that from me," she shouts, slapping her fist against the floor. Neither girl seems concerned by the outburst. The cabin grows silent, and for a long while, we just stare at each other. "He stole her from me,

Hazel. Your husband stole my daughter, and he put her in your arms, and you are the only one who can do anything about it."

"I can't..." I can hardly breathe.

"You have to." She stands, steps forward, and takes my hands. "You have to."

I shake my head. I'm not strong enough. "I didn't ask for this. I didn't...I didn't do anything wrong."

Her green eyes line with tears, then they overflow, cascading one by one down her cheeks.

She's the one who did something wrong.

She slept with a married man.

My married man. She...

My eyes scan her bruises and scars. Up close, I can see even more.

The sound of tires on the gravel draws me out of my thoughts, and Nancy's hands tighten on mine. *He's home.*

My heartbeat thunders in my ears, chills lining my arms. I look at her directly, urgently, trying to keep her calm. "Where are your boys?"

"School." She's shaking in my hands, trembling so much I feel sick.

"I can't get you out of here without him seeing." I don't have time. I don't know what to do. "Maybe we could tell him. Talk to him." But even as I say it, I know we can't.

Thoughts twist violently in my mind.

Silent tears paint Nancy's cheeks as she crosses the

room and bends down to hug her daughter one last time. "He's going to kill me. Do you understand that? He's going to kill me, and...and you're going to let him. Promise me you will take care of her. Promise me—"

"Shut up!" I cry, crossing the room and grabbing her arm. When she winces, I release it, feeling as if I might pass out. "We are not going to let that happen. Do you trust me?"

"Why would I?" She scowls, rubbing her arm.

"Come with me."

In my bedroom, I shove aside the cedar trunk filled with blankets and lift the door to the cellar. I know the rules here, of course I do. She is not supposed to know Foxglove's secrets, but what choice do I have? Leave her to Charles? I can't stomach the thought.

Please don't punish her, I beg.

"Go down through here. There are tunnels. You can escape. Go to the back wall, the far corner, and push in. It will give. Follow the corridor and take the stairs. Just please, *please* don't ever tell anyone about this."

"Wait. What?"

"There's no time. Go. Or else wait in the cellar until I can get rid of him. Either way, you'll be okay. I promise, it'll be okay. Just stay quiet."

"What? No." She looks terrified. Perhaps of the dark. Perhaps of what I might do, that I might change my mind. "Please don't leave me down here alone."

I glare at her. "It's the only way. Do you want to see your daughter grow up? Conrad and Cory, too? They'll be home from school soon. Do you want to make it back to them?"

Her chin quivers as she nods.

"Then get down there and be quiet."

I'm sliding the chest back into place when the front door opens a few minutes later. She'll be okay. It's dark down there, but it's safe. As long as she is quiet, she'll be okay.

I rush back into the living room, lightning flowing through my veins.

I have to stay calm if I'm going to survive this. I have to be smart.

The girls have stopped painting when Charles finds them. He bends down, looking over their artwork. "Well, aren't these pretty?" He winks at me, then stands and kisses my cheek. "Just like your mama."

I lean into his kiss.

It could be this easy. I could choose him. Choose this. I could tell him where Nancy is and let him handle it. I could choose this family and get everything I want.

I squeeze my eyes closed, imagining it. The girls could be mine. Even if I don't tell him about Nancy, I could keep her down there until he leaves again and send her away. She isn't strong enough to fight me. I don't owe her anything.

"Mommy? Who was that lady?"

Billie's tiny voice rips my eyes open.

"What lady?" Charles asks, frozen. Defensive already.

"The lady Mommy was talking to."

My breathing grows shallow. *Think. Think. Think.* "Oh. She's talking about earlier. A woman came by; she was trying to sell makeup. I sent her away. Told her we're not interested." I reach out and brush a bit of Billie's hair from her face. "It's all okay, honey."

She draws out a long pause, eyes searching mine, and I pray with everything in me she'll let it go. To my great relief, she just sticks her tongue between the corner of her lips and goes back to painting.

Charles watches me. I force a smile, willing it to reach my eyes as I try to mask the doubt clawing at my throat.

"Supper isn't on the table?"

"Just about. I didn't expect you home for another hour."

"Finished early." He kisses my cheek again, patting my bottom. "Billie, get this all cleaned up and help your mother set the table while Daddy hops in the shower."

When the bathroom door closes moments later, tears line my eyes.

I know, no matter how much I'd like to lie to myself, no matter what happens next, this is the last time it will ever be like this.

After the girls go to bed, I ask him. I need to know the truth. I need to either hear him say it or watch him lie to me.

"Have you heard from Nancy lately?"

He doesn't look up from his seat next to the fireplace, still flipping through his newspaper. "Nancy?"

Is he honestly pretending not to know which Nancy I mean?

"I used to see her around town. You know, before. I just...I can't believe she doesn't ever want to see Violet."

He's still for a moment, then slowly closes the paper and turns his head to look at me. "Where is this coming from?"

"It's just a question." I cross the room and crouch down, gathering the girls' toys from the floor.

"Well, I don't know what to tell you." He opens the paper again, sleepy gaze returning to its pages. "Motherhood doesn't come naturally to every woman."

I feel the sting of his words, even for a woman I don't particularly care about. A debt to the sisterhood wells in me. I drop the toys into a basket in the corner, out of the way. "She always seemed to be a good mother to Conrad and Cory. They're good boys."

He stands up then, and takes a step toward me. I've crossed a line. I've pushed too hard.

"Where is this coming from? Do you not want Violet anymore?" His voice is too loud, and I worry the girls might not be fully asleep. What if Violet overheard him ask that terrible question? If I don't *want* her—as if she's a mutt we can take back to the pound.

"How can you ask me that?"

"If you want me to take her back to her mother, just say the word."

I blink, swallowing the bitter lump in my throat. My gaze flicks between his eyes, searching for the man I thought I knew, not this stranger in front of me. "Would you do that?"

His brows draw down, a muscle tensing in his jaw. "What the hell is wrong with you, woman? You been drinking?"

"You know I don't drink."

He scowls, voice like gravel as he turns away from me. "Well, maybe you should."

"I think you do enough of that for the both of us."

He whips back around, staring at me as if I've started speaking another language.

I shake my head, disgust bubbling in my core like I've just downed a glass of rotten milk. "Don't think I don't know you've been sneaking whiskey again. I smell it on you. Just like before."

"You're insane." He waves a hand at me. "Delusional, just like your damn mother was."

Delusional. Mad. Insane. Crazy. All the insults they've thrown at my mother and her mother and many, many mothers before them.

The Wilde family—disappearing through walls, appearing out of thin air and shadows. I've heard the rumors. I know what people say about us, what they've always said. Just like I know at least one of my ancestors fell victim to the witch trials.

When they can't understand us, they hurt us.

But I don't need magic to do the right thing. "I want you to leave."

He scoffs, looks at me as if I'm dirt, one brow rising. "What the hell's gotten into you?"

"I want you to leave, Charles."

"You leave." He steps closer to me. "This is my house, woman."

"Foxglove has never belonged to a man. It will never belong to a man." I square my shoulders. "It will never belong to you."

He grabs hold of my arm. "*You* belong to me."

"*Let me go.*" I fight the words out between gritted teeth.

"Damn you." His face is so close to mine, a bit of spittle hits my cheek.

Maybe this is what I needed to see. Him this angry. Him ready to hurt me. Maybe I needed to know the monster was always there lurking.

I shove him away, trying to storm out of the room, but he grabs my wrist.

His grip is too tight. "Where do you think you're going?"

I sink my teeth into his knuckles, biting down until he jerks away with a roar. I stumble backward. In a rush to escape, my foot catches on a chair leg, and I crash to the floor.

A low chuckle builds in his throat. His lips tug into a terrible grin as he steps forward, the toe of his socked foot on the hem of my dress. "Someone's feeling mouthy tonight."

"Cut it out, Charles." Fear grips my throat with icy fingers. Why did I do this? I didn't need proof. I saw it already on her skin.

"Don't think I will." He lowers himself to the floor, looming over me. "See, someone needs to remember just who the man of the house is around here."

"Oh, and you're going to show me?" I bite back, jaw tight.

His expression twists into something unreadable. Menacing. A rock settles in my stomach.

"Like you showed Nancy?"

He goes eerily still, doesn't even blink. "What did you just say to me?"

I scoot farther away until my shoulder scrapes the fireplace. The walls close in around me. With nowhere else to go, I try to stand, to run.

Charles launches forward, grabbing my neck and shoving me back to the ground. His hands go to my windpipe, and I struggle to suck in a breath. I claw at the air, desperately searching for his eyes, his face, but he manages to stay just out of my reach.

I'm not strong enough, though maybe I've always lied to myself and said I was. My hands fall to the floor, searching blindly for something, *anything*, I can use.

His grip tightens on my neck.

My vision blurs, thoughts disappearing like smoke.

My hand connects with something above my head,

something metal, and I send the fireplace tools in every direction.

In a second, I have my chance. He sees it coming moments before it hits. My hand clasps the fire poker, the ornate, wrought-iron pattern of the handle fitting perfectly in my palm.

I meet his eyes, and I swing.

The shovel slips in my hands, splinters stabbing the raw skin on my palm. I bite the inside of my cheek to keep from cursing out loud, the burning impossible to ignore.

I stab the earth again, angrier this time, and the metal strikes stone hidden just below the surface. A sharp jolt shoots straight up my arms, into my bones.

I brace myself and try once more, but the ground is unrelenting and hard as brick.

Just like he was. Set in his ways from the very day I met him. Unyielding.

The quilt wrapped around his body behind me is an old one, hand-sewn by my great-grandmother and passed down through generations. The faded pattern is stained dark now—from both his blood and the creek water I dragged him through to get here.

I can't stand to look at it. Nor at him.

"You always did weigh too much," I say to the bundle without turning back. *In words. In secrets. Apparently in fists.*

My palms are raw and blistered. In my rush, I didn't think to grab my gardening gloves. It feels as if I've been digging for hours, though I have no idea how long it's actually been.

Could be minutes.

Or years.

I'm not sure my body knows the difference anymore.

Around me, the woods are too quiet. No birds, not even the wind chime singing on the breeze from the porch. Just the sound of my tired breath and the dry scrape of my shovel.

I drop it, cursing and wiping sweat from my brow with my arm.

The shovel clangs against the ground, and I press my hands to my thighs, gasping for breath. My arms are filled with sand, and my dress clings to my skin with sweat. There's a tear in my sleeve, and I realize it must have snagged on a branch at some point while I was dragging him through the forest.

He won't be buried like the others, between the new willow and the old oak. He doesn't deserve it. I wouldn't dare lay him to rest with my mother.

I want to cry, to succumb to something other than blind rage, but the tears won't come.

It's not grief I feel in this moment.

This is something else.

It's the sound of a door slamming shut, leaving nothing but an echo in its quiet wake.

"You would've known how to do this," I whisper,

staring down into the half-dug grave. I know they would have—*the others.* The Wilde women who came before me. Who built this house and protected us all.

I can't even dig a grave.

I sink onto the ground, dropping my face into my hands.

That's when the wind shifts. I feel it first on the back of my neck. There's a sudden breath, sharp and cold. The leaves on the ground around me shudder. The air seems to thicken, and I smell a storm coming, damp and metallic.

It comes on quickly.

Rain. And not just a drizzle. There is no warning. No gentle heads-up. There is only the storm.

It pours down as if the sky has been holding its breath all spring, waiting for this moment. Like it's a bucket filled to the brim, suddenly tipped over.

The trees groan, flowers in the meadow whip this way and that. And right before my very eyes, the soil all around me, under me, turns soft.

I sit in disbelief, soaked to the bone as I watch the earth melt.

It's impossible, but it's real.

I know, but I don't.

Foxglove is helping me in that way she does, a way I've only heard stories of until this moment.

Our land doesn't speak to us, not in words, but it knows. It remembers. It remembers my mother's warmth and my gran's playful manner. It remembers their fire. It remembers our stories and our scars, the blood on the floor after each baby has come into this world. The whispered secrets floating to the rafters. The tears. The laughter. The love.

It remembers us, just like my gran told me all those years ago.

I don't wait. I move.

I grab the shovel and begin to dig. The earth shifts easily now, yielding like warm dough. A better woman than I might say a prayer, but when the grave is deep enough, I just let him fall in.

I pour the dirt back over him in a hurry, in silence.

By the time I'm done, my hands are slick with mud. My dress is ruined by the act. One more thing he'll take from me.

It doesn't stop raining, even when I'm finished. Doesn't stop taking him deeper into the earth, and for that, I am grateful.

Within minutes, the spot where his body rests has vanished, the ground unmarked. It doesn't look like a grave, only dirt. Like nothing ever happened here.

He will disappear from this earth and no one will even realize he's gone. Not a soul will miss him.

The storm begins to ease on my walk back to Foxglove, the thunder farther off in the distance. The woods are dark, but the moonlight leads me.

I don't look back, only forward, though I move without haste.

When I get back to Foxglove, I will light the fire. I'll

wash the dirt and blood from my hands and change out of my dress, then toss it into the flames and watch it burn.

When there's nothing left but ash, I will open the cellar and hand Nancy our daughter.

Her daughter.

And I will make her swear to never, ever come back to Foxglove again.

CHAPTER FORTY-TWO

CORINNE WILDE - PRESENT DAY

We run.

Oh, do we run. I've never moved so fast in my life. Never moved so quickly that I feel as if I'm ripping my muscles as I go, tearing my lungs straight out of my chest.

She must've been forced to stop near the patch of flooded road Conrad and Benji mentioned and decided to walk the rest of the way, walk home to us.

If he hurts her—if EJ hurts my baby—it will be my fault. My fault for asking for the divorce. My fault for moving us here. My fault for not asking enough questions when Mom ignored me. My fault for not checking Taylor's phone more often. My fault for not saving her.

We reach the door, and I turn the handle.

No.

No.

No.

No.

No.

I'm falling, falling, falling.

I crash to the ground. "It's locked. He locked us out."

Lewis pulls out his keys, but reality is already setting in for me. "You don't have the new key." I curse, stepping back. "You don't have the new key."

My fault.
My fault.
My fault.

"Taylor!" I pound on the door, shouting. Begging. "Taylor! It's Mom! Let us in!"

Nothing.

There is no response.

"The tunnels," Mom whispers in my ear, pulling me back.

"There's no time. We have to go through the window," I cry.

"I'll do it." Lewis takes off his rain jacket, wrapping it around his arm as he walks around the house to the kitchen window.

"Be careful," I call after him. Once he's gone, I turn, looking at Conrad and Benji. At Greta. "You guys should go back to the road. I couldn't live with myself if anything..." I stop, looking down to compose myself as panic claws at my chest.

"What are you talking about?" Greta asks.

I take both of her hands in mine, my voice tight with emotion. "I need you to do this for me, okay? I need you to go back to the woods and wait for the police. Find them and bring them here."

"What?" Conrad asks.

"No." Greta's face is fierce, haunted. "Stop it. I'm not leaving you. Not now. *No.*"

"Please. Please go and get help." I'm crying then as I hug her. "We need someone to help them find us. To tell them what happened." I squeeze her tighter. "I need to know that you're safe."

"We can help you." I can't tell her tears from the rain painting her cheeks.

"Please," I beg. "I have to save her, and I need you to save me. We need the police, or we'll never make it out of this."

I watch my words wash over her expression, over all of their expressions.

Slowly, reluctantly, Benji tugs at her arm. "Come on. She's right."

Greta doesn't move, but Conrad gives me a look that says they'll be okay. He juts his chin forward, toward Foxglove. "Go. We've got her."

"Be safe," Greta says, chin quivering. "Please be safe. Find our girl."

I don't wait.

I can't.

Together, Mom and I run toward the meadow. I should send her away, but I need her. I need her help navigating the tunnels and navigating this man.

At the base of the old oak tree, she shoves a large rock

aside, revealing an iron door set into the earth. My heart hammers in my chest.

This is impossible.

The door's groan pierces the air as she tugs it open, then pulls me inside. Our footsteps echo on the stone stairs, and when the door closes behind us, we're swallowed whole by inescapable darkness.

A shiver crawls down my spine as the heavy silence presses against my skin, my lungs. This place is nothing like I imagined, and I only wish I could see it better.

See it at all.

My fingers brush the cold stone walls as we ease down the spiral staircase. At the bottom, Mom takes my hand without a word, guiding me until I feel the walls pressing against both sides of my body.

The path we follow is narrow, suffocating, the air dusty and damp. I think of the women who have walked this same path. I wonder if they were as terrified as I am, if they had as much to lose.

Mom is limping as we move through the passage, and I wonder if she twisted her ankle just now, running through the meadow or on the stairs.

Or if it's pain she's been hiding from before. From EJ.

His name burns me, and I pray we reach him in time.

She slows her steps, and I worry momentarily she's hurting too badly to go on, but then I hear voices.

"Please."

Taylor.

She's crying. Begging.

I'm going to be sick.

Mom holds a hand against my chest. I try to shove past her, but she stops me, gripping both my shoulders.

"*Wait,*" she whispers, voice so low I barely hear it. A breath more than a word.

All thoughts cease. Time stops. The world shrinks further, darkness closing in around me. I can't wait. My baby is on the other side of this wall.

She's crying for me.

She needs me.

"Why are you doing this?" Taylor asks, and to my surprise, she sounds stronger than before. Angrier.

It takes several seconds for him to respond. "You were never meant to be a part of this, you know? I had a plan for you to be tucked safely away. You can thank your grandma for that. Your parents."

"You're Austin," she says firmly. There's no shock in her voice.

"Bingo." He laughs. "Don't look at me like that. You're not exactly Miss Innocent here."

"I have no idea what you're talking about, psycho." After a beat she yelps, and my heart tugs. He's hurting her.

"How do you think your parents would feel if they found out you were the one who ruined your things so your mom would want to leave? Or that you texted your dad when that didn't work, pretending to be your mom in hopes he'd come here and you could convince him to bring you home? Honestly, nice touch. *Austin* was proud, and so am I. And if we can get them back together, we both win."

My chest tightens.

"What do you even want Foxglove for?" she cries, voice feral, panicked. "You said this place sucks."

"That's for me to know. Now keep quiet. I'll be back." I hear footsteps upstairs, and I hold my breath, squeezing my hands into fists.

Someone's up there. Lewis.

The sound of EJ climbing the steps echoes through the shadows. He closes the cellar with a soft thud. Once we're certain he's gone, Mom moves her hand and shoves the wall aside.

Taylor is on the ground, hands tied behind her back. She spins around, panic flickering across her features. "What the—"

"*Shh, shh, shhhhh,*" I whisper, throwing my hands up to keep her quiet. "It's us. It's us."

I hurry forward, desperate to hold her. To prove that she's real. That she's here. Hurt—with a bloody gash across her lip—but alive.

"Where did you come from?" she whispers, eyes wild.

My stomach knots. "We'll explain everything. But first, we have to get you out of here."

CRACK.

We all flinch as the sound tears through Foxglove. I can't breathe, can't hear. My ears roar, thoughts collapse. Reality shatters. *A gun. That was a gun.*

Upstairs, Lewis cries out with a guttural groan I feel deep in my chest. I squeeze my eyes shut as the sickening thud of someone hitting the floor reaches my ears.

No.

My vision flashes, blotting with black ink like a Rorschach test.

"Take her." I shove Taylor toward Mom, my voice trembling. "Please."

She resists, unmoving. "I'm not leaving you."

"Me neither," Taylor snaps, eyes wide with fear. "What's happening?"

I clutch Taylor's rain-soaked hair in both hands, pressing a desperate kiss to her forehead. "I love you."

Taylor's hands go to mine. "Mom, you're scaring me."

"Go with your grandmother." My tone doesn't leave room for negotiation, however quiet my voice is. "Go now, and I will come find you, okay?" My eyes lock on Mom's. "Get her out of here. Go back the way we came and find the others. Wait for the police."

Mom's gaze flicks to Taylor, then back to me. "Come with us. I can't leave you here. I won't."

Before I can answer, something warm hits my cheek. I look up, brushing it away, then glance down at my finger.

A bitter lump hardens in my throat.

Even in the dark, I can see the crimson painting my skin. *Blood.*

"Corinne!" Upstairs, Lewis coughs, spits, and wheezes in rapid succession. "Corinne, please! Help!"

Taylor goes stiff, then yanks out of Mom's arms. *"Dad!"* Her wide, furious eyes drill into mine.

Above us, he groans again, his ragged breaths leaking through the floorboards. Taylor bolts, shoving Mom aside and slipping past me before I can stop her.

She doesn't know.

She doesn't know that it might not be him.

"Taylor, wait!" I shout after her. My arms shoot out, fingers clawing for her ankle, but she kicks me away.

She climbs the stairs in seconds, with me just behind her. When we reach the cabin floor, she rushes ahead. I lunge to stop her, but I'm not quick enough.

In the living room, she freezes mid-step. I nearly crash into her as the terrible sight snaps into focus.

My blood runs cold. The edges of my vision turn black, as if being burned by a match.

Lewis lies motionless on the floor next to the fireplace. Unconscious or...*worse*. All around him, the floor is puddled with thick blood, creeping across the floorboards like a shadow, and slowly dripping into the cellar below.

"*Dad! No!*" Taylor runs to his side, dropping to her knees. Her hands tremble as her eyes dart desperately, searching for something—anything—to fix. Her voice breaks. "This is all my fault."

Before anyone can respond, EJ steps out of the closet

across the room, a smug grin tugging at his lips. He holds up his phone and taps the screen.

"Corinne, please! Help!" The message plays again, clear and chilling. And still in Lewis's voice.

"Let them go," Mom's voice cuts through the air as she appears behind me. The muscles in my chest squeeze tighter. She winces, leaning heavily on her good foot. Her pain is hidden, but I can see it.

"No can do," EJ says in a cheery, singsong voice.

"What do you want?" I grit out, jaw clenched.

"She hasn't told you?" His surprise is fake, a performance unworthy of an Oscar.

"All this for money?" I glare at him. "Why?"

He chuckles darkly, running a hand over his buzzed hair. "Money? I mean, come on. We're not talking about a five-spot, Rinnie Ren, but don't insult me. I don't need the money. Would it be nice? Sure. But I'm already successful. I certainly sell more than your little friend."

He sneers, eyes gleaming with something vicious. Of course he had to bring Greta into this. "No, this isn't about money," he says, his voice curdling. "It's about justice."

Mom steps in front of me. "Justice?" Her voice is sharp, uncertain. "What are you talking about?"

EJ's smile twists into something darker. He looks down, then back up from behind his heavy brows. "I'm talking about my mom, Billie." There's a pause, cold and deliberate, and Foxglove seems to hold her breath right along with us. "Or did you think I was genuinely attracted to you?"

CHAPTER FORTY-THREE

BILLIE WILDE - 1980

The house is quieter than I've ever heard it. The wind chime sings in the wind, but there's not a sound to be heard inside. It's the kind of quiet that settles into your bones. Where every creak of the floorboards, every shift of the wind, feels like a whisper in church.

Even the dust is still.

Michael is at the door, adjusting his coat and holding one of my bags. I don't remember even packing it. Last night was a blur.

The sun is barely up, the sky still strangely gray rather than pink. Like Foxglove knows it's losing me today, like it's saying goodbye.

I stand by the window, looking out at the meadow as a sort of sadness washes over me. I didn't expect it. Yesterday, I was glad to be rid of this place. Today, it feels like someone has carved a hole deep in my chest.

Maybe it's just a trick of the light, but I swear from here, I can almost make out the place where the grass once flattened in the meadow—where I used to lie beneath the sky and dream of someday.

Back then, Foxglove felt magical. Special. It felt like home.

Now, I've never felt so far away. As if we're already in the car. As if it's nothing but a memory.

"Are you ready?" Michael's voice breaks through my thoughts. He holds out a hand and I take it. His palm is warm, strong. He makes me feel safe in a way I never have before.

I smile at him and wonder if he understands, if he's ever felt this quiet longing for a place that is no longer yours. A place that never can be again.

He must understand, though. He's left his home, too. We're going to be married. To live in the city. Away from here. Away from everything we've ever known.

I take a step toward him and feel something inside me, like a tug of a string being pulled in my chest. It's always been there. The familiar weight of Foxglove's walls. Of my mother's expectations. They both want me to stay, but I can't. This place is no longer meant for me.

I squeeze my eyes shut as I hear it, the steady, deliberate shuffle of footsteps behind me.

Mom.

I feel her before I see her, standing there at the end of the hall. Her face is unreadable—too calm almost, when I know she's anything but. There's a storm gathering behind her eyes. Her hands are clasped together, and I know Michael doesn't see the slight tremor she's trying to hide, like she's holding onto something too tightly.

Maybe that something is me.

"Don't do this, Billie." Her voice is raspy from both sleep and age, but every bit as cutting. It can still make me as nervous as it did when I was a child.

"You've left me no choice."

"No choice." She laughs under her breath. "You don't know a thing about having no choices, girl. I promise you that."

"Is that what you tell yourself?" I release Michael's hand, standing between them. "That you had no choice?" I can't say the rest, can't bring up my father and what she did to him. Can't bring up the fact that she's lied to me all my life about what happened, how he died.

"I told you the truth because you needed to hear it." Her voice slows down, begging me for something I don't understand. "Because you need to understand that even the most powerful love can change. Even the person you think you know best…can become a stranger."

I blink, unable to point out the irony of her words. "I love him. That's all that matters."

"I have no doubts. You don't know him."

"I don't know *you*."

She huffs, her shoulders rising with a deep, drawn-out breath. "Be mad at me if you want, but Foxglove is yours. You belong here. This house, her land—it's in your blood. The Wilde name is yours, and it means something. It's all we have. All we've ever had."

I swallow hard. "It's just a house, Mom. Just a name." The next words come easier than I expected them to. "And neither are mine anymore."

"What did you say?" She looks at me as if I've slapped her.

"I will be taking Michael's last name. I have to build something of my own."

"Of his." She spits the words as if they were venom.

I press my lips together, pushing a breath through my nose as I do my best to stay measured, calm. "I can't be bound by the past anymore. Even if you refuse to leave it."

Her eyes narrow, something flickering in their depths. Anger. Hurt. "The Wilde name is something more than just words on a page, and you know it. Don't do this. Don't throw everything away because you're upset with me."

I stand straighter, feeling the heat of her disapproval but unable to resist what comes next, fueled by my anger. "The Wilde name will end with you."

She takes in the words like a blow she hadn't braced for, flinching with a sharp intake of breath. Then her lips wrinkle with indignation.

"No." The single word is uttered with finality, firm and absolute. A command. "Change your name if you want, but you cannot change your blood. You are Wilde. You have always been Wilde."

Behind me, I hear Michael shift. I suspect he's wondering whether to intervene, to speak on my behalf.

My pulse races as I meet Mom's gaze. She's getting older; her eyes are tired. But she still has fire left in her, plenty for this fight in particular.

It's her pride. Her name.

Her beloved home.

But it's just a house.

"I don't belong here anymore. I love you, Mama. I always will. But I can't stay. We are leaving. Today."

Her breath hitches, and for a long, painful moment, I'm sure she's going to yell at me—something she's never done, not even as our world collapsed in on itself over and over again. *My father. My sister. My aunt.*

I cannot stay. I know the truth in my heart. I cannot live with her knowing what she's done, who she is.

In the end, she doesn't yell, though. She just stares at me, fire in her eyes, and gives a sharp nod. "Then go. To your city. To your new name." Her eyes flick to Michael, then back to me. "I hope it brings you whatever it is you're looking for."

Tears sting my eyes, but I fight them back. "This isn't goodbye. I'll come back to visit. I'll call when I can."

She isn't listening, though. She turns away from me, her soft frame disappearing down the shadowy hall.

I turn to Michael, ready to break, and he holds out a hand. We step onto the porch, and I refuse to look back. When the door shuts behind me with a soft thud, it sounds a lot like goodbye.

I suck in a deep breath, blinking away tears. It's done. I'm free. I knew goodbye would hurt, but it's over. *There's no going back.*

Even as I think it, as I force the thought into my mind, etching it across my brain matter, something in me fights against it. This all feels too heavy for me to bear, and I find myself wanting to turn around, to run to my mother and fling myself into her arms. To stay.

But I don't.

I let Michael lead me to the car, his kind, worried eyes trained on my face. We pull away from Foxglove in silence, and I know, once I leave, there's truly no coming back.

I've chosen this new life. It's what I want. But still, I feel as if I'm losing something.

I give in and look back over my shoulder just once as we pull down the gravel road. And Foxglove—the house that has been home to so many Wilde women before me—stays behind, watching and waiting as the last Wilde woman drives away.

Later - 2024

My favorite little bookshop on Jefferson is booming today, filled with customers excited for their big sale. All around me, people shove books into baskets, stocking up on adventures. I'm a browser. I can't grab based on covers alone. I take my time with each story, read the back cover, then the first few pages. I feel the weight of it in my hand.

Each story is a commitment, and I want to feel drawn to it. Like I can't possibly read anything else.

On the endcap, my daughter's novel sits, and I stick one in my basket without thought. I think I have about fifty copies now. She'd be embarrassed if she knew, but I can't help it. I'm so proud of her. Of whom she's become. The life she's built.

I stop at the next shelf, lost in thought.

"You're eyeing that Atwood like she owes you money." A voice slips behind me, warm and casual, as if we're old friends.

I turn, expecting to see someone I know, but instead I find an unfamiliar face. He's tall. Forty-something, maybe. That smile—that boyish little grin—confuses me at first, then charms me.

Normally, a man who looks like that staring at me might make me blush, but I don't. Maybe I've grown out of it, too old for girlish habits.

Still, I find myself standing a little taller. A little straighter.

"She might. I own two copies already, but not this cover." I tap it with my finger. "I think I need it."

He chuckles and grabs two copies, placing them into his basket. I blink at him. "One for you, one for me."

And that's how it starts. A conversation in the fiction aisle. A gifted book. A coffee after, across the street. A walk back to my car that seems to last both forever and not nearly long enough. Then a dinner invitation.

Which leads to another.

And another.

EJ doesn't ask how old I am, not at dinner, nor when he comes back to my house a month in. I don't volunteer it, but I figure he can tell. He traces his finger across the lines on my face, the silver in my hair. He makes me feel beautiful *because* of them, not in spite of them. He doesn't judge or get annoyed when I forget words mid-sentence and have to pause. He looks at me like he really sees me, like he wants to.

I forget how much I missed that, how good it feels.

Michael and I had a messy divorce, but I loved him dearly. Sometimes I wonder if we might've fixed things, reconciled someday. If we could've had one of those post-divorce rekindling moments they make such a fuss about in all the rom-coms.

But we never got the chance. He's been gone nearly a decade now. Some days I still wake up reaching for him.

I didn't think I needed anyone else. I'm happy. With Corinne, Taylor, and Lewis. With my books and my painting. I'm fulfilled.

I don't need anyone, but *want*...that's something else entirely, isn't it? EJ makes me feel desired again. Interesting again. Alive.

When I brought up the idea of him meeting my daughter, I worried he'd think it was too soon, but he was overjoyed by the idea. He's different from most men his age. Serious. Committed.

And so, here we are. At dinner with my only daughter.

"She's fiercely smart," I warn him as we wait for her arrival. "Like her father was. But sharper-tongued than either of us. She's also protective in the way people become when they lose a parent too early. A grandparent, too." I wonder what Hazel would think of EJ. She'd probably tell me I've lost my mind.

"She sounds amazing," EJ says, kissing my hand. "Like her mother."

"She can be shy when she first meets you."

"I can handle it." He lifts his glass to his mouth with that charming smile of his.

I add the last two points I should warn him about silently, wringing my hands together in my lap.

She doesn't like surprises.

She especially doesn't like when people haven't earned their place in our lives.

"Oh." I pause, thinking as he watches me. "Don't be offended if she's a little cold at first. When she meets people, it takes her a while to open up, but once she trusts you, you're stuck with her for the long haul."

"Then I'll just have to earn her trust."

He never seems bothered. Never worried. He adjusts the watch on his wrist, but not in a way that seems like he's rushing. It's just a habit.

His phone buzzes, but he silences it. He could be

busy as a bee with showings and listing appointments, but he always makes time for the things that are important to me.

When Corinne enters the restaurant, I spot her right away. I stand, hand over my shoulder.

I wonder if she'll notice the sapphire earrings Michael gave me years ago for one anniversary or another. I want her to know I haven't forgotten him. This was never about that.

She's right on time, dressed in a black dress with dark lipstick. Beautiful as ever. She kisses my cheek, then turns to EJ, who stands and holds out a hand.

Her smile is cool, polite, but her eyes are not. She takes his hand. "You must be EJ. My mom's told me... almost nothing about you." Her words aren't sharp, but there's no warmth to them. She's caught off guard by his age, I know. I should have warned her.

EJ, if he's offended, takes it in stride. His charm oozes out as he smiles, shakes his head, and gestures for her to sit. "Well, she's told me quite a lot about you." He compliments her book next, telling her he read it and found it "intriguing and unique in all the right ways."

He lifts his glass to his lips, then pauses to add, "A bit cutting too, if I'm being honest."

She nods. "Thanks. I never meant for it to be polite."

We switch subjects, eating and talking about everything under the sun. EJ tries, bless him, but Corinne fences him with every word, shutting down his charm and dodging his compliments as if they were knives.

When he steps out to take a call, a heavy silence falls over the table. I let out a sigh full of anticipation, watching her.

When she doesn't say anything, I prod. "Well?"

"He seems nice." Her voice is neutral, not giving me any indication of how she truly feels, though I suspect I know.

"He *is* nice," comes my quick reply.

Her eyes dance over my features. "Do you like him?"

I don't have to think about it. "Yeah. I do."

"And he likes you?"

I bristle. "Yes. I think so."

She tilts her head slightly, and I can see she's holding back.

"What? Just say it."

"I don't... I..." She presses her lips together. "He gives me bad vibes. Men like him, they know how to read a room. Are you sure he's interested in you for you? Does he think you have money or something?"

The back of my neck heats like a stove burner. "Men like him." I puff out a breath. "And that means what, exactly?"

"You know what I mean."

"No, I don't. Tell me."

She sighs, then unfolds and refolds her napkin on the table. "Well, he's attractive, for one thing. But also young. He probably gets attention from a lot of women. Why is he spending so much time with someone—" She cuts herself off.

"Someone what, Corinne? Someone old? Someone my age? You're right, how dare I hope he could possibly be interested in me?"

"You know that's not what I meant." She looks hurt, but so am I.

"Isn't it?"

She takes a breath, her next words careful. "I just don't want to see you get hurt. Or…or taken advantage of."

Her words sting, her lack of faith in me hurts even worse. Like a bruise I'd forgotten about until she'd pressed down on it.

"I'm not stupid just because I'm old."

"Mom—"

I cut her off. "I've been judging character longer than you've been alive, Corinne. I think I would know if he wasn't who he says he is."

She blinks, silent, and looks away. "I'm sorry."

"I invited you here because I was excited for you to meet someone important to me. I should've known this was how you'd react. Should've known you couldn't just be happy for me."

She opens her mouth to say something, maybe to tell me I'm wrong, but then EJ is back.

He sinks down in his chair, smile fading as he senses the tension. "Everything…all right?"

I can't bear to look at Corinne, so I turn my gaze to him instead, my voice tight as I fight back angry tears.

"Corinne just had something come up. She's not going to be able to join us for dinner after all."

Concern washes over EJ's face, and I'm furious at her for doing this. For embarrassing me and hurting him. "Oh, no. Is everything okay?"

We look at her then, and she hesitates. Something flickers behind her expression—regret, maybe. But she says nothing. Just stands from her seat and walks away.

CHAPTER FORTY-FOUR

CORINNE WILDE - PRESENT DAY

EJ glares at me, pacing the room with slow, deliberate steps. His hands are clasped tightly behind his back, so I can no longer see the gun.

"My grandmother," he begins, voice low and cold, "she told me stories about this place. About this cabin. About the man who broke her. The family who stole my mother from her."

His eyes flare with something darker than rage. Sharper, somehow. It's like I can feel it crawling across my skin. "She told me about the cellar, where *your* grandmother, Hazel, locked her away. Made her wait in the dark. In the cold. Alone, for hours."

He stops pacing and turns to face me fully. His voice drops low and dangerous like distant thunder rolling in. "She told me about the tunnels she searched for but never found. She warned me about the infamous Foxglove. And all about you, of course. *The Wilde women.* Hiding out here with your money and your power. Your secrets."

A crude smile twists his lips as he steps closer. "My grandmother may not have found the tunnels, but I remembered her stories well enough. Once I got inside, it wasn't hard to find them. And after you gave my uncle a key to watch over the place, I only had to steal it and make a copy to start coming here whenever I wanted."

He leans in, voice dripping with venom. "It was all going well. I could come here, show clients around. And then...*you* came along."

"You had no right to be here," I say, keeping my voice steady despite the fury in my gut.

"No right?" He scoffs, rubbing a hand over his chin. "This house is mine as much as it is yours. It belonged to my mother, too."

"Violet," Mom whispers, voice barely audible. "Your mother was Violet?"

He jerks his chin, eyes lighting up. "So you do remember."

"You're wrong. Foxglove has never belonged to men," Mom spits back at him, fists tight at her sides. "It would never have belonged to Violet because it wasn't Charles's to give away. It passed from my mother to me. From mother to daughter. My mother did what she had to do to protect me. If Violet was your mother, she did it to protect her, too. And Nancy. Without my mother, you might not be here at all."

I stare at her, stunned. My mind scrambles to keep up. "You remember Violet?"

"Bits and pieces," she admits, eyes flicking back to EJ. My chest twists with confusion. "It doesn't change anything. You've wasted your time. Foxglove is not yours, and it never will be. Long before you were a twinkle in your father's eye, men have tried to take this house from us. Every single one has failed."

Mom takes my hand.

I've always believed Foxglove has a heart. I don't mean it as a metaphor or something poetic and beautiful, but something real. A beating thing buried beneath the bones of wood and stone and rot.

As a child I could feel her breathing, and as I stand here now, I swear I feel it again.

This time, it's beating in erratic, wild tandem with mine as I watch Lewis bleed out on the floor, waiting for this argument to end.

"He's going to die. Please stop this," I beg, pointing to Lewis on the floor. "You don't want this. It isn't worth it. Please."

Next to him, Taylor sobs silently, one hand pressed to the bleeding wound in his back, the other—just as bloody—covering her pale face, her open mouth. She looks like she might pass out.

EJ leans back, his free hand clasping the other wrist at his waist. He looks pleased with himself. "Sure. All you have to do is...let me have the place. I've already got the papers drawn up. Sign them, and you'll be free to go."

I hesitate, looking at Mom, searching for any hint of what she's thinking.

He leans back on his heels, then bounces forward impatiently. "Come on. Just a little signature and all of this is over. One signature, and your bad karma?" He snaps his fingers, as if to say *poof*. "Gone."

Mom's eyes narrow.

"It's the least you can do, and we both know it. I don't care what stupid little rules you think you have. This place should be mine after everything you've done." He clicks his tongue, shaking his head. "Your family, you just take and take and *take*. My grandmother is back in this place she hates because she's sick and needs my uncle to take care of her. My mother already died—poor and hungry and alone. All while you sat here on your millions, on what should've been hers. On what should be mine." He jabs a finger against his chest.

"No," Mom snaps. "The house is Wilde. No one else's. Violet was my father's, but she was not ours, even though we loved her. I'm sorry to hear what happened to her, I truly am, but this is not the way to get justice. It's not the way to make her proud."

"Well then." He raises the gun slowly, pointing it at her, one corner of his mouth fighting a smile. "I guess you can either sign the papers...*or* leave the place to your husband in death. The choice is yours." His eyes dart to me, his hands following until the gun points directly at my chest. "But first..."

My breath catches in my throat, pulse pounding, and then—*Taylor*.

She moves like lightning, the fire poker held high in her hands. With a crack that echoes through the cabin, she slams it down, the metal colliding with the top of EJ's head.

The sound of wind fills my ears, drowning out everything else.

I watch in slow motion as he stumbles backward, dizzy and disoriented. The gun slips from his hand and clatters to the floor. His head slams into the carved stone mantel—right where our name is etched: WILDE.

His blood paints the E.

He stumbles again, dazed and bleeding, and the whole room feels wrapped in a sudden, breathless fog where nothing else exists except waiting for him to fall. To die.

For a moment, I think it's over.

He looks ready to crash to the floor, but he doesn't. His eyes cross, then find focus again, and he roars back to life. He rushes forward and grabs Mom by her collar, tossing her to the floor.

She lands with a dull thud, curling up on herself. She cries out, winces, breathes. I'm just grateful she's still alive.

"Mom!" I scream, scrambling to reach her—but EJ stops me. He grabs my wrist and twists it so hard I hear a pop. I yelp, and Taylor shouts.

"Stay back!" I warn her. *The police should be here. Where are the police?*

I spot the gun on the floor under the chair, but I can't reach it. It's too far away, too hidden. If I tell Taylor to grab it, EJ might get there first. I can't say a word.

"Taylor, run!" I shout, begging. It's her only chance to save herself. "Please."

Both his hands wrap around my neck, squeezing, and my knees give out. My back hits the floor so hard it knocks the breath from my lungs. The room spins, my vision blurs.

"You're just like the rest of them," he hisses, lowering his face to mine. He's covered in his own blood, yet still just as strong. "You stupid bitch." He lifts my head off the floor, slamming me back down. The yelp that escapes my lips is involuntary. "You stupid *witch*. This house will burn to the ground before I let you keep it."

He lifts my head again, his facial muscles tense and twitching with rage as he prepares to slam me down once more. I won't survive this. I can't breathe, can't think.

My hand—desperate, fumbling—slaps the floorboard beside me. *Please,* I beg. To whom, I don't know. The universe, maybe. Myself. Foxglove. Grandma. *Please.*

There. A give. A space. A floorboard, bowed and loose. It shifts beneath my palm. I grasp the board, preparing to strike him, but he's too quick.

He sees what I'm doing, releases me with one hand, and rips the board from my grasp, hurling it across the room.

Taylor screams, and I realize she didn't run. She didn't go. He'll kill her if I don't kill him first. He'll kill us all.

I search, begging. Begging Foxglove and my ancestors and myself. The woods and my mother and the women who came before. The meadow and every single piece of folklore and magic that has been passed down through whispers and tears. Daughter to daughter. Blood to blood. I think of my grandma. Of Hazel Wilde. *Dust to dust.*

And then—cold. My fingers connect with something cold and hard.

I don't think, don't question, I just trust. As his hand returns to my throat, as I feel him squeeze, feel him lift, as my vision blurs, I look at my daughter. She's crying over her father—terrified and alone.

My eyes fall to my ex-husband—the man I once loved, the man I once hated—bleeding out, probably dead. And then to my mom—eyes closed, curled up in pain.

Then, in one fell swoop, with every ounce of strength I have left, I swing.

The old, rusty knife comes into view for me moments before EJ sees it. He turns his head, terror splashing onto his expression, and I connect the blade to his eye. The metal slices straight into his flesh, piercing the empty black pupil without resistance.

He falls back against the floor. His scream rips through the room, white-hot and full of terror—a pure, animal sound. He covers his face with trembling fingers, unsure what to do, how to stop the pain. Curses fly from his lips, bellowing as he tries but fails to pull the weapon from his eye.

Blood spurts, and his skin swells.

His face is almost unrecognizable in an instant.

My hands find my throat, and the breath that floods in feels like mercy, the sweetest balm on a terrible wound.

I don't need to watch him die to know that he will.

The blood pouring down his face tells me no one could survive this.

Still sticking out of his eye, the knife's blade is long and rusted, the handle made of blue stone. It's simple and beautiful, probably centuries old.

From where I sit, gasping for breath, I stare at it and wonder how it got there—and why. Buried beneath a loose floorboard all this time, waiting for me to find it right when and where I needed it.

As if Foxglove knew I would.

I shake the thoughts from my head and rush to Taylor, pulling her away from her father and into my arms, squeezing her against my chest. I ease back, hold her face in my hands, and brush the hair from her cheeks with my thumbs. "Go check on your grandma for me, okay?"

She nods through her sobs and moves out of my way. I reach for Lewis next, my hand lingering over the wound. I don't even know where to start. What to do.

The police should be here.

Across the room, Taylor helps Mom sit up, and I hear her groan.

"Corinne?" she calls.

I place my hands on his back, and he's warm, but barely. His back rises with shallow, quick breaths. "Please don't die on me," I whisper, lowering my mouth next to his ear. "Please."

Mom scoots over beside me, grimacing with pain. "Corinne." Her voice cuts through the chaos, commanding even as it trembles. She winces, inhaling sharply through her teeth, one hand on her hip. "Taylor, towels. We need every towel you can find."

Taylor snaps into action, but we both know it's pointless. The gunshot went straight through his stomach, through his back. There's too much blood.

Towels won't help.

Nothing will help.

Tears hit my cheeks as I kiss his forehead with shaky lips. A lump of dough sits lodged in my throat as I whisper, "I love you."

It's "I'm sorry and thank you and goodbye" all rolled into one.

Taylor brings the towels, and we cover the wound, but his blood soaks through, warm and sticky. His face is pale as a sheet, mouth slack. I hope he can hear me, that he knows he's not alone.

If I hadn't sent Benji away, maybe he could help. Maybe he could do something.

My fault.

My fault.
My fault.

As I look at my daughter, then at my mom, I know we're all having the same thought, each shouldering some of the blame.

"Come on, baby," I whisper, sobs tearing through me. "Stay with me. Please. The police are on their way. Just—just please keep breathing. Please."

I can hear myself panicking. I know I'm scaring Taylor, but I can't calm myself down. He's too still. The wound is too bad.

This wasn't supposed to happen.

None of this was supposed to happen.

Mom's hand touches my arm. "Corinne."

I snap my head to look at her.

"I need you to get up." Her eyes are steady, voice low and firm.

"What?"

She winces again, eyes squeezed shut. "Go. Go to the cupboard."

I brush tears from my cheeks, sniffling, desperate to understand. "What are you talking about? Lewis is bleeding out. We have to do something. We have to save him—"

"Go. Now." She's calm. Too calm.

I rise, confusion gnawing at my chest, and cross the room. My fingers are icy as I pull open the cupboard door.

"The back wall," Mom says, her voice tight with

pain. "Press the bottom-right corner. You might have to press kind of hard."

Is she just trying to distract me? Buy time while Lewis dies out of sight?

I press against the panel.

At first, nothing happens. Then, with a soft click, the wall shifts inward and back out, revealing a hollow space hidden behind the cupboard with five wooden shelves.

A false panel.

The scent of dust hits my nose, then herbs—lavender, rosemary, mint. There's more, so many more, but I can't pick them out. My heart pounds in my ears. "What...is this?"

Mom is quiet, breathing through her teeth. "Look for...something to help."

"What does that even mean?" My hand scans the shelves. There are tiny vials and aged tins of different shapes and colors. A stone mortar and pestle. Tinctures sealed with wax or cork stoppers. Bundles of canvas bound tightly with twine. A half-burned candle.

I rummage carefully, reading over labels written in faded ink. Some of the handwriting is scratchy, rushed. Another hand wrote in looping cursive.

> *For pain*
> *To stop a quickening*
> *To aid digestion*

To ease a cough
For a full night's sleep
For a sore throat
To cure a headache

For rash
To bring down a fever

For swelling
To quiet restless thoughts

I stop when I reach a dark-brown bottle, almost black. The label is yellow and curled up on itself. As I run my finger across it, revealing its use, the room's temperature drops twenty degrees.

To stop the bleeding

I pick it up with shaking hands.

Yarrow to stop bleeding. Grandma's soft voice floats through my mind—so real and so close I glance over my shoulder. But she's not there, and this isn't her handwriting.

I don't even know what it is. I don't know how they'd know...

How could they have known we'd need this?

A peculiar and oddly warm sensation settles on my skin, just like before with the knife.

I stare across the room at Mom. "What is this?"

"It will work" is all she says.

I don't know whether to laugh or cry. This feels ridiculous. "It's...it's *ancient*. We can't just... What is it? Is it even safe?"

"Bring it to me. We don't have much time."

The moment I place it into her waiting palm, Mom sets to work without explanation. She pops the cork from the bottle, and the scent hits my nose all at once—sharp, earthy, bitter. Almost smoky, like pine tar and old rain.

It's a smell I recognize but can't quite place. So much and nothing at all.

Mom pushes herself up onto her side, reaching toward him. She takes the last clean towel and pours some of the liquid onto it, instantly staining the orange cloth a dark brown. She hands it to Taylor and lifts his shirt. "Hold this on his wound. Do not take it off." We both stare at Mom in disbelief. She's practically unrecognizable right now, led by something I don't understand. She doesn't pause, turning to me. "What are you waiting for? Open his mouth."

I hesitate, but only for a moment. I nod at Taylor, who does as she was told, placing the towel on Lewis's back. Mom leans in and, together, we turn his head just so, tilting his chin down.

Lewis lies motionless, unaware of what's happening or what we're doing. Unaware of most of what's happened.

His lips are pale, chest barely rising now.

I hesitate. This is Lewis. It feels too risky. I'll never forgive myself if this makes it worse.

"Maybe we should wait," I say, but no one is listening.

Please, the word swims through my mind. Just one more request today.

I stare down at his face. My ex-husband. The father of my child. The man who broke my heart into tiny pieces and somehow managed to keep me whole at the same time. Who showed up for me, for our daughter, when he didn't have to. Who held me and helped me through this terrible night.

I don't know how to feel looking at him now. All our history is tied in knots, blocking my throat.

Mom tilts the vial to his lips, pouring the dark brown liquid into his mouth. Some spills down his chin and onto the floor, but more lands on his tongue.

She covers his mouth with her palm, forcing his lips closed. I wince, hating this.

His throat jerks. Bobs with a swallow.

Then...stillness.

Mom corks the vial and hands it back to me. I hold my breath. My heart hammers against my ribs as I clutch it close to my chest. "Do you really believe this'll help him?"

Mom looks at me. Her eyes hold a sort of understanding that feels as old as this house. As old as the earth underneath it. "What matters is what you believe."

The room goes silent, painfully so. And then—a sharp intake of breath.

In front of us, Lewis gasps. Coughs. Sputters.

His back arches, like something has grabbed him under his belly. Taylor jerks back, but just as quickly, she returns the towel to his wound. He spits blood, groans, and collapses again. I don't know if this is better or worse.

If we killed or healed him.

But he's breathing. I watch his back like a hawk.

My hands go limp on my lap. "Should something be happening?"

Before she can answer, I hear it. Sirens.

Far away but closing in fast. Flashing red-and-blue lights begin to strobe across the curtains.

Police.

EMTs, hopefully.

Help.

Mom pats my hand with a soft nod. "Put that away."

I push up from the floor and cross the room back to the cupboard, wiping the neck of the bottle clean with the hem of my shirt. It feels something like a ritual. I whisper my thanks, my prayer, and tuck it back on its shelf. Then, I press the panel closed, sealing the secret away so it remains invisible.

Just ours.

The hospital smells like antiseptic and coffee that's been heating too long.

I'm in the waiting room, hunched over in a cracked plastic chair, fingernails still caked with blood.

The adrenaline from earlier is gone now, and I feel hollow—like my skin is a container for something afraid to move. To breathe. To look anyone in the eye.

I'm petrified the doctors will tell me we gave him something poisonous. That I made this worse. As the hours have dragged on in this seat, my worries have intensified.

What was I thinking?

What was Mom thinking?

How did she even know about the panel? Where did it come from?

The waiting room is still and quiet. Behind the desk, a nurse types quickly at a computer. An old man sleeps in a chair across from me, a blanket pulled over his knees.

At the end of the room, a door opens. Every person that's awake in the room turns their head.

A doctor walks out—her eyes red-rimmed and exhausted, an iPad in her hand. "Corinne Wilde?"

I stand, rushing toward her. My heart and head pound in unison.

"Lewis is stable." The doctor doesn't look up from the chart right away. "Surgery was a success. The internal bleeding has stopped. He's unconscious. Weak, but alive."

My heart sings. "He's going to be okay?"

She lets out a long breath. "We really don't know how, but yes. Based on where the bullet hit, the damage it caused—particularly to his stomach...the amount of blood loss—he should've coded. He shouldn't still be alive." Her tone is matter-of-fact, but also...concerned. Confused. "But then he just...stabilized."

The memory flashes in my mind. Mom's sure tone, steady hands. Her words: *What matters is what you believe.*

The doctor's eyes narrow slightly, like she's trying to make sense of it. "Honestly? People don't come back from this type of injury. At least, not without serious complications. And yet, he doesn't appear to have any. We'll know more once he's awake, of course, but for now, well, he's a very lucky man." She meets my gaze, eyes serious but soft. "It's a miracle he survived."

I swallow hard, and there's a sudden buzzing in my ears. Cold sweat beads at my temples.

"A miracle," I repeat.

She nods, brows rising as she tilts her head. "That's one word for it."

CHAPTER FORTY-FIVE

CORINNE WILDE - 2008

The trip to Foxglove has never seemed to take so long.

The wind blows hard at our backs, shoving at the car as if it's pushing us forward, hurrying us along. We pass the familiar spots, and my heart seems to know where we are. That we're going back.

Lewis holds my hand over the center console, his gaze fixed ahead.

"I feel nervous for some reason," I admit, squeezing his hand.

He glances at me, a half-smile tugging at the corner of his lips. "You? I feel like I'm trying to impress a house."

I laugh. "What?"

"The way you talk about this place...it matters to you. It's special."

I flip down my mirror and glance at Taylor, asleep in

her car seat. She's so tiny still, her face peaceful and innocent, unaware of the world we brought her into.

Sometimes the guilt of that can be a lot. Of everything I know she'll go through, and all the things I can't predict.

I can't help feeling protected by Foxglove, though it is just a house. Just stones. Still, I think of all the stories Grandma used to tell me about it. The way the house holds memories, how the earth there knows us—our names and our blood. How it wraps us in its secrets.

I want Taylor to know those things, too. However imaginary. I want her childhood to be filled with the magic of the old cabin the way mine was.

I shift in my seat as Foxglove comes into view over the gravel road, and it's as if it's smiling at me. The goldenrod dazzles, blowing in the breeze, a gentle reminder that some things stay the same.

"One day this place will be yours, baby girl," I whisper, the words meant for me more than anything. It's a promise to us both.

The cabin sits at the edge of the clearing, its silhouette outlined against the sky. In the distance I see the meadow, and my throat grows itchy.

I never realized just how much I've missed it.

Foxglove draws me like a magnet, and something tightens then loosens in my chest as we pull into the driveway.

Lewis takes a sharp breath beside me, his fingers gripping the steering wheel as he puts the car in park. He looks a bit like he can't decide whether to go inside or slam the car into reverse and floor it.

"Look." I point to the meadow, to the wildflowers waving hello. "See, she likes you."

He shoots me a skeptical glance and rolls his eyes playfully, but it seems to do the trick of easing his nerves. He steps out of the car, and I hear the crunch of his boots on the gravel.

I unbuckle Taylor from her car seat, cradling her tiny body in my arms as I follow him onto the porch. It seems as though a lifetime has passed since I last walked through this door. I'm an entirely new person now. And I've brought an entirely new person with me.

Inside, the scents of cedar and rosemary, of earth and dust, fill my nose. The old cabin is just as it has always been—cozy, weathered, safe. As we move through the house, the smell of warm wood hits me, along with fresh herbs drying on the beams above my head and smoke from the hearth—though it has remained unlit for many years now. The combination of scents brings me right back. It's something that seems to have always been here, something as old as Foxglove herself.

Despite the years I've been away, Foxglove doesn't feel empty or forgotten. Strange as it sounds, she seems just as alive and lived-in as she ever has.

Lewis watches me from the corner of the room, a mix of wonder and incredulity flickering in his eyes. "You really love it here."

"When I was little, my grandma used to tell me

stories about this place. She said it was 'special, more than just wood and stone.'" I repeat her words just as she'd said them, remembering every bit of her tone and cadence. "She said Foxglove has a soul, and we're all a part of it. That's why Foxglove doesn't leave us, even if we leave it. It's home. She always made it feel a little magic."

His eyes scan the room with seriousness, and I love that he isn't teasing me about something that feels so important.

"I like it," he says softly. "I get why you do."

I move past the worn sofa and the shelves lined with dusty knickknacks and old photos on my way to the fireplace. I stop in front of it, feeling intense reverence for this moment and this home as I lift Taylor, showing her the word carved there in stone.

"Wilde," I read. "That's you, my love. And me. I'll make sure you know this place." I brush her cheek softly with my finger. "It's your home and always will be."

Lewis comes up behind me, his arms sliding around my waist as he rests his chin on the top of my head. He doesn't say anything, doesn't need to. This space isn't his in the same way it is ours, and he doesn't get it. But he's here. That's what counts.

We stand next to each other in front of the fireplace in silence, and I'm filled with wonder and curiosity about the women who stood in this spot before me. I wish I knew their names, their stories.

I read the word in front of me again and know that I

will always have a part of them, and they me. Foxglove is our home, and we will always return to it.

CHAPTER FORTY-SIX

CORINNE WILDE - PRESENT DAY, ONE WEEK LATER

The warm scent of chamomile-and-mint tea fills Foxglove, hitting my nose the second I walk through the door. I know the recipe by heart. It's the one Mom made me as a child whenever I was sick or sad, the one that feels like a hug from the inside out.

"Any change?" Mom asks from where she stands in the kitchen over the sink. She's washed so many dishes lately, scrubbed so many floors, that her hands have been dry and cracking. Bleeding.

I drop my purse onto the couch. "He was sleeping for most of the visit. The doctors say everything's healing better than they expected. Hopefully he'll be cleared to come home soon."

Mom pauses at the counter, watching me. "Want some tea?"

I take the mug from her hand when she holds it out.

On the far side of the room, the fire crackles, throwing shadows across our cozy space in the dim evening light.

"Are you ever going to tell me what that was?" I ask, casting my eyes toward the cupboard. I've been too afraid to open it since we saved Lewis, too afraid of what I'll find. Or what I won't.

I know I didn't imagine it, I know it was real, but sometimes I start to question everything.

Mom's lips tip up with a smile that says I may never know all of Foxglove's secrets. That's why it surprises me when I hear her say, "I'll tell you whatever you want to know. If you're ready."

"I want to know, too," Taylor says, leaning forward in her chair by the fire. She closes her book, and I start to argue, to list all the reasons she's already been through enough and doesn't need to worry herself with anything else, but Mom puts a hand on my arm like she senses my incoming protests.

"Walk with me. Both of you." Mom places the chipped mug down on the counter, the steam curling toward the ceiling like a ghost, then holds out her hand.

Cautiously, I take it.

We walk together through the living room, where Taylor joins us, looping her arm through her grandmother's.

Medically, Mom is bruised, but not broken, and I guess the same can be said for all of us.

Outside on the porch, I draw in a deep breath,

tasting the rosemary and lavender in the air. The meadow grass rustles in the breeze, so loud it sounds like whispers.

"Where are we going?" I ask as we step down off the porch and into the yard.

"I thought we'd visit your grandma." Mom's voice is low, and I can't help thinking of the last time the two of us were here together, saying goodbye to Grandma, but also to Foxglove.

It feels like a lifetime ago.

We cross the meadow slowly, the weeds and flowers grasping our legs as if welcoming us, calling us forward.

"Do you remember much about her?" Mom asks, eyeing me curiously. There is wisdom etched across her face that I haven't noticed before, lines worth of stories I want to hear.

"I remember everything. She was always singing. And she knew every flower, and that every plant had a purpose. She could sense when a storm was coming, even before the weatherman. She was patient and could make anything. Do anything. She could make any meal delicious."

"And she loved you," Mom reminds me, her eyes sad. "And I kept her from you. More than I should've."

My stomach drops. I can't argue with the truth, but that doesn't mean I want Mom to hurt over what she can't change. "I knew she loved me."

Mom runs a thumb over my hand as we reach Grandma's grave. Together, the three of us sit down on the grass, and instinctively, our hands go to the earth, side by side.

"My mother—Hazel," she tells Taylor, "your great-grandmother, used to say the women in our family are born with roots rather than bones. That the forest is inside us, as well as around us."

Taylor gives her a quizzical smile. "She loved nature," she deduces.

"She loved this place." Mom runs her hands through the grass. "Foxglove isn't just a house. A building. It's... it's a promise." She nods, confirming something to herself. "It's a living thing. It knows who we are, and more than that—it remembers us."

With her last words, she turns her face up to the sky, eyes squeezed shut. A tear skirts down over her cheek, following the wisdom lines almost as if her face were being caressed by a gentle hand.

The wind blows through the trees, and they seem to lean toward us, like they're listening, too. Like they're confirming her words.

"I never told you why I left Foxglove," Mom says, dropping her head forward to look at me. "But it's time you know now."

I wait, anxious to know, but also scared. I fear the truth will hurt worse than the wondering.

"I was a little younger than six when your grandfather, Charles, died. I don't remember a lot about him, but I remember his smile." Her fingers trace her own lips in memory, her eyes looking through me rather than at me. "He had a charm like sweet poison. I think, even then, I suspected he had a darkness in him. I was a child. I didn't understand. But looking back, I know it's true. I believe my mother's story."

She runs her lips together, plucking three daffodils from the earth. Slowly, her fingers work to braid them together, the movement happening without thought. "When I was ready to marry your dad, my mother sat me down and told me the truth. About love. Marriage. About this place. About...about what happened to Charles."

The earth is eerily still around us. Even the flowers and trees have stopped moving. It's as if everything—us included—is holding its breath.

"He was a dangerous man. Not just to your grandmother, not just to me and Violet, but to others. To Violet's birth mother especially. And her boys. Conrad." She nods her head toward the woods in the direction of Conrad's house. Our new, dear friend. "His brother, Cory, too."

Mom places the braid of flowers on Grandma's grave. "She did what she did because she had no choice. Or rather, because her choice was the only real one she had. She killed him, not out of hate, but out of fear. Out of love."

Taylor's inhale is sharp. My hand goes to my mouth. It's impossible to imagine my dear, sweet grandma Hazel who captured spiders and set them free in her garden ever harming anyone, let alone her husband.

"That's about how I reacted at first," Mom says. "She wanted me to know the truth because there was a point when she loved him. Trusted him. And in a split second, it all changed. She warned me against loving your father, warned me there were more important things." She pauses, collecting herself. "In the end, she was right in more ways than she could've known. But I'll never get to tell her that."

She ducks her head, and I rub her back, wanting nothing more than to comfort her. "I left here thinking she was a monster. I couldn't see then what I see now. She made an impossible choice...and in doing so, she saved *you*, Corinne. And *you*, Taylor. And your children, someday. That's the legacy of Foxglove. That's the legacy of Wilde women. We protect the ones who come after us. Even when it costs us everything. Even when we'll never see what comes next."

Mom squeezes my hand, then Taylor's. I don't know what to say or how to move on from this. All I know is that if Grandma had ever asked for, or needed, my forgiveness for making an impossible choice, she'd have had it.

She *does* have it.

Whatever decision she made, I believe it was the right one. I'm sitting here with the proof that it was.

The sun hangs low in the sky, like a shimmering coin resting on the edge of the earth, ready to disappear.

"I wasted so many years being angry at her. Afraid of

what it meant. Of what it made her. I took you from her, and her from you."

"That's not true—"

"You had the occasional weekend and your earliest summers together, yes, but you were meant to grow up here. At Foxglove. You were meant to have known your grandmother and this place in ways you never got the chance. The three of us should have so many memories together. Here. But I couldn't…I couldn't stay. Even when I wanted to. Even when I brought you, dropped you off. I couldn't bring myself to stay with you. I can never fix that. Never make it right. But…" She releases our hands again and picks up an oak leaf, running her fingers gently along the edges. "I know what I can do. I know what she would want. What she always wanted."

She places the leaf down on Grandma's grave. "This place…Foxglove…it's meant for us. It's watched us bleed and grow and grieve and survive. This land is woven with our choices. Every tree, every flower, every stone carries the bones of women who fought for the ones they loved. Who fought to give us this moment right here."

She looks at me then, her eyes shining. "I don't want to waste any more time. Not with you two. Not now that I understand our legacy. Not now that I understand her."

I wait, watching as she says so much with her eyes and no words. As we have a silent conversation, as words are passed between us with only glances and tears. "I want us to stay here—together. The three of us. I want you both to know the strength you come from. Not some fairytale strength, but the real kind. The kind that walks into fire if it means the next girl won't have to."

Silence stretches between as soft and gentle as the ribbons of flowers Grandma used to tie in my hair.

"The three of us?" I ask, watching her.

Mom nods. "You understand."

"What will that mean?"

"He can't stay here." Again, she reads me like a book. Understands the question I'm not asking. The one I'm not brave enough to ask. In truth, I don't know if I want Lewis to stay, or if that's even on the table for him. I don't know where we stand. But I don't like being told it's impossible, either.

"Foxglove is ours, Corinne. And I don't say that to be cruel. My mother was right, and someday, when you're older...you'll know that I'm right, too. It's not about exclusion. It's about protection. Foxglove isn't just yours, it belongs to future generations of Wilde women, and it is your duty to protect it for them. To guard its secrets for them."

"But surely you don't think Lewis would ever try to take this place." Even as I argue, my mind drifts back to that night, how I kept the secrets of the tunnels from him. Of Foxglove's worth.

"Foxglove doesn't know how to hold a man without turning him into something else entirely—even the best ones. It's our legacy. Our blessing, and our curse. This place was made by women, for women." She meets my gaze, eyes soft but steady. "What I'm doing now is for

Lewis's protection, too. Foxglove protects its secrets, with or without our help. If you love him, you'll listen to me."

I look away, blinking hard as Taylor moves to sit by me and leans her head against my arm.

"I know this is a lot," Mom says, watching us as her voice takes on a new tenderness. "And no matter what you choose—to stay or to go—you know I will love you. Always. But if you choose to stay, I'll teach you everything my mother taught me about this place. Even more than you can imagine or might remember. And someday, you'll tell your daughter." Her eyes shift to Taylor, then to me. "And your granddaughter."

Mom pushes up on her knees, kneeling in front of me like she did when I was a child, heartbroken over shattered toys and scraped knees. Her hands are rough and familiar as she takes mine. "I know you probably think I'm being dramatic, but I always kind of thought you understood this place. Maybe better than I do. You're like your grandmother in that way. It meant a lot to you, even when you were young. You believed in it. You still do."

"In *her*," I correct, though I'm not sure whether I mean Grandma or Foxglove. "I believe in her."

A gentle warmth spreads across her face, and for the first time, I realize just how much she resembles Grandma. "This place is ours. Our sorrow, our strength, our legacy. Our home. The Wilde women have always endured. And now…I don't want to just endure. I want to *live*. Here, with you. I want to laugh here. Cry here. Heal here. Teach here. Learn here."

"I promised Grandma I'd come home someday." Heat blooms under my skin as my fingers trace the soft grass over her grave again. I swear I can feel her here—hear her voice on the wind, feel her touch in the breeze that blows through my hair. "But our custody agreement makes that complicated. Taylor has school. Lewis would never understand—"

"So make him." Mom's eyes dart between mine. "I want you to remember who you are, Corinne. Remember that you come from fire, flowers, and bone. You are Wilde. The storm and the shelter, in equal measure. Just like your grandmother, and hers. There is a long line of women who came before us who want you here, who have done everything—sacrificed everything—to make sure this place stayed standing for us. Because even in the darkest parts of our history, love has always been the root."

Her words hit me square in the chest, and no one speaks for a long time. The ground underneath me seems to hum, like it hasn't since I was a little kid. A low, living sound. Familiar.

The last of the sun is disappearing, painting the sky with flecks of light.

Taylor leans forward next to me. She brushes my hand with hers, and I take it, holding tight. Her eyes are full of tears and something fierce—fire, maybe. But lighter. *Dawn.*

She is the future they all dreamed of.
She is the freedom they fought for.

"Mom, I want to stay," she says softly, like she's worried I might be mad. "I want to learn everything. With you. Dad will let me. We'll talk to him together."

I can't believe her words, can't believe what they mean to me. Slowly, I nod, my lips trembling. *Is any of this real?* "Then we'll stay."

"Really?" Mom asks.

"Together," I vow, wrapping an arm around my daughter's shoulders.

The meadow relaxes, as if exhaling, and I can feel its relief on my skin. Smoke rises from Foxglove's chimney in the distance, still there. Still strong. Still home.

Somewhere deep in the woods, an owl hoots—low and ancient. It sounds menacing, but it's not. It's not a warning this time. It's a welcome. A celebration.

The three of us move closer together without saying a word. There are no words needed. We are three generations bound not by blood alone, but by the unbroken promise of protection and love, passed down like a sacred heirloom from mother to daughter and beyond.

All around us, the forest sings. The moon appears, watching, and Foxglove and her land—our land—remembers.

CHAPTER FORTY-SEVEN

CORINNE WILDE - ONE YEAR LATER

I close the door to the cabin—my door now, our door—and turn the lock. The click settles something deep in my chest, a small anchor thrown into place. The wind howls outside, but in here, there's only quiet. The good kind.

This house has seen so much noise.

Mom hums in the kitchen. It's the same tune she's hummed since I was a girl, something wordless and familiar. Taylor is upstairs in the loft, singing to herself while she reads next to the window—the very spot where I used to sit and pretend I could hear the trees whisper. Maybe I could. Maybe I still can.

Foxglove is officially our home now. We live here together, the way we promised we would that evening by Grandma's grave. Three generations of Wilde women under one roof, just as it's always been—only now, it's us. Our turn.

Lewis still visits—sometimes with groceries, sometimes to stay for supper. Taylor remains the center of his world. I think I was once, too. Maybe I could be again. But these days, I'm not sure I want to be the center of anyone's world.

Not after everything.

The idea of marriage feels far away now, like a book I finished long ago and left on a shelf.

I'm happy. Free.

Not free to see anyone else, necessarily. But to see myself. To learn who I am.

Greta comes by whenever she can—often with snacks, always with memories and laughter. Occasionally she's here when Conrad and Benji stop by, and we have spontaneous picnics in the orchard, drinking fresh cider and staying out late enough for the fireflies to join us.

No one was more devastated to learn the truth about EJ than Conrad, and some days I get the feeling he's still trying to make it up to us. To pay for his nephew's sins.

There's no need, though. Lewis, Greta, Conrad, and Benji have become our family, and even though we aren't conventional, I like to think that comes with my name.

Wilde women have never been normal, and we've learned to embrace the words that were once hurled at us, the ones that haunted us.

Mom is teaching Taylor and me everything she knows—everything passed down from her childhood—and I'm discovering there's very little her remedies can't heal.

It's been fun to discover Foxglove's secrets, but

there's a peace that comes with knowing they belong only to us. And that they'll be there to protect us should danger ever come calling again.

I've spent more time this year thinking about that night than I'd like to admit. The way Lewis's blood felt on my hands. The way Taylor sobbed. The way Mom fell —so fast, so sudden. The way she knew what to do. The way she saved Lewis.

The sound EJ made when the knife sank into his eye. *The knife.*

Sometimes I wonder if I should have left it where I found it, tucked it back under the floorboard to wait another hundred years or so. But I didn't. It lives in the drawer now, cleaned, sharpened, and wrapped in cloth, beside the old herbs Mom now keeps for salves and poultices. We're making good use of the hidden space in the cupboard, filling it with recipes and oils of our own.

I can't explain what happened. Not really.

There are moments when it all feels unreal. How the floorboard came loose just when I needed it. How my hand found the blade without looking. How Foxglove was hiding just what we needed to save Lewis. How the women who came before me knew just what to hide, and where.

Somehow, they planned for everything. It's impossible, and yet...

When I get too lost in my thoughts, I start to question whether it might've been...magic, I guess. I don't know the answer to that, even now.

I don't know if I believe in spells, in whispered words under moonlight, in curses or potions. I don't think I need to.

I believe in tea.

I believe in this house.

I believe in the women who walked these rooms before me—the ones whose names are written on doorframes, carved into stones out by the meadow, whispered in family stories. I believe in the others, too, the ones who've been completely forgotten by this world, though never by this land. Never by Foxglove.

I believe in the knowing. In believing. In trusting myself.

I believe in Foxglove.

And I believe in Wilde women.

We've buried husbands and secrets in this soil. We've fought off men who wanted to own us. We've raised daughters and fed them food and stories, even when we didn't always believe them ourselves. Even when we wished they were stories we didn't have to tell.

We stayed, and we survived.

Foxglove may not be everything, but she is our home. She is everything we need, and everything we have ever needed.

This land belongs to the Wilde women.

And we aren't going anywhere.

CHAPTER FORTY-EIGHT

TAYLOR WILDE - FOUR YEARS LATER

The cabin looks smaller than I remember when I return.

Funny, how that happens. The way your whole childhood can feel like a myth by the time you're twenty-two. The trees seem different now, or maybe I'm just finally standing among them with grown-woman bones.

Foxglove rises out of the field like a secret that refuses to be forgotten, stubbornly alive.

Just like the women who built her.

It smells like smoke and lavender, and I swear the wind slows as I open the door. Like it knows who I am.

Inside, everything is still. The same fireplace with our name carved deep into stone. The same board hanging above the window—another carving from a woman who came before me, another promise. WILDE WOMEN.

My shoes echo on the old floorboards. The board near the hearth is still loose. Mom never fixed it, and I didn't ask why. I step around it without thinking.

Grandma Billie filled it with all sorts of things, trinkets and treasures she couldn't bear to part with. Now, it's another secret, this one added by us.

I kick off my shoes, drop my bag on the chair by the fire, and move toward the door again, past the kitchen where dried herbs still hang in the window—faded now, though their scent lingers in the air. I'll bet Mom couldn't bear to take them down yet, and I'm quietly grateful.

I can almost hear her humming.

It's like she's still here.

If I close my eyes.

If I pretend for just one second.

And what place could be better for pretending than Foxglove?

I see her standing in the kitchen, filling the old cookie jar. Happy. Loved.

Grandma Billie. Stubborn, loud. Half sunshine, half steel.

She died quietly in her sleep, the way she always said she wanted to go. Mom called me at school yesterday, voice trembling like I hadn't heard since the night EJ died. I booked a flight as soon as we hung up.

Grandma Billie asked that we bury her in the ground by the old willow. Right next to her mother. And the others.

The same place where generations of women lie under wildflowers, their graves marked with stones and pieces of wood and carvings that can no longer be read.

It's kind of beautiful, I think. A way of returning to a home where we all might be waiting someday.

A Wilde woman belongs to Foxglove until the end.

And after.

I cross the porch and head for the meadow. I walk the path barefoot, same as always, letting the grass brush my ankles. It's late spring, and the air carries the scent of the old cedar tree and this morning's storm. The soil is soft—eager, almost. It's ready for her.

Mom's already there, waiting for me. She's kneeling beside the grave she dug, her hands muddy, shoulders heavy. I give her a lopsided smile, my chin quivering, tears welling in my eyes. Her broken expression mirrors mine as she reaches up and takes my hand, squeezing it once.

She has pieces of silver in her hair now—like moonlight—and it's beautiful and magical, but it also makes me scared. I can't help watching her, noticing that she's aging. Remembering we can't stop it.

It's the first time it's worried me. Made me think of losing her someday.

We place Grandma Billie beside her mom, Hazel. Beside Hazel's mother, and hers, and hers. We don't know how far back the names go. It's sad how many have been forgotten through the generations, whispered only between daughters in the dark.

But I take a bit of peace from knowing the earth here remembers. That pieces of their legacies, their lives, are scattered here. That we still interact with them in ways we'll never know.

That they live on within us. Within Foxglove.

We scatter rosemary. Place a sprig of foxglove on her chest. Mom braids some of the wildflowers together. We cry.

The wind shifts through the grass, dry and noisy.

I hear it then—faint, but clear. Maybe it's just my grief, my wish, but I swear I hear her voice. Then, the echo of a child's laugh, a lullaby hummed in another time, pages of books being turned, chopping of vegetables and grinding of herbs, stories being read, the rustle of skirts on floorboards of passages known only by us. The voices of all the women who've lived here.

Billie. Hazel. Ruth. Martha.

My grandmothers and aunts whose names are written on the doorframe of the closet. Lyddie. Hannah. Josephine. Katherine. So many others we can't see. Can't remember. So many others we'll never know.

I hear them all.

Their lives are in this place—in the carved letters, in the beams of the house, the roots of the trees, the seeds they sowed, the dust between the stones. They're in the cracked dishes and the worn spots on the floor, in the hidden doors and the soft creak of the loft stairs. In the moon I look at each night standing where they once stood and in the smoke of the fireplace that has filled Foxglove for hundreds of years, feeding us, protecting us, warming us.

They are in the safety they left for us—knowing what

would come for us without ever really knowing. Without ever seeing if they were right.

They are in me.

Later, after the sun has fallen low, I sit alone on the porch, my legs curled beneath me, watching the trees sway in the pink-and-amber sunset. The lavender, rosemary, and wisteria dance in the breeze, almost like they're waving hello.

The old cedar tree stands strong as ever, and in the wind, I can see just a hint more of the rusted mailbox than usual. Between the goldenrod and pokeweed, I see our name, painted on by my great-grandmother perhaps. Or one of the women before her.

Wilde.

The word hums in my chest, like a spell. Like a wish.

It's strange, but I swear I hear Foxglove breathing with me.

I don't know what comes next. I don't know who I'll be.

But I know where I am. Here. Home.

People will forever try to lay claim to Foxglove, just as they always have. Centuries ago, the Wilde women battled things I can't imagine to keep this land. Men and dangers I'll never know. Generations later, we're still fighting, and I'm not sure the threats have changed all that much. Men and their greed will always want her, but she will never be theirs.

I vow it to Foxglove, hoping she's listening.

This place—this old, haunted, sacred, holy place—belongs to me now.

And I belong to it.

Wilde women live here.

And we are never going anywhere.

WOULD YOU RECOMMEND WILDE WOMEN?

If you enjoyed this story, please consider leaving a quick review. It doesn't have to be long—just a few words would mean so much to me. Who knows? Your review might be the thing that encourages a new reader to take a chance on my work.

To leave a review, please visit:
https://books2read.com/wildewomen

Let everyone know how much you loved
Wilde Women on Goodreads:
https://bit.ly/wildewomen

STAY UP TO DATE ON EVERYTHING KMOD!

Thank you so much for spending time with me within the pages of this story. If you enjoyed it, I'd love to invite you to sign up for my VIP Reader Alerts so we can be sure you don't miss any exciting updates.

Sign up for my newsletter here:
kierstenmodglinauthor.com/nlsignup

Sign up for my text alerts here:
kierstenmodglinauthor.com/textalerts

ACKNOWLEDGMENTS

This story came to me in waves.

While I used to say I build my stories "from the twist out", meaning I start from the twist I want to write and structure the story around it, lately I've been most inspired by the interesting relationships within stories.

So it's no surprise that the first initial spark for WILDE WOMEN (it was actually called FOXGLOVE at that time) was Corinne and Lewis fresh out of a divorce and having to stay together during a terrible storm. That idea latched onto me sometime more than a year before I wrote the first word and I couldn't let it go.

The next spark came in December of 2024, when my grandpa asked me to make him a family tree of his line of our family. As I was going back through our lineage, I was struck by the devastating reality that, at a certain point in history, all the women in our line stopped being listed by their names. They were just Mrs. HUSBAND'S FULL NAME. As I wrote their married names over and over again, my heart was heavy. I couldn't help thinking about these women and how we'll never even know their first names. They remain erased from history, and it's something I've thought quite a lot about ever since I discovered it.

The final piece clicked into place for me in January of 2025 when we lost my granny unexpectedly. My granny was my best friend and the rock of our family and, needless to say, it was a catastrophic loss. I still miss her every day. A few days after we lost her, once my mind found its focus again, one heartbreaking truth stuck out to me: How much history did we just lose? I can't count the number of times I've asked someone in my family a question only to be told, "Granny would know that. Ask Granny." And she always did. She knew the names of every person in every photograph, she knew how we were related to everyone, she remembered the birthdays and the stories and the lives of not only those still with us, but those long gone. There's so much I wish I could ask her now, so much I wish I'd written down or recorded in some way because there's no chance to get it back again.

And so, with those pieces all swirling in my mind, I began to plot this story—one meant to honor forgotten women throughout history, meant to feel like a warm, familiar hug from the women we've lost, and meant to keep you guessing all the way until the end.

The first draft of this story took place only in present day, and only from Corinne's POV. But as I typed those final words, I knew something was missing. In fact, I think I knew it much earlier. The long gone Wilde women had been speaking to me from early on in the story, but I just couldn't imagine writing all I needed to if

I included them. For one thing, I'd never written anything historical and I was worried I'd be terrible at it. For another, I knew if I wanted to write it the way I needed to, we wouldn't stay with any of the women for long. Would that make it hard for readers to connect with the characters? Would they love them the way I wanted them to if we only saw one brief moment in their history?

When the first draft was finished, there was no denying it. My story was missing something—*several* somethings.

I often tell myself while writing, if I end up hating it, I can just throw it out and pretend it never happened. *That's what backspace is for.*

And so, with that in mind, I gave in and began to write the past.

Oh my goodness, did the women from the past have a lot to say. Their stories poured out of me in a way I've never experienced. I loved their similarities and their differences. I loved seeing the different ways the women reacted to Foxglove and her secrets. I loved their hobbies and their humor. I especially loved watching the grandmothers interact with their granddaughters.

I loved the secrets, the coincidences, the magic that wasn't quite magic, and most of all, the love within the pages. The idea that these women went through so much to protect Foxglove for granddaughters they'd never meet. The idea that they'd protected future Wildes in ways they'd never get to see.

I loved the fact that so much changed throughout the generations and yet, so much stayed the same.

I loved that, by the end, it didn't matter so much that we only saw brief glimpses of the women's lives. By the end, they were one collective voice speaking to the experience of women throughout history.

I loved asking myself the question—was Foxglove actually magic? Or did it just provide the Wilde women with the freedom, safety, power, and confidence women traditionally didn't have? What would an entire generation of women who'd grown up knowing they had somewhere safe to live look like? Somewhere that was just theirs, forever.

Perhaps most of all, I loved those final chapters, wrapping up this story with such weighted scenes. I loved that the weight was amplified by the history we learned and I loved that we ended the way we started.

Selfishly, I *did not* love saying goodbye to this book. I spent way too much time inside the world of Foxglove and the Wilde women. I kept coming back to these pages, looking for ways to improve things, changing this word or that, adding a new paragraph, a new facial expression, a new line. I jotted down words and phrases that came to me at the most random times, thoughts and feelings that I wanted to include somewhere. That I *had* to include somewhere. I wanted this world to feel as special here on the page as it does in my head and in my heart and now, as I pass it onto you like my own sacred heirloom, I hope it does.

As always, WILDE WOMEN exists only because these people embrace my wildness every single day:

To my husband and daughter—thank you for making our home such a beautifully wild mosaic of laughter and love. I'm so grateful I get to do life alongside you both. From (way too) early dance parties to our famous movie nights, you make every moment better. Love you both to the moon and back.

To my editor, Sarah West—thank you for always rolling with whatever wild story I place on your desk next, and for making each one a thousand times better.

To the proofreading team at My Brother's Editor—thank you for being the final set of eyes on these wild pages.

To my loyal readers (AKA the #KMod Squad and the Modglings)—Ahhh! Where do I start? Every single day, I'm grateful to have you in my (dark, twisted, cobweb-filled) corner. I'm thankful for your trust in me, and for showing to catch me every time I leap. Every time I worry my next idea is too weird, I remember that you guys just keep proving me wrong. That you just keep showing up, just keep cheering me on. Just keep celebrating my weirdness. All my life, I've dreamed that someday someone would read my stories and now, so many of you showed up in full force, unfolded your chairs, and have never left my side. I'll never be able to put into words what that means to me. Thank you for every social media shout out, every review, every email, every recommendation to a friend, every book club, every video, every time you attend one of my signings, and every time you gift one of my stories to a new reader. Thank you for this wild, magical life you've given me. And thank you, as always, for meeting me on the page.

To my book club/gang/besties—Sara, both Erins, Heather, Dee, and June—thank you for the laughter, tears, and everything in between. I'm so grateful for our sisterhood and wild inside jokes. For the bathing murders, murder dogs, murder mystery parties, spidery cannibal murders, Tarantino murder scenes, and ...crafts? What can I say, we've got range. ;) Love you girls to pieces.

To my bestie, Emerald O'Brien—thank you for being here through everything. For being my cheerleader, sounding board, and best friend. The one I come to for advice and whenever I need to vent. The one who is always on my side. I'm forever pinching myself that I have you here on this wild journey with me. Love you, friend. Same moon.

Last but certainly not least, to you, dear reader—thank you for buying this book and supporting my art. Whether it's Book 1 or Book 51, when I sit down to write my stories, my first thoughts are always of you. I wonder which parts of the story will give you goose-bumps. Which parts will make you gasp. I wonder which characters you might relate to. Which characters you might love. Which ones you might hate. As I dive deeper into each story, I write as if I am the reader, guessing as you might guess and throwing curveballs to keep you turning the pages. With this story, I hope you were reminded of the people you've lost. I hope the words I've written within these pages were like a warm hug from someone you miss. And, of course, I genuinely hope that it kept you guessing and entertained the whole way through. Whatever path led you to this story, I want to thank you for giving it a chance. Thank you for seeing it online or on that shelf in your local bookstore or library, thank you for listening to that post you saw on social media, or finally giving in when your friend said you had to read it. Or, if I'm lucky enough to have had you with me for a while, thank you for coming back like you always do. It means everything to have you here. Out of all the books in the world, I'm so glad we were able to meet here on these pages for a brief moment in time. It is the greatest joy of my life to write these stories for you. As always, whether this is your first Kiersten Modglin book or your 51th, I hope it was everything you hoped for and nothing like you expected.

ABOUT THE AUTHOR

KIERSTEN MODGLIN is a #1 bestselling author of psychological thrillers. Her books have sold over two million copies and been translated into multiple languages. Kiersten is a member of International Thriller Writers, Novelists, Inc., and the Alliance of Independent Authors. She is a KDP Select All-Star and a recipient of *ThrillerFix*'s Best Psychological Thriller Award, *Suspense Magazine*'s Best Book of 2021 Award, a 2022 Silver Falchion for Best Suspense, and a 2022 Silver Falchion for Best Overall Book of 2021. Kiersten grew up in rural western Kentucky and later relocated to Nashville, Tennessee, where she now lives with her family. Kiersten's readers across the world lovingly refer to her as

"KMod." A binge-watching expert, psychology fanatic, and *indoor* enthusiast, Kiersten enjoys rainy days spent with her favorite people and evenings with her nose in a book.

Sign up for Kiersten's newsletter here:
kierstenmodglinauthor.com/nlsignup

Sign up for text alerts from Kiersten here:
kierstenmodglinauthor.com/textalerts

kierstenmodglinauthor.com
www.facebook.com/kierstenmodglinauthor
www.facebook.com/groups/kmodsquad
www.threads.net/kierstenmodglinauthor
www.instagram.com/kierstenmodglinauthor
www.tiktok.com/@kierstenmodglinauthor
www.goodreads.com/kierstenmodglinauthor
www.bookbub.com/authors/kiersten-modglin

ALSO BY KIERSTEN MODGLIN

<u>STANDALONE NOVELS</u>

Becoming Mrs. Abbott

The List

The Missing Piece

Playing Jenna

The Beginning After

The Better Choice

The Good Neighbors

The Lucky Ones

I Said Yes

The Mother-in-Law

The Dream Job

The Nanny's Secret

The Liar's Wife

My Husband's Secret

The Perfect Getaway

The Roommate

The Missing

Just Married

Our Little Secret

Widow Falls

Missing Daughter

The Reunion

Tell Me the Truth

The Dinner Guests

If You're Reading This...

A Quiet Retreat

The Family Secret

Don't Go Down There

Wait for Dark

You Can Trust Me

Hemlock

Do Not Open

You'll Never Know I'm Here

The Stranger

The Hollow

Bitter House

The Guilty One

The Hidden

Where the Darkness Goes

The Last Trip

Nine Pines

Wilde Women

ARRANGEMENT TRILOGY

The Arrangement (Book 1)

The Amendment (Book 2)

The Atonement (Book 3)

THE MESSES SERIES

The Cleaner (Book 1)

The Healer (Book 2)

The Liar (Book 3)

The Prisoner (Book 4)

NOVELLAS

The Long Route: A Lover's Landing Novella

The Stranger in the Woods: A Crimson Falls Novella

Made in the USA
Middletown, DE
17 October 2025